Jasmine

By Richard Cook

ISBN-13 978-0615553573

ISBN-10 0615553575

Jasmine

First Paperback edition: October 2011

Cover design: Alexa Melone

For information:

http://www.booksbyrick.com

booksbyrick@gmail.com

This book is dedicated to:

All the people in my life who believed in me and
encouraged me to put my stories on paper.

My father who taught me to embrace the unknown and try
new things.

All those who I've come into contact with over the years
and whose stories I enjoy telling.

To women everywhere; you give us life, bring softness
and beauty to the world, and make life worth living.

Contents

Prologue

Jasmine stood, as she did every morning, at attention, facing the picture of the cute, almost loveable donkey. His hat was cocked to one side as he stood in the barnyard. Jasmine was not alone. Her best friend, Mary, stood next to her between the salon chairs, also at attention. Like a precision drill team, they looked at each other, then snapped their heads back to the photo. Their arms rose slowly, yet deliberately, from their sides, extending out in front, fingers clenched tightly into a fist. You could almost hear the snare drums pounding out their slow and steady beat.

Their arms were extended, fists pointing at the photo, when they abruptly stopped. Arms trembled as they stood in the empty silence of the shop. The ladies' heads turned, once again, to each other. A hint of a smile caressed their lips. Jasmine and Mary had repeated this ritual every day since the divorce. In perfect synchronization, heads snapped back to the picture. Suddenly, wrists turned, and their middle fingers, in unison, snapped to attention and performed the Fred Salute.

Hatred of Fred had gotten Jasmine through the last ten years. Little did she know just how much her life was about to change. Nothing she had known would be the same again.

Jasmine

Life

Jasmine fumbled through her purse, digging for the key. *Where is that key?* she wondered. The three plastic grocery bags swayed on her arms, hindering the search. She pressed on, fingers probing the array of things she had accumulated since the last time she cleaned out her purse. She listened for the sound of the keys knocking together, revealing their hiding place as the purse swayed.

It was the start of another week at the shop. Finally, Jasmine's fingers touched the cold metal of the keys and out of the purse they came. *I need to clean this thing out,* she complained to herself as the key slid into the lock. With a flick of her wrist, another week began at Jasmine's.

Walking quickly to the counter, Jasmine set the bags down providing relief to the hands that were starting to ache under their weight. Jasmine paused as she always did, and surveyed the small shop. There were two stations, each with a chair holding a neatly folded cape, the sinks sparkled as the light hit the porcelain, hair dryers, and other tools rested neatly on the towel covered shelf. Off to one side, the bottles of gel and hair spray stood expertly arranged according to height. The magical mirror was spotless and awaited the customer's gaze. The two stations were identical. A workspace that evolved over the fifteen years of giving customers what they wanted.

The narrow hallway was somewhat less inviting, leading to the restroom and small office in the rear of the salon. The picture of the shop mascot, Fred, hung predominately between the chairs. This was a momentous day. It had been fifteen years since she'd created Jasmine's.

Jasmine had always loved doing hair. In high school, she had colored and cut the hair of all of her friends, as well as her mom's. The exceptionally brave allowed her to experiment with a Toni perm. She'd worked hard to get those cute spit curls and long, flowing tube curls that she had seen in magazines just right. Jasmine had many successes and a few failures as she learned her craft. Hair had always been a passion for her. After high school, she attended beauty school and graduated as a licensed hairdresser.

Jasmine had spent most of her life married. She and Fred met at a club one night, and the connection was instant. She knew he was the man for her, and, after dating for several months, he finally proposed. They married and settled into a warm and loving life. Fred was everything to Jasmine. He could make her laugh when she was down. His touch would send bolts of electricity to all the right places, and he was always able to make her feel special.

Jake was born shortly after they married, and was the light of their life. As he grew, her love for both of the men in her life grew even stronger. Jasmine and Fred stood together through all of the joy, trials, and drama that came along with raising a rambunctious boy.

Together, they celebrated the triumphs and overcame the struggles of just living. They were a team. Fred held her the day her precious Jake went off to the army, cradling her as their baby left home. On that terrible day, when the letter came, it was Fred who held her, and got her through the agony of their loss.

They had been together more than 25 years when Fred came to her one day and said he wanted a divorce. He had found someone new in his life and was leaving. Her life came crashing down. The relationship had not been strained, in her eyes, and she was caught totally by surprise. The devastation was total and immediate. Jasmine turned to her friend, Mary, and her work in order to get through the pain.

Many days, she could not even get out of bed. She just laid there and cried. Mary covered for her friend, doing every customer's hair. Oft times working until her fingers could no longer hold the scissors. Mary would then return to Jasmine and sit with her as she cried. It was Mary who finally got Jasmine to move on, and move on she did. Jasmine built a thriving business with extremely loyal clients that were more like family than customers.

She did, however, resign herself to one fact. Fred was her one true love. There could never be another Fred, and, as time passed, she began to sink deeper and deeper into social isolation. She didn't even notice the UPS man when he delivered packages to the salon. She was silent as the ladies discussed their love lives while spending time in the chairs or under the dryers. She patterned her life after that of the nuns she had spent time with in grade school. Men were all around. They were just not something that she was interested in.

Jasmine had actually become bitter towards men in general, in particular Fred. She needed a focus point for her pain, and Fred was it. One day, she was shopping in a thrift store and there on a shelf among what could only be called junk, was a photograph of a broken down donkey. *An ass, now that's perfect*, she thought to herself and bought it. She placed the photograph on the wall in the shop, and each and every day, she would look at it and remember. She would remember the pain a man had caused in her life and vowed that it would never happen again. Never would she allow herself to be so dependent on a man.

Mary was the one who got her started.

"Don't you think it's about time you found someone to share your life with again?"

Jasmine was not interested in sharing her life again, but she was a little bored at night. It took several prods from Mary, but, finally, one night, she and Mary sat at the computer together, with a bottle of white wine, and Mary introduced her friend to the wonders of the internet. It was pretty innocent at first, but as the second glass of wine turned into the third, and the first bottle into the second, things started to get a bit interesting. The two women were acting like schoolgirls again. Schoolgirls who had just found another steamy romance novel and could not wait to get to the good part.

By the end of the night, Jasmine had several sites with true potential added to her favorites, and she would never look back. In the weeks and months that followed, Jasmine learned the hard way how to tell a fascinating man from a sleazy one. Slowly, she added people to her chat list.

She considered them friends since they shared common interests and were fun to talk with. She began to look forward to meeting her friends on-line and talking about anything and everything.

Then, one day, she connected with Luke. There was just something about him that made her want to be with him more and more. They began sending each other short text messages during the day and would spend hours at night chatting on-line. Soon, Luke was the only one she wanted to talk to\, and she let nearly all of her other on-line friends drop by the wayside.

Months passed, and, then, one fateful night, she thought to herself, *I wonder what it would be like to meet him?* She kept the thought to herself, but spent many satisfying late nights dreaming of what an evening with Luke might be like. How would his hands feel as they caressed her skin? Would the touch of his lips ignite the fire within her? His image became the focus of her special nights. Then, one night, her dreams got the best of her. She just inserted it, the question she had been frightened to ask for nearly a month. Her fingers trembled as she typed out the simple question.

Jasmine:

Luke do you ever think about what it would be like to meet somewhere?

Jasmine felt a jolt of electricity shoot through her body as she pressed the ENTER key, sending her message into cyber space. Her breathing quickened as she leaned back into the chair staring at her monitor awaiting his response.

Luke:

Yes, I have, Jasmine, but this is the Internet. I wasn't sure what you would think of me if I suggested it. Our towns are not that far apart, maybe forty-five minutes. Would you like to meet for coffee some day?

Jasmine's heart skipped a beat as she read Luke's response. She paused for a moment; then, once again, her trembling fingers continued.

Jasmine:

I've just been thinking about it lately. How does this Saturday sound?

Her entire body exploding in goose bumps as she could feel her heart pounding in her chest.

Luke:

That sounds wonderful, Jasmine. I'd love to. Where shall we meet?

Jasmine thought for a moment. *It has been so long since I've been out on the town; I don't know where to go.* The paper was open in front of her on the table, and she spotted an advertisement for a pub. It was in a section of town she drove through on her way to the grocery store.

Jasmine:

There is a pub on Main Street called O'Toole's. We could meet there. What do you think Luke?

Jasmine could feel her growing excitement, as the now familiar tingles swept over her.

Luke:

That sounds wonderful! About 7:00 then.

Jasmine:

Get a table in the back so we can talk.

Jasmine typed with her fingers now trembling uncontrollably.

From that message on, Jasmine knew her life would never be the same. She had taken the leap. She would meet this man that had captured her imagination. The two continued their conversation until Luke had to leave.

Jasmine immediately reached for the phone sitting beside the computer. Her fingers flew over the keys, and she tapped on the table as she awaited the connection. Finally, the phone began to ring, and ring, and ring again. *Come on, pickup, pickup* she thought to herself.

"Hi, this is Mary" came from the phone, and an excited Jasmine nearly shouted into it.

"I did it, Mary; I did it! I've got…"

"I'm not home right now; please leave a message at the beep."

Jasmine could not believe her ears. She was so excited she could hardly breathe, and she got the machine! Jasmine hung up the phone. This was way too important for the answering machine. Mary would just have to wait until morning to find out.

That night Jasmine treated herself to a bath. Not just any bath, but a real bath. She lit candles, poured wine and turned on the soft music; she even treated herself to a facial. She laid there, her legs and arms floating in the steamy water, and dreamed. She dreamed of being with this man who had reawakened her sleeping womanhood, her repressed desires, and allowed her to, once again, dream of being with a man.

The Awakening

It's so hot in this mall. Why do they keep these places so hot? Maybe it's just me that's hot! Jasmine thought as the conversation continued within herself. *I get to see him in six hours, and I just need something to keep my mind off him.* Jasmine had fantasized about Luke so many times that she knew exactly what it would be like to be with him. *It's been so long since I've done this. I'm not even sure what I'm doing.*

What was it about him that moved her to want to meet? There is just something sweet, yet powerful in his voice. When he spoke, he was sexy and funny all at the same time. She couldn't help the feeling. She just wanted, no needed to meet him. Jasmine's head was alive with a spirited conversation between herself and herself.

The many nights of discovery while chatting were wonderful. Mary was right; there is life beyond her door. Jasmine began to doubt herself as she strolled through the mall. *I'm not sure I can truly MEET a man after all this time of being alone. I'm not a young girl any longer.* She paused as she caught her reflection in the storefront window. She studied the woman in the window, taking note of every detail.

I bulge in places I didn't bulge years ago. I've had a child and raised a family. I was a wife, lover, and, sometimes, nursemaid to a man. Jasmine continued to wander the mall and consider what she had gotten herself into.

Will the feelings of hurt and betrayal I felt during the divorce ever go away? Do I really want to bring a man into my life? It's very strange, how he made me feel while we chatted on-line.

Their discussions had awakened feelings in Jasmine that she had kept hidden for years. Suddenly, she found herself craving those feelings again.

They chatted about everything. At first, it was the weather, hobbies, movies, music, culture, her son, and then, what it was like to be alone. They even talked about sex.

It was so natural though. When she stopped to think about it, she knew others would not understand. Jasmine discussing sex with a "stranger" over the Internet! Her friends would die if they knew. Oh, it was innocent at first, talking about what she found attractive in a man, giggling about what made her tingle. It's a good thing he couldn't see her face as the blazing red took over when she spoke of things she barely admitted to herself.

When Jasmine spoke to Mary about her chatting, Mary simply laughed and said she was a big girl and that it was only natural that Jasmine spoke of big girl things. But sex? She had never discussed sex with anyone, not even Fred. What was she thinking? Jasmine felt young and tingly as they spoke of their thoughts and desires. What was it that made her want to tell this man her innermost secrets?

Now she was going to actually sit across the table from him. A date! Jasmine was not sure she even remembered how to date. All she knew was that she wanted to be with him. Jasmine wanted the tingling to continue. When she spoke with Luke, she felt special, truly special.

Jasmine's dreams had changed and nearly always centered on him doing "things". Things she used to enjoy. Visions that caused her to lock the bedroom door, shut her eyes, and enjoy the soothing results of pleasuring herself. It had almost become an obsession since that first reawakening in the tub when she dropped the spray head, and its jets touched her in that "special" place. The jet of water took her breath away, and brought back memories of the euphoria she had experienced while taking those long, private, baths.

Now she just needed to kill some time and make the clock spin faster. Perhaps a little shopping would pass the time. *Maybe I should find just the right outfit for tonight? Jeans?* Jasmine asked herself. *No, that just won't do for tonight.*

Luke said he's partial to frill. Frill, my God, I haven't had frill on this body for 10 years! He'll get jeans and like it.

Jasmine felt a bit lost without Mary. She would know what outfit to get. It was not like Mary to miss something so important. Normally, the two ladies would be shopping together. Had Mary not been doing 75 in a 45, she would be here rather than in Traffic School! She just loses her mind when she gets on that bike.

Jasmine scanned the area and spotted a rack of skirts. *These skirts look nice she thought to herself, classic black and split up the side. Black is slimming. The straight shape and the slit could work nicely, if I choose to work it. A skirt and turtleneck; I'll be warm and safe. Wow. These lace blouses are gorgeous and they button up to the neck. Oh, they have lavender! Maybe a skirt and lace blouse; yes, that will do. He'll like that.* Jasmine was suddenly aware that her nipples were hardening, and there was a feeling of heat inside of her. Giggling to herself, she grabbed the blouse and skirt and headed for the changing room.

Once in the room, Jasmine quickly latched the door. Stripping off her clothes, she prepared for the rough ride that was typical of trying on new outfits. Removing the skirt from the hanger, Jasmine suddenly came face to face with her reflection. She turned left, then right, then left again.

The bra she was wearing was basic white. The thick cups and wide straps provided the support needed to keep her breasts under control. The straps of the bra were pulled so tight that by the end of the day her body screamed for release. Her matching white underpants pulled tightly across her buns, yet somehow, were still slightly baggy in the butt. Their high wasted design covered every inch of what they should; even her belly button was hidden from view.

How did I get here, she wondered? *What would Luke think if he ever saw me like this? I've been wearing the same bra for nearly three years. My God, I'm wearing my mother's underwear! I'm not that old... why do I dress this way? I need to start with the basics for this outfit!*

She pulled the skirt over her hips, closed the clasp and tugged the zipper up. The hem hit just below her knees. *Yes, I like it. It's a bit snug, but...* Jasmine turned to look at herself in the mirror. As she did, her leg peaked through the slit. *Oh now that is sexy.* She slid her hands down over her hips and onto her thighs. She pressed the fabric against the goose bumps on her legs to smooth it. She felt pretty. The decision was made.

Jasmine slipped the blouse up her arms and began to close the delicate buttons. She noticed the telltale signs of her excitement showing through. *My God, this is fun* she thought with a grin as she continued to fasten the small buttons. She lifted her head as she closed the last one at her throat. Jasmine looked at herself in the mirror. An approving smile came to her face. *Now it's off to lingerie.*

Jasmine weaved her way through the racks of bras and underwear; she could not believe what was there. She'd avoided these racks for so long. Now, here she is, looking for sexy underwear once again. Suddenly, something occurred to her. *When did panties become underwear? Panties are sexy, underwear is functional. I want panties not underwear!* Jasmine's breathing was more labored, and her body seemed to have come alive with chills as she envisioned herself in each style she passed.

The dampness forming was unmistakable. Jasmine could feel the flush in her face as she picked up a pair of thong panties. *How can I wear this? That small string would go right up my butt, I would feel like a slut.* Then she grinned to herself as she pictured Mary standing there beside her. *Maybe you want to be a little slutty tonight. Well Mary, maybe... but these are just too much.*

She put them back on the rack and continued shopping. *Something with a little lace perhaps?* Jasmine picked up a pair of bikinis. *Now these are panties.* She held them up. The black lace was so delicate, but the cut was tiny compared to what she had been wearing for as long as she could remember. She gently stroked the lace with her fingers as she imagined what it would be like to wear something so beautiful. *These are nice and would match well.* Suddenly, she realized she was holding them high above the racks and jerked them back down to the privacy of her cart. Jasmine grabbed a couple of sizes, not sure just how they would fit. *Now for a bra.*

Jasmine looked and looked, but the only one that matched had those low cut cups. *I cannot imagine,* she said excitedly to herself, *but what the hell! Normally, I need a C cup, but this looks way too small, so I'll grab the C, D, and even DD. They all look too small, but we'll see,* as she placed them into the cart, being careful to pull the skirt over the top. After all, no one needed to know what she was trying on.

As Jasmine approached the dressing rooms, she noticed the twenty something clerk smiling. Reaching the bottom of the cart, her hand caresses the soft fabric as she dreamed of her man and her desires. Her long fingers curled, gripping her selections as she handed them to the clerk. The clerk smiled, accepted the selections, and guided her to a vacant dressing room. She placed the delicate lingerie on a hook, then turned and pulled the door closed behind her.

Oh my God, Jasmine wondered in panic, *was that a grin I saw on her face?* She could feel a flush come over her once again. With a click, the door was secure. Jasmine quickly disrobed then reached, with a trembling hand, for the first pair of panties. She slid them slowly up her long legs and over her underwear as a chill shot through her. *Is it cold in here?*

With the dainty panties in place, she looked at herself in the mirror, turned once, then again. *Damn, I just cannot tell with these granny panties on underneath* Looking quickly side-to-side, as if someone could see what she was about to do, she slipped off the new panties and then her own underwear. She quickly slid the panties back up her legs.

What a sight! The way they seem to showcase her bottom; the lace clinging to its roundness. The triangle in the front seemed to mold itself to her body. *Do they actually make my legs look longer, maybe even thinner? We will need to trim a few things*, Jasmine giggled.

She reached behind her and deftly released the clasp of her bra and let it slide effortlessly down her arms. With a quick flick, the heavy white bra landed on the changing room bench. She caught a glimpse of herself in the mirror and paused. *My goodness, I remember when the girls were much higher on my chest. Guess that was a lot of years ago. Time is just cruel.*

Jasmine cupped each breast, lifting them and pushing them together. She looked longingly at herself and took a deep breath. She recalled when a bra was something she wore to be pretty. Somehow, over the years, something had happened. She wasn't happy about it, but the effects were there none the less. She pulled her hands away and heard a distinct "flop" as her breast took up their natural position.

What the hell! she thought to herself. *It is what it is.* Jasmine then reached for the first bra. She stretched the delicate lace across her chest and reached behind her back, slipping the hooks together. Then she slid it up her torso and lifted each breast into place. She tried to position herself into the cups, but no matter how she did it, the bra just didn't seem right.

These cups are just way too small, but look at the pushup! She turned to the side, and once again, remembered the days when her breasts actually were this perky. A smile came across her face, but her breasts seemed to spill over the top like nothing she had ever felt. With that thought, she removed the bra and reached for the DD.

This cup doesn't look right either, she commented to herself. She looked into the mirror holding her arm high in the air. It gapped under her arms leaving her uncomfortable as her breast sped across her chest.

Well, maybe the D? No, that's not right either. Disappointment began to come over her. She looked at the C lying on the bench, and with a grin, tried it again. She felt young and sexy when it was on her body, and that is exactly how she had felt since chatting with Luke. Jasmine gazed at herself in the dressing room mirror. Her eyes stroll up and down her body as she turned one way, then the other. Jasmine could actually see the tops of her areolas peeking out from the cups. This was the first time in years that her nipples had not been staring at the floor.

As Jasmine's eyes took in the view from the mirror, she realized that she was not looking at that lonely lady that stayed home every night. She was a vibrant, sexy woman. *I look it, feel it, and damn it, I'm going to be it! I'm not my mother, and I won't dress like her!* Her mind flashed back to those arguments she had with her mother over fashion while in high school. A smile grew across her face.

Jasmine hurriedly removed the garments, taking care to fold them neatly. She then dressed, grabbed her selections, and left the dressing room. Quickly, she returned her selections to the bottom of the cart and once again, pulled the skirt over them.

I'll need a pair of panty hose. Jasmine strolled past the racks and noticed a garter belt that matched the underwear. *Well,* she thought to herself, *I used to wear one, a hundred years ago.* She checked the sizes and snatched one up. Under the skirt it went, and she could feel the flush in her cheeks. In the hosiery department, Jasmine found a pair of nude, silk stockings in her size. *These are expensive,* she said to herself, but decided that for this special occasion, she would be going all out, and under the skirt they went.

The bottom of Jasmine's cart now had an apparent lump under the skirt. She took a look around to be sure no one was watching her as she continued on her mission of rediscovery. *What's left: shoes! Yes, I need new heels.*

The store was crowded, but it didn't take long to find a nice pair of strappy heels to complete the look. A little flashier than normal, but this was not a normal outfit. The heel was a little high, but when Jasmine got them on, they fit perfectly. She headed for the checkout.

Jasmine wheeled her cart up to the checkout."May I help you ma'am?" echoed across the store and her heart leapt into her throat. Jasmine slowly raised her head, and she came face to face with an 18-year-old boy with a smile on his face.

Oh-my-God! Jasmine thought to herself! *How can I let a pimple-faced adolescent boy ring me up? He'll touch my things, and probably picture me in them! No, I won't do it. There must be another cashier somewhere?* Jasmine mumbled something about forgetting an item and took off at top speed. The wheels of the cart begged for mercy as she headed for the cover of the clothes racks.

Once there, she paused. Her chest was heaving, and her hands were shaking as she again imagined that BOY touching her special purchases. As she regained her composure, she pointed the cart to the far end of the store and the other checkout lines, hoping females manned them. *Thank God,* Jasmine sighed to herself, as she quickly slipped into the checkout line.

"Did you find everything?" the sales girl asks.

"Yes, thank you" she replied, as the clerk scanned, folded, and slid her treasures into a bag. Jasmine handed the clerk the credit card, and with a swipe, was on her way. Realizing the time, she was suddenly on a mission.

Jasmine arrived home and headed straight for her room. Hanging her new skirt and blouse in the closet, she laid the rest of her purchases neatly onto the bed. Quickly, she striped her clothes off and headed for the shower. The warm water soothed her body as it cascaded downward. Jasmine let the water spray over her hair, face, shoulders, and down her torso. The streams felt wonderful, and she could feel herself relaxing. Her mind wandered as she stood there, eyes closed, trying to remember how it felt to have a man's hands roaming over her sensitive skin.

Yes, I want to feel that again, and I will feel that again, Jasmine said to herself with conviction. She recalled her chat sessions when she intimated exactly what she missed: the soft stroking of her hair and warm kisses on her shoulders.

Strong hands caressing her back and drawing her close into someone she cared for. Jasmine was quickly drifting off into her fantasy of discovery.

Lips, soft and moist, pressing against her own. She missed the deep, steady rhythm of his heart beating while she nuzzled into his chest. The slight tickle of his chest hair on her face. These were the things she missed most.

Her hand rose, gently cupping her breast. She began massaging the sensitive orb with soft, feathery strokes. The warm water cascaded over her. Suddenly, she jerked herself back to reality. Time, we have limited time. She washed her hair, then her body. Once this was complete, she splurged and grabbed a new razor. Almost without effort, she shaved her legs leaving them silky smooth.

Stepping out of the shower, she dried herself. Jasmine took a deep breath and thought, *now for the other trim. It's been years since I've done this and it shows.* Jasmine pondered as she looked back on the days when she wore a two-piece swimsuit. Taking her time, she worked carefully, but when she was done, she was pleased with the results.

Jasmine sat and looked at herself in the dressing table mirror. *Young. That's the only way to describe how I feel,* was Jasmine's comment to herself. *Look at me though; I'm not young anymore.* The woman staring back at her had raised a child, run a household, and even fixed a leaky faucet. *Experience,* she laughed to herself but then the demons of doubt snuck into her brain.

I have no business meeting a man. It's been years since I dated. There, I've said it; dated. What will he think of me? We've grown so close over the computer. He seems to be such a wonderful and caring man. Sexy too. Let's not forget sexy. He's awakened feelings I've kept locked away for many years, Jasmine thought to herself.

My God, I've even had dreams about him! Adult dreams of a man softly stroking my body while whispering in my ear; "I want you." Dreams of him holding me in his strong arms, kissing me with soft, moist lips and then carrying me off to his bed. Those are the dreams I'm having.

Jasmine's stomach was alive now, like a schoolgirl about to meet her boyfriend. Her hands were trembling. *I can hardly hold my hairbrush,* she thought.

Suddenly Jasmine snapped back to reality and hurried to dry her hair and put on her makeup. *Time, where has all of the time gone?* The sun had gone down and she needed to get in gear, or she would be late.

Jasmine took one more look in the mirror. Her hair was perfect. Could this be an omen? She untied the waistband of her robe, let it slide off her shoulders and placed it across the back of the dressing table chair. *Now, let's get dressed.* Again, the demons returned. *Oh, come on now,* she thought to herself as she looked at her foundations. The excitement she was feeling could not be denied. The flutters in her stomach, the moisture, it all said she had chosen well. Jasmine was past rationalizing this. She wanted to knock his socks off.

Jasmine slowly slipped on her new panties and bra as she noticed her hands were shaking uncontrollably causing her to fight with the hooks. She lifted and positioned her breasts into the cups, noticing her body awakening to the excitement of the evening.

Sitting in the chair at the dressing table, she slid the stockings up one leg, then the other, and fastened the garters. She stood to pickup her blouse as she caught a glimpse of herself in the mirror across the room. *Wow, I look good!*

Between the high cut of the panties and the stockings, her legs seem to go on forever. And they look thinner, much thinner. A smile came to her face as she looked at what she'd created. *Not bad for a woman my age,* Jasmine said to herself.

She carefully removed the blouse from its hanger. It was so light as it glided onto her arms. The lace was soft and felt so wonderful against her tingling skin. She closed the buttons one after the other until she raised her chin and fastened the last one tight against her neck.

She reached for the skirt, opened the clasp, and slid the zipper down. Carefully, she stepped into the skirt and pulled it up, wiggling side to side as she coaxed the skirt over her hips. She fumbled with the clasp until the hooks joined. Her fingers tugged at the zipper, and the skirt was on. She then gathered the skirt around her waist, gripped the hem of the blouse, and tugged everything into place. Jasmine let the skirt drop and the fabric tumble down against her thighs. Jasmine reached for one shoe then the other. She struggled a bit with the straps, but finally, she was dressed.

Looking over at the full-length mirror, she saw the beautiful, vibrant woman he keeps telling her she is. She turned one way, then the other. Yes, she had chosen well. But Jasmine noticed something seemed out of place. It's subtle, but it's there. She reached up and unbuttoned the top button of her blouse. Then the second. And the third. The image looked better as each button opened. She had cleavage, and she daringly showed it.

Jasmine opened the fourth button. Oops, too far! After all, she wanted him to notice her, not her cleavage. There needs to be something for his imagination. *Yes, this is what I want him to see,* and Jasmine turned to leave the room.

On her way out she stopped and gave her neck a short spritz of perfume, then her wrists, and finally the important spritz between her breasts. Out of her bedroom, down the steps and into the living room she went. Jasmine grabbed her small purse and headed for the door listening to the click of her heels on the tile wishing her good luck as she left.

The photos they exchanged should let him know exactly what she looks like, but, what if the photos he sent are not representative of him? What if he is really older than you; much older? She remembered when she was selecting photos to send to him. The first one was a "few" years old… like 10. Her hair didn't have a hint of grey. Then she got to know him better and sent the more recent photos. He loved all of them.

Each photo resulted in a very flattering compliment. Even the ones of her in her one-piece swimsuit at the beach were met with compliments. *He knows what he is getting and he still wants me? I definitely want him,* Jasmine thought as she walked to her car.

Luke Meets Jasmine

Waiting for her to arrive is like torture, Luke thought to himself. He had been staring down the narrow passage between the bar and the tables against the wall for nearly half an hour. He nervously checked out every woman entering the pub in hopes that she matched the photograph clutched in his hand.

There were many girls in the pub that night, mostly thin college girls looking for their boyfriends or trying to find a boyfriend. They were all the same; perfect hair, the unspoiled figure of an adolescent yet to experience life, and the same bounce in their step.

These were children trying to find their way into womanhood and not having a clue what it was to be beautiful on an individual basis. The only originality they could muster was whether to wear the tan furry Uggs or the black furry Uggs.

Luke was there to meet a woman. Not just any woman, but the lovely lady he'd been chatting with on-line. The pub was getting crowded, and it was becoming hard to see up the long corridor to the door as more and more of these girls began to fill up the pub.

Should I move to a table in the front or stay here? Luke wondered. She had asked him to meet her at the pub and to get a table in the rear.

Suddenly, as if Moses were standing at the water's edge, the sea of children divided. *There she was. This had to be her. Shoulder length hair, lace blouse and black skirt. No this couldn't be her. Where are the 20 extra pounds she said she was carrying? She had obviously left them at home. This was a woman, someone with confidence, and style.* This woman was an alpha female. Lower ranking females sensed it, giving her the space and respect she deserved. Luke watched in disbelief as she moved towards him. He nearly spilled his drink when she stopped at his table.

"Hi, are you Luke?"

This cannot possibly be her. Luke's heart was in his throat as he rose to his feet, came around the table, and extended his hand.

"Yes, nice to meet you. Please have a seat."

He then pulled out her chair. Jasmine felt flushed and a bit disoriented. It had been ages since someone pulled a chair out for her. Luke just stood there holding the back of the chair. Jasmine smiled, swept her hands across her skirt smoothing it as she took her seat. She lifted herself slightly as Luke slid the chair up to the table.

The two talked with Luke hanging on to her every word. They talked about the weather, their children, and other people in the pub until Luke couldn't take it anymore. He had to be alone with her. He asked if she wanted to get something to eat. Jasmine reached out, touched his hand.

Time seemed to stop for Luke as chills shot through his body. His eyes were drawn to her hand. Her long, slender finger lay across his. Luke felt a shudder coursing though him. He had never felt a touch like this before.

"Sure, I know a nice Mexican restaurant a few blocks from here."

He stood, took hold of her hand once again, and watched as she gracefully rose from the chair. Luke turned and led the way through the crowd toward the door.

He used his broad shoulders to separate the crowd. She clutched his waist and drew herself into his back as he nudged people out of the way. Jasmine's head lay against his back, and her hands on his sides seemed to stroke, not squeeze, as he navigated the sea of people.

The feeling was so wonderful that Luke slowed his pace in order to savor the moment. Something began to stir inside his body, and he fought to remain in control. He wanted to just stop right there in the middle of the crowd, turn and kiss her.

You're a gentleman, he reminded himself. *She is a lady, not some tramp.* Luke needed to just slow down and see if he was sensing what he wanted or if she was giving him clues about what she wanted. Only time would tell.

They broke from the crowd, and a small sense of disappointment was felt by Luke. He reached back for her hand and guided her next to him. The night air was brisk, and Luke felt a chill, as goose bumps rose on his arms. Was this due to the cold or the incredible woman whose hand he was holding?

"It's only a few blocks," Jasmine said, and the two began their journey.

Luke was having trouble walking without bumping into the others on the sidewalk; he just couldn't keep his eyes off of Jasmine's lovely face. He listened intently as she told him about how much she enjoyed coming to the restaurant district.

Her lips were full and moved effortlessly as she spoke each word. In no time, the couple reached the restaurant. The hostess seated them at a window table overlooking the street. The waiter appeared and took the drink order, then left the two alone once again.

The chatting continued as they both tried to calm themselves and get their nervousness under control. It could only be described as infatuation, as Luke listened to Jasmine continue to tell him about her life. He could have listened to her all night long. Her voice was like a beautiful symphony.

He watched the words float from her lips to his ears, like notes from a page of music. The waiter interrupted the symphony's third movement.

"Are you ready to order?"

Luke realized he hadn't even opened the menu. He quickly found a burrito and placed his order.

"I'll have the nachos."

Finally, they were alone once again. Luke's hand slowly moved across the table, towards Jasmine's, his fingers taking care not to be too bold. His finger tip touched hers, and once again, he felt the electricity shoot through him. Slowly, their fingers entwined until her fragile hand was in his, and the conversation continued.

Jasmine smiled while trying to conceal her own nervousness. She felt warm and somehow safe with her hand in his. The pounding in her chest began to slow, and she could feel herself beginning to relax. They had spent many hours "talking" on the computer and there really were no secrets being revealed here, only the method of communication was different.

Luke would say something witty and Jasmine would giggle. Jasmine would say something funny and Luke would laugh.

The two watched the young college kids as they paraded past the restaurant, noting how similar the girls look. Creative and individual they are not.

"Look, that one has brown furry Uggs not black like the others" Jasmine remarked.

"Yes a true individual" Luke responds with a chuckle.

They spent several minutes speaking to each other about their lives, likes, and dislikes, until, once again, the waiter appeared, this time with a tray of food. He set the food onto the table and again, they were alone.

Reluctantly, Luke released her hand, so they could eat. The food was good but gone in a flash. They had taken more than an hour to eat, but it passed so fast that it was like they were in a time warp.

Jasmine laughs, Luke speaks, Luke laughs, Jasmine speaks, and suddenly they were ready to move on with the night.

Jasmine began to fuss with her purse, but Luke snatched the check and smiled.

"No date of mine will ever pay a check, the man pays" Luke stated forcefully, and then realized he may be coming on a little strong and chuckles to soften the comment.

"Well, okay for this time, at least." Jasmine had grown used to paying her own way, but the feeling of being treated was nice also.

Luke placed cash onto the table, rose and extended his hand to Jasmine. He assisted her as she rose from her chair, leading them out of the restaurant. Arriving at the curb, Luke was suddenly horrified that he had not prepared for the evening. Now, bashfully, he admitted to Jasmine that in his excitement to meet her, he had made no plans for the evening.

Jasmine sighed softly and realized this was the first time she had seen the vulnerable side of Luke, and she loved it. This was a truly sweet man.

"Do you have a favorite place we could go?" He asked sheepishly.

"There is a club over there" she replied with a grin on her face.

"I've driven past it many times and have always wondered what it was like inside. Some of the girls at work talk about it and it sounds quite interesting. They have three floors for dancing, so you can choose what type of music you want to listen or dance to."

"Would you like to go? It's been a long time since I've been inside a dance club."

"Sure, sounds like fun" and they were off on another adventure.

Luke led Jasmine across the street maintaining his tight grip on her hand. Loud music emanated from the open door as they approached. With Jasmine in tow, Luke pushed his way through the crowd to the dance floor. Most of the dancers were college age kids, moving in ways Luke only wished he could move.

Jasmine and Luke look around the room; each remembering what it was like years and years ago when they were in college. There were couples staring starry-eyed at each other as they moved together, girls dancing apparently alone showing off not only their dance moves, but themselves, as they twisted and turned. Groups of kids gyrating together as they let the beat of the music flow through them.

Luke spotted a set of stairs that appeared to lead to an upper level. He navigated them through the dancing masses over to the steps, and up they went.

The couple reached the top of the stairs, and Luke found a pair of stools along a rail overlooking the dance floor and grabbed them. He helped Jasmine up onto her stool.

"What would you like to drink?"

"Rum and Coke, please" was her answer.

Luke quickly disappeared back into the crowd. When he returned, he stopped in his tracks as he gazed at this beautiful woman. Jasmine was looking down at the dance floor with her foot tapping and her head bobbing to the music.

Luke watched for a moment as her hair bounced, her body moved with such grace that he just stood there in awe. A patron bumped into him knocking him back into reality.

He walked over, slid her drink along the small bar railing until it was in front of her. He grabbed his stool and pulled it over close beside hers. The rhythm of the music was pounding and soon, like Jasmine, Luke's whole body was caught up in the beat.

The two sat and sipped their drinks trying to talk with each other, but the music was so loud they could barely hear. Luke scooted his stool still closer, spreading his legs wide apart and closing the space between them. His hand came to rest on her back. They watched the dancers as his strong hand gently pulled her closer. They were nearly cheek-to-cheek as the fragrance of her perfume filled Luke's head.

"Would you like to dance?" he asked nervously.

"No thanks, I just want to watch and listen for now" she replied.

Jasmine's body felt so good to the touch, that his big hand began to move over her. It slid slowly down to her waist and then up again feeling her ribs and the soft contours of her torso. Luke's left knee joined the exploration as he scooted his stool even closer to her.

The fire that burned inside of Luke was now out of control. He knew he wanted her. He wanted her now, but does she want him? Luke could feel the outline of Jasmine's bra clasp and could not help but wonder if he would be fortunate enough to open it tonight.

His hand seemed to have a mind of its own as it slipped further around Jasmine. It slid down and onto the left side of Jasmine's shapely bottom. *Will she object?* Suddenly becoming concerned that his advances may be too much too soon, his hand froze waiting for some sign of acceptance.

After a long pause, Luke continued his exploration pushing his hand forward onto the top of her thigh then pausing again. *Did he feel a slight pressure against his body?*

She seemed to lean back into him. His hand continued its journey of exploration and started up her torso once again. His fingers traced the soft curves as Jasmine's side melted into her chest. Up and up his hand continued its journey under the cover of darkness in the club.

Suddenly, once again, he freezes, and a soft moan escaped his lips. The sound was hidden from Jasmine by the loud music. Luke could feel the subtle curve of her breast.

My God, I can feel the beginning of her breast, Luke thought to himself. His hand started to tremble. He swore he could hear the rapid beating of his own heart over the pounding music.

The softness and the sensations beneath his finger tips rushed to his brain. His arm tightened as he drew her even closer to him. *This is it,* Luke thought excitedly as he leaned forward and placed that first tentative kiss on Jasmine's cheek.

She turned quickly. Their lips meet for the first time. Soft moist lips pressed together. His right arm extended and cradled her even more as the two somehow maintain their balance on the stools.

Luke's hand slid up and into Jasmine's hair as he tried to pull her even further into their passionate kiss. Her lips part almost immediately as they introduce their tongues to each other. Their tongues seem to dance together as the couple explored each other for the first time.

Luke's tongue explored the inside of her lips, tracing them as he felt her tongue moving into his mouth. The kiss seemed to go on forever. Luke could feel her hot breath on his cheek as she exhaled. Then the coolness as she struggled to draw oxygen into her body. Luke, too, struggled to breathe as his chest rose and fell. Finally, their kiss ended, and Luke looked deep into her eyes.

"Would you like to get out of here?"

Jasmine replied with a simple nod of her head. Luke nearly kicked the stool across the room as he jumped to his feet. His hand extended, helping Jasmine to her feet, then pulled her into him. Once again, they were lost in a passionate kiss.

This time, their tongues seemed to battle for position. Jasmine's was in Luke's mouth exploring, then Luke's was in Jasmine's again. This went on and on as their breathing turned into panting.

Luke's powerful arms locked them into the passionate embrace. Reluctantly, they broke and headed for the club's door.

Once outside, Luke pulled her close to him, and they began to walk. He spotted a store that was closed. The storefront picture windows would provide some shelter from the night's cool breeze. He guided her into the recess, lifted her hand while starring deeply into her eyes, and softly kissed it.

"I wanted to see if you were having the same thoughts as I."

The smile and sparkle was all he needed to see. He pulled her close, and once again, their passion was communicated though a kiss. The feeling was incredible. The softness of her lips and the heat from her body made it impossible for him to control his passion any longer. His lips parted, hers followed, as he received another passionate kiss from Jasmine; the incredible woman he'd waited so long to meet.

Luke slid one hand down her back to pull her even closer the other hand up to her head as his fingers ran through her hair. Their tongues danced as Jasmine's hands roamed over Luke's back. He felts her pulling him tighter. The kiss seemed to last for hours. When they finally broke, they were both gasping for air.

Oh my God, Luke suddenly screamed to himself. *We're moving too fast, we need to slow down. We've only just met, physically,* he reminds himself. All of those long nights chatting with Jasmine could not have prepared him for this incredible woman he was now holding in his arms. He looked deep into her eyes once again and whispered to her.

"You are an incredible, wonderful, and beautiful woman. May I see you again?"

She seemed to take a moment to compose herself, then smiled up at him and with a simple answer.

"Yes."

The couple pulled themselves together and walked to Jasmine's car. Once there, she unlocked it, and Luke stepped in to open the door.

"This night has been incredible," he whispered, as he held her soft hand in his.

"Thank you for such a wonderful evening," Jasmine responded, as she felt her heart pounding within her chest.

A soft kiss on her cheek and Luke held her hand as she gracefully slid behind the wheel. He pushed the door shut and watched, as the woman of his dreams drove off into the night.

Could I be More Alive?

Jasmine guided her car towards home, her mind racing and her body tingling after her incredible night. All of her fears had been wiped away by this wonderful man. His presence put her at ease immediately. His respect for her could be felt the first time their eyes met. The passion, my God, the passion in this man's kiss took her breath away. Jasmine's hands were still trembling as she tried to concentrate on her driving. Her mind returned to the touch of his hand and how it was somehow soothing and yet fiery at the same time.

The butterflies in her stomach could not be ignored, and she pulled the car to the side of the road in an effort to regain her composure. She sat alone in the darkness as she cradled her face in her hands and tried to relax. Jasmine's chest was heaving, her hands shaking, and her stomach was fluttering. She felt as if she couldn't control herself.

Oh my God, am I going to be sick? Jasmine's hand gripped the door handle, just in case. Beads of sweat formed on her forehead, and she was really not sure what would happen next. It was as if she were a teenager again, wondering if mom would notice the flush in her cheeks when she walked in the door.

Her fingers began to trace her lip, touching it ever so softly as she remembered the feel of his lips on her own. It had been years since the last time she was kissed by a man. The memories of the evening poured back into her consciousness. This indeed was a very special night with a very special man.

Calm slowly settled over Jasmine. The flutters in her stomach subsided, breathing slowed, and the trembling was gone from her hands. The thoughts of the night were still vivid in her mind, as she smiled to herself.

With a quick look over her shoulder, she was back on the road headed for home. Jasmine glanced at the clock nestled in the dashboard, ten thirty. She wondered if it was too late to call Mary.

I need to talk to someone. Her hand searched the purse for her cell phone. Finding the phone, Jasmine flipped it open and pressed the speed dial button for Mary. Her mind wandered back to the events of the evening and the wonderful time she had. A smile came across Jasmine's face as she recalled the feel of his hand as it gently held her own.

"Hello," snaps her back to the present as Mary answered the phone.

"Mary, its Jasmine, is it too late?"

"No, never. So how was it?"

"Oh my God, he was a dream, so polite, so interesting, I had a wonderful, wonderful time."

"Well don't stop there, tell me all about it."

"Where do I start?", she said as she turned into her driveway.

"You sure it's not too late?"

"Jasmine, shut up about the time and tell me everything. Don't leave a single thing out" Mary demanded.

"OK, but I just pulled into the garage. Let me park, and I'll call you right back when I get in the house."

"Well, OK. I'll be sitting here next to the phone."

Jasmine snapped the phone shut as she pressed the button on the garage door remote, closing the door behind her. The car door creaked as if to complain about having to be up so late. She exited the car and headed into the house.

On her way through the kitchen, Jasmine dropped her purse onto the counter, pulled the refrigerator door open, and grabbed her favorite bottle of wine. Reaching into the cupboard, she pushed aside the "every day" wine glasses, reaching the back of the shelf. Jasmine carefully retrieved one of the crystal wine glasses her grandmother had given her years ago, and headed for the recliner. The pure tone made when the bottle touched the wine glass's rim was a clue that perhaps her hands had not yet stopped shaking.

These shoes sure are cute, but they just have to come off, she said to herself releasing the tiny buckles and kicking them to the side. Jasmine sighed and stretched her toes in relief. *Oh that feels wonderful.* A quick sip of wine and she reached for the cordless phone and started dialing. After only a single ring, Mary was on the line.

"Well let's hear it" she demanded.

As she sat back into her favorite chair, wine in one hand and the phone in the other, Jasmine started to tell Mary about the entire night.

"Where do I start?"

"Start at the beginning, I want to hear every detail."

"I was so nervous getting ready," Jasmine responded.

"My stomach hadn't flip-flopped like that since I was in high school."

She could hear Mary struggling to disguise her cackling.

"Finally, I got myself together and headed for town. When I got to the pub, I couldn't believe I had told him to meet me there. The place was overflowing with 20-something tarts with perfect hair, perky boobs, and hourglass figures. What was I thinking?" she screeched as she took a gulp of wine.

"Why didn't I pick some place where I would be most comfortable, like the frozen food aisle at the grocery store? I paced back and forth in front of the pub for at least five minutes trying to work up the courage to go in. Finally, I took a deep breath and decided, by God, I have thought of nothing but Luke for weeks now, and I was not going to let a sea of little girls keep me from meeting him!"

Her friend had completely lost it and was now struggling to breathe as Jasmine continued.

"It was awful, my hands were trembling, the butterflies in my stomach had turned into condors, and I swear my knees were shaking. But I made up my mind I was going to do this. I put on my best strut and went in. I could feel all of the girls turn and look at me, checking me out to see if I was a threat to them. I knew the look, I'd given it plenty of times when I was married to Fred. That catty smile that says, Welcome, but keep away from my man! I just held my head high and didn't even give them the time of day. I knew that somewhere at the back of that pub was Luke, and nothing would stop me from finding him."

"MARY!" Jasmine shouted in exasperation, "Stop laughing!"

Her friend attempted once again to hide her total enjoyment of the story.

Once I broke out of the crowd, there he was. My God, Mary, he was so handsome. His mouth was agape, and I choked back a chuckle when he nearly spilled his drink. His picture did not do him justice. When he stood to greet me, he just kept getting taller. He was over six feet and had the most wonderful naturally curly hair. He looked as if he had combed it back, but the unruly curls went where they wanted to go. His face was clean-shaven, and his wonderful blue eyes just seemed to draw me in."

Jasmine had to stop and take another drink of wine. She could feel her own excitement rising as she continued her story.

"His smile was so inviting, much nicer in person than in the photo he e-mailed to me. He wore a nice button up shirt and khaki pants, all freshly pressed. Then he smiled. Mary, oh my God, I wanted to run and jump into his arms. He came out from around the table and pulled out my chair! Do you know how long it's been since someone pulled a chair out for me?"

"Slow down Jasmine. You are talking so fast I can barely understand you."

"I sat down, and when he walked back to his seat, I got my first peek at that butt of his. You know I've always been a "butt woman." It was round and wonderful. I just wanted to reach out and pinch it just to make sure it was real. My head was spinning. I could feel my heart racing, and I haven't had that much movement in my stomach since I was in labor!"

"Jasmine, he sounds wonderful," a more composed, yet still giggling, Mary responded.

"When he spoke, his soft, yet deep, tone immediately settled both my nerves and my stomach. I hung on his every word. His voice was low and confident. It seemed to penetrate right to my soul. It was like we were in that pub alone. We sat there for I'm not sure how long, talking about anything and everything. I was willingly drowning in those pools of blue and feeling wonderful."

Once again, Jasmine took a drink of her wine. She needed something to moisten her throat as she continued.

"Finally, he asked if I was hungry, and I took a chance. I reached out and touched his hand. The electricity shot, well, you know where, and I had to fight, not to gasp. All those times we chatted on-line, my fingers trembled as I typed; dreaming about what it would be like to be with him. Oh my God, I nearly had an orgasm right there at the table!"

Jasmine was so excited at this point she was leaning forward in the recliner. She looked more like a football fan watching his team during the last two minutes of the game than a woman discussing her first date in ten years.

"He was so romantic on-line, but he was even more romantic in person. His hand was soft and warm. I couldn't help myself; my thumb started stroking the back of his hand, feeling every hill and valley as it moved. I suggested Jose's for dinner, and he said ok."

Mexican? You could go anywhere you wanted, and your suggestion was Mexican?" Mary questioned.

"He was up in a flash and helped me with my chair, then took my hand and lifted me to my feet. He was such a gentleman. He plowed his way through the crowd with me in tow, and I reached around him and held on tightly. My God, Mary, the power I could feel in his body as he pushed his way through the crowd. When I pulled myself tightly against his back, I felt like I was on the back of Fred's Harley again. Once we got outside, Luke took my hand and we walked to Jose's, talking the entire way. He was just the same as he was on-line: charming, funny, and such a gentleman."

Jasmine reached over and refilled her glass. Her mouth was dry, and the more she spoke, the more excited she got.

"When we got to Jose's, I reached for the door, and he said, "No, please allow me," and opened the door for me. The hostess showed us to our table, and once again, he helped me with my chair. I felt so special. He's just such a gentleman. You know how long it's been since I've felt special? The longer I was with him, the more I wanted him. I've fantasized about him so many times during the long nights after one of our chat sessions. I could not help the tingles I was feeling, nor did I want to. It was wonderful to feel excited again, fidgeting in the chair as the electricity shot through my body. It's been so long since I wanted a man. Since my divorce, I've made a life out of pushing men away, not wanting their attention. But Luke, my God I wanted him. I wanted to feel his hands running over my body. My nipples were on fire, and my panties, damp the entire night. It was like I was alive again."

"Jasmine, slow down" Mary said in a soothing voice.

"You've only just met him. Take your time and really get to know him before you do something crazy."

"From Jose's, we went to that club I heard about, with the three floors of dancing. It was great. The sound of the music, watching the couples, imagining it was us out there. He asked me to dance a couple of times, but I just wanted to sit and enjoy the music. He took me up to the second floor balcony where we got a table along the rail. We could see the band and watch the couples as they moved on the dance floor. Luke got us drinks, and then he sat on the stool next to me. He kept getting closer and closer until finally he was snuggled in so closely, he actually had one leg on either side of me."

"Wow, now that's hot" Mary said breathlessly.

Hold that thought Jasmine, I need to get something to drink. Jasmine took the time to pour the last glass of wine from her bottle.

"Ok, continue Jasmine."

"He wrapped his arm around me, and I thought I would die. I could feel his muscles flexing as he pulled me in. His hand was stroking up my back and then down my side. My heart was racing as I sat there, very still, actually never wanting him to stop. I thought I felt Luke's hand ever so lightly stroke across my bottom. Soon he placed it gently onto my outer thigh, and I thought I would scream. I dare not move for fear I might just throw him to the floor and take him right there in the club. My nipples were pressing so hard into my bra that I thought they might just jump off my chest. When his hand was on my thigh, I have never been so wet. I could feel him leaning into me, and I just had to kiss him. When I turned my head, there he was, and I did it! I kissed him! Oh, his lips were so soft. I could feel him tremble as we kissed. Mary, this is it! He is the one, I can feel it! While we were kissing, the world stopped. There was no band. The other people in the club seemed fade away. Not a sound in the world, just us, locked in the most passionate kiss you could imagine. So many nights while we chatted, I wanted to feel him kiss me, and now that I was feeling it, it was unbelievable."

The phone fell silent as Jasmine paused. Her mind wandered back to the club and Luke's arms wrapped around her.

"Jasmine!" Mary shouted into the phone, "Don't stop now. What happened next? I'm sitting here panting. I have to know what happened!"

"He helped me off of the stool, and we left."

"You left? Where did you go? Did you...?", Mary stammered.

"Mary, I wanted him. I wanted him in the worst way. When we got outside we started walking towards our cars. My whole body was alive with excitement! He pulled me into a doorway and we kissed again. The passion locked within this man is indescribable. I was completely under his spell. I would have made love to him right there on the street if he'd wanted to."

Mary could feel her friend's excitement as she told her story. It was almost like Mary was standing next to her as she and Luke embraced in that dark doorway.

"Suddenly, he pulled away. His eyes met mine, and it was like we were wired together. I'm sure he could see my soul. Somehow, I could feel his need to slow down. The passion within him was fighting with his rational side. I watched as he got himself under control. He told me I was a wonderful and beautiful woman. Then asked if he could see me again."

"Well, what did you say?" prodded Mary.

"My mind was totally blank, and my mouth refused to work. Finally, I took a deep breath and replied yes. With that, he took me by the hand and walked me to my car. My knees were weak, my heart was racing. Somehow, he got me into my car, gave me one last kiss and stepped back. He waved as I drove away. Mary what an incredible night I had. He is even dreamier in person than on-line. Luke was such a gentlemen, and so attentive and considerate. I need to send him an e-mail and thank him for tonight. My hands just need to stop shaking so I can type. I'll see you in the morning. I need to go write my e-mail and get to bed. Thank you; I never would have met Luke if you hadn't shown me the net."

With that Jasmine, logged onto her computer and sent Luke a message, trying to convey in words what she had felt that night in her heart:

Dear Luke,

I wanted to thank you for a truly wonderful evening. I can't remember the last time I had so much fun. The pub was great, meal excellent, club wonderfully exciting, not to mention the stimulating company, lol.

You are even more than I expected after so many hours of chatting.

I hope we can get together again soon.

I'll be on-line tomorrow evening and hope to see you there.

Jasmine.

Will He Call

Mary was waiting at the shop the next morning when Jasmine arrived. Jasmine walked through the door with a bounce in her step and a smile that stretched from ear to ear. She was a very positive person, always wearing a smile, but this smile was different. This was the smile of a woman smitten.

Mary had started Madge's perm, and the aroma of perm solution was strong in the air. Dianna was seated, patiently waiting for her wash, cut, and color. Both Madge and Dianna were regulars and well aware of Jasmine's adventure the night before. The fact that they had both scheduled their appointments for the day after her big date was no coincidence.

The ladies waited while Jasmine stood next to her chair, turned to the wall and snapped to attention. She raised her hand, gesturing the morning salute, perhaps with a little extra attitude today.

"Oh, thank God you're finally here!" Madge said as she leaned forward in the chair.

"Mary just keeps telling us to ask you. We know she knows something, but she won't spill her guts!"

Dianna put down her magazine, jumped up, and scurried over to Jasmine.

"Good morning, Jasmine. Tell us. Oh, please tell us! Did he look like his picture? Was he tall?"

Madge being a little more mature got right to the point.

"His butt, did he have a nice butt? Come on Jasmine, spill it!"

Jasmine just smiled, put her purse into the cabinet, turned, and gave Dianna a coy smile.

"Well now, that was a cut and color wasn't it Dianna?"

"Now come on." injects Mary.

"We've been talking about this for a week." she said with a wink.

Jasmine was determined to relish in the attention. It had been nine long years since she had been on a date, and she was not about to kiss and tell. *Well, not without a little drama,* she thought to herself. Each time she thought about last night's adventure, she felt a little tingle come over her.

"Was he as gentlemanly as he claimed to be?" asked Dianna.

"Let's just say I didn't open a single door or pull out a chair the entire evening. And let me tell you something ladies, his picture did not prepare me for just how blue his eyes were. They are so blue, I just wanted to climb into them and stay there," Jasmine beamed.

"His butt; did he have one of those butts that just made you drool?" insisted Madge.

"Oh Madge, every butt makes you drool," Mary laughed.

"You bet it does. Hank's butt is beginning to sag a bit, and I really like a firm grabbable butt. Did you kiss him?" Madge asked in her typically blunt way.

"Madge! Stop that," Jasmine remarked as she continued to wash Dianna's hair.

Dianna sat up from her wash.

"Did you say you kissed him?"

"I said no such thing," Jasmine said indignantly.

Mary just smirked, choking back a laugh.

"Lie back down, Dianna, you're getting water on the floor," Jasmine ordered in a mocking tone.

"When I saw him sitting there in the pub, he looked like a dream. From his curly hair down to his broad shoulders, he just took my breath away. Yes, he looked just like his picture only better. When I walked up to the table, he immediately stood up and moved my chair for me." Jasmine said with a starry look in her eyes.

"Wait a minute," Dianna said, rising up again.

"Darn you! I can't hear with the water running! What did he do?"

"Oh just sit up, Dianna, I'm done rinsing anyway," Jasmine said with a laugh.

"I said, he pulled out my chair," as she wrapped a towel around Dianna's head.

"Oh my God did you sleep with him?" Madge asks leaning forward hanging on Jasmine's answer.

"Was he good? Did he have a nice butt?"

"Madge, if you don't behave, I won't tell you anything!" Jasmine answered sternly.

"Madge, you really need to get that husband of yours some Viagra® before you drive us all crazy," Mary said with a giggle.

"He was just so handsome. His broad shoulders, and oh, that curly hair! But what really got me was his soft smile and deep blue eyes. The photo he sent me did not do him justice. When he started to talk, his voice pierced me and sent little electric shocks to all the right places. It got so hot in that pub, that I just had to get out for some air. Thank God he asked me if I wanted to get something to eat."

"He was up in a flash, helping me out of my chair. The pub had gotten very crowded, so he had to push his way through. I just wrapped my arms around his waist and held on as he plowed his way through the crowd," Jasmine said with a sigh.

"Plowed, I would've been thinking about him plowing something too," Madge giggled.

"Whack her with that brush Mary!" Jasmine demanded.

"Ouch," echoed across the salon, as Mary carried out the order with a laugh.

"But it sure was nice to wrap my arms around him and snuggle into his back. I drew in a deep breath and filled my head with his wonderful scent."

Jasmine paused as she relived the moment.

"Once outside, we walked and talked until we got to the restaurant. I felt like I was in high school again, reaching out to him every chance I got just to touch him. I felt like I was on fire if you know what I mean? I just could not take my eyes off of him, nor did I want to."

Jasmine was glowing, as she told her story, and each one of her friends was sharing her joy in their own way. Madge enjoyed the excitement and anticipation of what she was sure would come next. Madge had complained often that her husband just wasn't physical anymore. She was the most senior of the ladies, and at 65, was wondering how to recapture some of her youthful wild times.

Dianna dreamed that she was the one being wowed by this handsome man. Dianna was in her mid forties and usually just listened, but listened intently every time someone told one of their stories, especially Madge.

Dianna had married her high school sweetheart and immediately started her family. She spent her life as a housewife and mother. She had never ventured past the city limits, living an extremely sheltered life. Dianna often wondered what it would have been like to travel and do some of the things the girls talked about.

Mary was still quite wild. She would often take off on her Harley and just ride, seeing what the world would bring to her. There had been many men in her life, some close, some not. Mary was a free spirit in the purest sense of the word. There was nothing she wouldn't try… once.

Mary was happy for her friend, and relished in the transformation she had finally accomplished. It had taken many months, but she had finally gotten Jasmine out of her isolation. Jasmine had avoided intimacy for so long, but Mary knew there was a wonderfully exciting woman locked inside and she wanted to let her out. Mary knew just what a wonderful exciting woman her friend had been before the divorce, and was determined to see that woman again.

"So, what is new with you, Dianna? We barely said hello this morning," Jasmine said wanting to pay attention to her customer.

"Is your daughter still doing well in school?"

"She made national honor role again last semester. Every time she's been eligible, she's been selected"

"Wow, that's great Dianna. You should be so proud. Does she have a date for the prom?" asked Jasmine.

"Not yet, but she has her eye on a boy that she is hoping will ask her."

"I'm sorry, Dianna, but let's get back to Jasmine's night with the hottie," Madge interrupts.

"Now Madge, don't be rude, Dianna was speaking," Jasmine said as she tried, in vain, to keep the conversation under some sort of control.

The ring of the telephone interrupted Jasmine. She put down her scissors to answer.

"Good morning, Jasmine's. How may I help you?"

A very strange look came over her. She quickly turned away from everyone.

"Well, good morning to you; too," she swooned into the phone.

Everything in the salon stopped. Mary stared. Madge and Dianna sat up in their chairs. Each lady strained to hear the conversation.

"Well, I had a wonderful time, also," Jasmine said in a low shy voice.

"Why, yes, I can be free then. Sure, I'm looking forward to it. Great, see you then. Bye."

Jasmine hung up the phone and leaned back against the counter for a moment. Not a word was spoken in the salon as each of the ladies waited to hear what had just happened.

Suddenly, Jasmine's eyes widen. Her smile grew to fill her face.

"He wants to take me on a picnic lunch in the park tomorrow! Oh-my-God, he called! I just knew he would!"

Jasmine could not contain the excitement she felt as she twirled Dianna around in her chair.

"Mary, pinch me. Am I awake? This must be a dream!"

Jasmine's mind and emotions were out of control with excitement as she danced around the salon. Each of the ladies beamed as they shared in Jasmine's excitement.

"Is he picking you up?" asked Mary.

"Yes, at 11:30 tomorrow. Can you watch the salon for me Mary? Joan is scheduled for a perm. Can you cover it? Mary, please say you can cover it!"

Mary hesitated for a bit, if only for dramatic effect, and then, smiled at her friend.

"Of course I can Jasmine, you know I'll cover for you no matter what it takes."

"Thanks, Mary, you are a life saver."

The questions about the call continued.

"Can he dance?" Dianna asked.

"Who cares if he can dance? His butt, does he have a nice butt?" Madge said excitedly.

The conversation continued all day long in the salon as customer after customer came in and insisted on hearing about the night before. Each time Jasmine told the story, she seemed to float a little higher off of the floor.

The last customer finally left, and Jasmine twisted the lock on the front door. Together, they had made it through another successful day at Jasmine's. Mary swept up, as Jasmine counted out the money in the register and prepared the deposit for the day. Mary came over to her friend and the two ladies embraced.

"I'm so happy for you Jasmine. He sounds wonderful."

"By the way," Mary's voice got quite serious for a minute. Jasmine gave her friend a puzzled look. She recognized when she was about to say something serious.

"I know, I know!" Jasmine interrupted. "Go slow, and be careful. I will Mary. It will be difficult, but I will."

Mary chuckled.

"Well, that wasn't what I was going to say, but, that too."

Jasmine paused and waited for her friend to speak.

"I've been meaning to ask you if I could do something special for my neighbor, Toni. She is about to begin chemo. She asked me if I would cut her hair for her. She would like me to shave her head rather than watch it fall out. She's embarrassed and doesn't really want to answer the questions that will surely come if she has it done during normal hours. Would it be OK if I do it for her after hours on Saturday?"

"Is this someone I know, Mary?" Jasmine asked with deep concern in her voice.

"No, she is my new neighbor, and while we were talking at the mail box, she found out I was a stylist and asked if I would do this, quietly, as a favor to her."

"That is so sad. Of course you can, Mary. Take your time and lock up when you're done."

Lunch Anyone

Jasmine arrived at the shop the next morning, as she always had, with one exception; she carried a fresh outfit neatly assembled on a hanger. She had left her room a shambles, having tried on everything she owned. She wanted just the right look for the picnic later that day.

Jasmine wanted to look her best for Luke. She had to dig deep into her closet to find what she wanted. Long ago, she had pushed her cute clothes to the back of her closet.

She finally settled on her black jeans and red shirt. She had put on a few pounds since the last time she wore them, but they did fit. The shirt was a bit clingy, and the jeans a little snug, but, when she put the outfit together and looked into the mirror, she liked what she saw.

The way the clothes hugged her many curves made her smile. Tiny, dangly, red heart earrings, red socks and her casual black shoes completed the outfit. She was sure today would be another wonderful adventure with Luke.

The day moved along with the speed of a snail, as she kept checking the clock. It seemed like she was stuck in slow motion. Jasmine was in the middle of cutting Bridget's hair, her 9:00 appointment, trying to concentrate on what Bridget had to say. Her mind kept wandering back to thoughts of Luke and the wonderful things that had happened on their date.

"So Jasmine, what do you think?" asked Bridget.

"Sorry, Bridget, what did you say?"

"Do you think I should get a perm next time?"

"No, Bridget, you have lovely silky hair. I think you look terrific. We'll just try a different style next time, if you would like. Think about what you would want, and we'll do it."

"Mary, is that clock broken?" Jasmine whispered.

Jasmine took a breath and continued with Bridget's cut, trying not to look at the clock.

"Jasmine," Mary called across the shop. "Phone for you," Mary said with a wink.

Jasmine's eyes lit up, and she nearly ran the ten steps to the phone, sliding like a pet cat and crashing into the cabinet as she reached for the phone.

"Oh yes, Mary just dropped something," Jasmine said with a wink towards Mary.

Mary just shook her head choking back the laughter.

"Oh sure, Mary dropped something" came loudly across the shop accompanied by laughter from the girls.

Jasmine shook her hand at them and continued.

"Hi. How nice of you to call."

Jasmine swooned around like a teenager as she listened.

"Sure that sounds great, I'll be ready. See you soon."

As her hand set the phone onto its base, the girls start firing questions.

"Who was that?"

Jasmine just smiled and ignored them all as she turned towards Mary. A beaming smile filled her face. The flush in Jasmine's cheeks made it obvious to Mary who was on the phone. A glance at the clock said time was short.

"How are you coming with Bridget?" Mary whispered to Jasmine.

"Nearly finished, if I can just concentrate; just the comb out is left" answered a somewhat flustered Jasmine.

Jasmine returned to Bridget, and with a little mousse and some expert comb work, she was complete. Jasmine swiveled her around, so she was facing the mirror. The hand mirror moved skillfully from side to side, so she could see the back. A smile and nod and another masterpiece was complete.

Jasmine unsnapped and swung the silk shawl off of Bridget's shoulders. Hair clippings showered to the floor, and Bridget was on her way. Jasmine smiled and thanked her for coming. She collected the money and shut the cash drawer. As soon as the door closed behind Bridget, Jasmine was on a dead run for the office.

She kicked the door shut and striped off her work smock and slacks. Quickly, she raised an arm and checked her deodorant; all is well. Jasmine grabbed her red shirt and slipped it over her head. She struggled to pull up her jeans, but with a few jumps and tugs, they slipped over her hips. Sucking in her stomach, her fingers finally manage to pull her zipper shut.

Huffing and puffing, she looked at herself in the mirror. A quick check of her makeup, and she exploded from the office leaving her clothes flung everywhere. The office looked more like a teenage girl's bedroom than an office: clothes, hairspray, and makeup strewn everywhere.

Jasmine paused in front of Mary. She waited impatiently for the approving comment. Mary pointed at her chest with a grin. Jasmine realized that she forgot to button the blouse. Shaking her head, she quickly closed up the shirt and headed for the door.

She tried not to hover, but she could barely stand the wait. Jasmine paced back and forth, peaking through the curtains, looking back at the clock then to the curtains again. Jasmine walked back to her station and nervously straightened the bottles on the shelf.

She looked over at her friend for reassurance. Her hands were shaking, her stomach fluttering as she attempted to deal with her excitement.

"I need to change! These pants are just too tight. They make my butt look huge! And this shirt, what was I thinking? You can see every bulge. The last time he saw me it was dark, now it's light! I just have to change that's all there is to it!"

Mary smiled a reassuring smile.

"Jasmine, now calm down, you look terrific."

Mary grabbed a red scarf from a small rack on the counter and tied it into Jasmine's hair.

"It's a bit windy today. He will love what he sees; beside, I think it's too late. A car just pulled up out front."

"Oh my God!" Jasmine cried out.

"Where is my purse? Got to go ladies!" and she headed for the door.

Luke's outstretched hand was about to touch the door knob when Jasmine pulled it open. Luke jumped back as the door swung out of reach.

Caught off guard, he quickly composed himself. He was struggling not to look too anxious, and here was Jasmine, blasting out the door like a kid on the last day of school.

He recomposed himself and smiled at Jasmine. She gave him a quick peck on the cheek, and they were off on their adventure.

Mary and the other ladies struggled to get a glimpse of Luke, but all they could see was a tall man walking away with an excited woman on his arm. It was eerily like watching Dorothy heading down the yellow brick road.

"This is like watching my daughter leave on her first real date," one of the ladies commented.

Mary just smiled and mumbled to herself, *You have a wonderful time, my dear friend. Find not only yourself, but what you've been missing.*

Luke opened the car door for Jasmine. She slipped into the seat, and they were gone.

The ride was short. Luke and Jasmine made small talk, discussing the weather, how their day had gone, even recalling the nice chat they had last night after work. Jasmine felt quite comfortable, and the butterflies in her stomach were beginning to quiet as they pulled up to the park.

Luke came around and opened the door for Jasmine, extended his hand, and helped her out. He then opened the trunk and gathered up a very large wicker basket. Across the top lay a red and black checkered blanket. The long handle on the basket was perfect for Luke to hold in one hand while reaching for Jasmine with the other. Hand in hand, they walked down the dirt path, passing lovely flowering bushes as they wound through the park.

"I thought we could eat by the lake, if you don't mind?"

"Sounds lovely," Jasmine replied as she enjoyed the firmness of his grip.

Her mind began to wander as she envisioned herself in another time. She was the lovely princess with her handsome knight. Hand-in-hand, they strolled along the edge of the kingdom. The lovely princess patiently waited for him to sweep her off her feet and whisk her away to his castle.

Jasmine loved to read stories of knights and fair maidens. Two of her favorites were the stories of King Arthur and Robin Hood. She could readily picture herself as Guinevere or Maid Marian.

Jasmine would often close her eyes and dream of her own knight one day coming for her. She loved romance and chivalry, but had long ago given up on these childish fantasies ever coming true.

Luke was a very old-fashioned man who believed in treating a woman as a lady. His desire was for a woman that wanted to be treated special. One who would allow him to open the door, wait for him as he assisted with her chair, and understand why he rose when she entered the room. Yes, Luke was old-fashioned and would often comment: *Chivalry is not dead! It is wounded badly, but definitely not dead.*

The couple strolled along the path, weaving in and out of nature's glory. Flowering bushes, canopies of green, and the occasional carpet of wild flowers graced the path. Finally, they crested a hill, and what opened up to them was so beautiful, it took Jasmine's breath away.

The lake was like blue crystal. The water shimmering in the noonday sun reminded her of the blue in Luke's eyes. Geese floated lazily along its edge. Thick green grass covered the bank and moved slowly up the incline toward a wonderful stand of maple trees. It was a postcard. A private postcard created just for them.

Luke led Jasmine to a beautiful spot a few yards from the water's edge. He stopped and spread the large blanket onto the ground.

"This is a special place for a special woman. Come my lady and sit with me."

With her hand in his, Luke helped her down onto the blanket.

Jasmine worked to settle onto the blanket next to Luke.

Why did I wear these jeans? My God I can hardly breathe and I'm not sure, but I think I heard the butt seam making noise. That's all I need is to have my butt explode out of my pants. O God let the seam hold, Jasmine prayed.

Luke opened the large basket and proceeded to lay out a fantastic lunch. There was fresh cut fruit arranged neatly on a plate; cheeses cubed and arranged in circles of color. Next, he pulled out sliced meats as well as sliced tomatoes, lettuce, and even onions. Finally, two large baguettes and a cutting board emerged from the basket.

"No picnic is complete without wine," Luke said.

He reached into the basket and pulled out two crystal wine glasses. A lovely bottle of sweet red wine followed.

Jasmine didn't know what to think. She had been expecting a peanut butter and jelly sandwich with a couple of Cokes®, not this. Luke is something special, she noted to herself, as she stared in wonder at this treasure she had discovered.

The two sat eating, laughing, talking, and sipping wine in the noonday sun. The more time Jasmine spent with Luke, the more he amazed her. Everything he did made her feel special, from opening her door to simply the way he looked at her and spoke to her. She felt like she had never felt before in her life.

He was so spontaneous and so creative. He remembered things that she had told him months ago during their chat sessions. Sweet red wine was her favorite, she loved baguettes. Little things, sometimes tiny things, that she scarcely remembered telling him, he took note of.

The afternoon could not have been better. The honking of the geese in the background, his deep laugh, and the warmth of the sun all combined to make Jasmine feel like she was alive. Even the geese had left the water and were milling around the shoreline. Their large bodies and long necks lost some of their grace as they moved onto the shore.

The largest goose, a big male, was honking loudly as it strutted along the shoreline. He seemed to be keeping the rest of the geese in line. His wanderings were moving closer to the couple, and his honking becoming louder.

"Think he wants us to move?" Jasmine questioned.

"We were here first. Sorry, my friend, you just need to go back to the lake. Shoo, shoo."

Luke motioned, trying to move the goose away. He had come extremely close now, and there was some concern that he may interrupt the wonderful day.

"I'll be right back," Luke said, as he rose and began to move toward the goose.

The goose moved off, and after a few steps, Luke turned back towards Jasmine.

"Look out!" screamed Jasmine.

Just as Luke turned, the goose lunged forward punching Luke in the side, knocking him off balance, and he crashed to the ground.

"I've had enough of this!"

Luke looked for something to use to shoo the goose away. He grabbed for the extra baguette and wielded it like a sword. Turning toward the goose, he proceeded to enter into a battle.

Suddenly, Jasmine found herself in of one of her daydreams. The dragon screeched and puffed its chest, as its long neck moved from side to side, attempting to identify the brave knight's weakness. The knight, with his mighty sword clutched in his powerful hand, stared at the beast watching its every move.

The dragon lunged forward as the brave knight countered with a powerful swing of his sword, narrowly missing the beast. The knight spotted weakness and thrust his sword toward the dragon's chest, only to miss as the beast flared its mighty wings and jumped to the side. The dragon emitted a powerful screech that seemed to freeze the brave knight momentarily.

A viscous lunge and the powerful jaws of the beast drew blood from the knight's arm. The knight retreated, momentarily taking note of his wound. A fire of determination could be seen in his eyes as he lifted his head and stared into the dark eyes of the dragon. A quiet pause came over the lake. Everyone knew the battle had taken a new turn. This would not be an easy fight, and the dragon had drawn first blood.

The knight retaliated with a powerful swing of his sword catching the beast on the side of the head, sending it whirling towards the water's edge. The knight, seeing his opening, brought the battle to the beast. With powerful swings of his sword, he kept the dragon off balance. Retaliatory wild lunges from the beast drove the knight back onto his heels. Amazing blocks by the knight foiled the snaps of the dragon's powerful jaws.

"Be careful," came from the maiden, as she feared for her brave knight's life.

The dragon had the advantage near the water, and quickly, the animal outflanked the knight. Now, with the water at his back and the fierce beast between himself and his maiden, the knight knew things were extremely dangerous. One false move could not only lose the battle, but, more importantly, expose the maiden to the beast.

He paused to ask God for his blessing; he knew that within the next few moments, he would surely either defeat the beast, or die himself.

"Oh Lord, guide my sword as I protect this fair maiden."

With the prayer, the knight concentrated on the beast's chest, focusing on that small place where its armor seemed to be weak. With all his might, he lunged, and the sword struck home. The beast screamed, then turned and fled the battle, heading somewhere we know not, a place where the beast could heal, and return to fight another day.

The brave knight staggered back to the maiden with his sword damaged; large pieces of the blade having been bitten off by the dragon's powerful jaws. His muscular arm, bloodied during the battle, needed loving attention. He gripped the weathered sword with his powerful hand. A trickle of blood moved between his fingers and onto the sword. The blood that was slowly dripping from his hand, bore evidence of just how vicious the battle had been.

She reached out, took the battered sword from his bloodied hand and laid it onto the soft grass. Holding his hand in hers, she placed a kiss upon it. The maiden pulled the scarf from her hair, wet it, and then gently wrapped her brave knight's wound. Staring into his eyes, she leaned forward and touched her lips to his.

Has her brave knight finally arrived? Could the many years of waiting and searching be over? Could this be the one she has waited for to fill her life, to finally make her complete? As her lips pressed to his, the warm rays of the sun showered down upon them. Her hand instinctively moved up and into his curly locks as she drew him closer. When she pulled away and opened her eyes, once again, she saw the shining face of her brave knight smiling tenderly.

"Are you alright?" Jasmine whispered.

"It's just a scratch. I'm so sorry about the way this turned out today. I wanted everything to be perfect, but hadn't bargained for this."

Jasmine pulled Luke close and kissed him again.

"This could not have been more perfect," she said with a soft smile on her face.

"Everything was wonderful, everything."

With that, they packed up the picnic basket, folded the blanket, and headed back for the car and reality.

Another Chance

That night, at the appointed time, Jasmine logged onto her computer. Her Instant Messenger opened automatically as Mary had set it up to do. There he was. Luke's icon blinked at her, indicating he was online and patiently awaiting her arrival. Their lunch had begun wonderfully, but ended in a very bizarre way. She could not recall ever experiencing something so beautiful, frightening, sweet, and yet hilariously funny, all at the same time.

Had she finally found the brave knight from her youth? Was this Sir Luke? The warmth that she felt simply seeing his icon was unmistakable. The trembling in her fingers, as she guided her mouse, could not be denied. Luke was definitely something special. Jasmine opened his IM window only to be greeted by Luke's message. Anxiously she slid the mouse over and clicked; opening the session.

Luke:

> Sorry for the way things turned out today. I had no idea a goose could be so aggressive. Will you allow me to make it up to you?

Jasmine:

> Are you ok, my brave knight, lol?
> How are your wounds healing?

Jasmine's smile beamed as she waited for his response.

Luke:

> Lol, yes I am. My ego is slightly bruised, but it too, will heal

Luke shook his head at the computer monitor as he blushed with embarrassment, and gently stroked his arm.

Jasmine:

> You were so brave out there defending me, and even though the powerful attacker put up a strong fight, in the end, my knight was triumphant, lol

Jasmine quickly returned to her childhood fantasy world, only this time, she had a face to put on her brave knight.

Luke:

> I did do quite well in my baguette fighting class in college. My superior intellect and cunning wit allowed me to dispatch the beast in short order. I only hope it didn't frighten my lady.

Luke recognized Jasmine's fantasy and played along as the two assumed their rolls.

Jasmine:

> She was concerned for her brave knight's life, but knew that he would somehow defeat the beast and return to her, lol.

Luke:

> Let me make it up to you Jasmine. I can be there in 40 minutes. We could go out for dinner and dancing tonight. It's still early.

Jasmine fidgeted in her chair and tried to be coy, not wanting to reveal to Luke just how badly she wanted to see him again.

Jasmine:

Well, I did just get home from work, and it IS Friday... Can you guarantee my safety?

I'm glad this isn't a video chat. The giggling, blushing, and fidgeting would definitely give away my true feelings. Jasmine wasn't sure she wanted Luke to know just how much she had fallen for him, at least not until she was more certain that the feelings were mutual.

Luke:

Yes, my fair maiden, I will guarantee your safety. I have dispatched the beast, and the village is safe once again.

Jasmine:

LOL, you are so funny

By this time, however, Jasmine found herself fully immersed in the fantasy of the knight and fair maiden.

Luke:

Will you come with me then?

Jasmine:

I don't know, I need to clean up, my house is a mess. I really should stay home.

Luke:

Oh, come now, surely those things can wait.

Jasmine:

Ok, but I need to go get ready. How about 7:00-- will that work for you?

Luke:

7:00 it is my lady. Your carriage will arrive precisely at 7:00. See you then.

Luke:

Jasmine, I've missed you

Jasmine:

I've missed you, too, Luke. See you soon

Jasmine shut down her computer and dashed for the shower. *Better put a fresh shave on these legs*, she said to herself as she grabbed a new razor, and her favorite scented body wash, and off to the shower she went. Jasmine performed the miracle, as only ladies can. She was out of the shower in a flash with a towel wrapped around her.

In a flurry of activity, Jasmine rushed to get ready. The ritual of hair, teeth, and makeup seemed to flow without a hitch. Not a lot of time left, and Jasmine felt the pressure as she stood before her closet. Selecting the outfit kept her scurrying as she raced to pull herself together. Settling on a nice skirt and blouse combination, the pile of clothes on the bed bore witness to the many discarded choices. Time was short, but finally, she was ready.

Down the steps she went, glancing at herself in the wall mirror, when suddenly, there is a knock on the door. Almost on cue, the mantel clock began to chime. *He is prompt, I'll give him that, Jasmine thought to herself. Do I holler come in like a trailer park hussy? Maybe, I let him stand there for awhile?* Jasmine paused at the bottom of the steps, wondering what to do next.

Outside, Luke took a deep breath and attempted to pull himself together. *I can't let her see me like this. Pull yourself together man!* Luke's inner voice gave him the pep talk he needed to knock on the door a second time.

Jasmine, on the other side of the door, gasped as she peered through the peep hole. *God, he's so good looking.* Finally, excitement overtook her, and she opened the door. In spite of her trembling hands and fluttering stomach, Jasmine presented a confident woman to Luke.

Luke could not believe his eyes. Jasmine was a vision as she stood in the doorway. Suddenly, he became aware that he'd frozen and snapped himself back to reality.

"Jasmine, you look ravishing tonight."

Luke extended his hand, and they were off. On their way to the restaurant, the couple playfully bantered back and forth. Once again, acting more like teenagers than the adults they were. The restaurant was lovely. The food was exceptional, but nothing could draw Luke's eyes from Jasmine. He was simply mesmerized by her beauty and grace. Jasmine kept her own eyes focused on Luke, letting herself become lost in his charm. She could barely breathe as he reached across the table and took her hand in his.

Jasmine slid her foot out of her shoe and began to move it towards Luke's leg. She'd never done it before, but found it quite sexy when she saw it in a movie. Slowly, she inched her foot towards Luke. She felt something solid and began to slowly move her leg up and down. When Luke showed no reaction, she was puzzled. In the movies, the man's eyes always bugged out, and he could scarcely breathe. Jasmine was reconsidering her advance when she realized she'd been stroking the leg of the table. It was she who suddenly smiled, nearly laughing out loud at herself.

"What's so funny, Jasmine?"

"Oh, I just recalled that goose."

Jasmine needed something to deflect his questions, and yesterday provided a cornucopia of explanations for a sudden smile. She removed her foot from the table leg and resumed her search. Finally, she found her target. Her toes worked ever so subtly. His leg felt muscular as she stroked. Her toes curled, not from effort, but rather, from pure excitement.

She watched as Luke began to fidget. She knew he was falling under her spell. Luke struggled to maintain his composure and mystique as a gentleman, but his red face and trembling hands gave him away. The two were but a few feet apart as they began making love with their eyes. Each recalled the passion of their last date. Each sought to pick up where they had left off.

Once they finished the meal, Jasmine and Luke strolled down the street, hand-in-hand, laughing and talking as they walked in the cool night air. Luke guided them down a narrow, dimly lit, street. He paused under a street light and pulled Jasmine to him. His hand cupped her cheek as he gazed into her eyes that sparkled in the dim light.

"You are so beautiful," he whispered. "I just had to look at you."

Luke then pressed a soft kiss onto her waiting lips. The couple embraced for a moment - a long moment. Luke, ever so gently, moved away, and once again, their adventure resumed. They rounded the corner, and a well weathered, neon sign flickered in the night. 'Jazz' is all it said. One of the Zs flickered, giving away its age.

"Wow, you really need to know where this Is, or you would never find it," Jasmine whispered, feeling the need to keep her voice down.

She was not sure why she whispered, but the scene seemed to demand it. Luke opened the door, and the wonderful melodies greeted them. The club was small inside. The lighting was low, the music soft. A bit of smokiness seemed to hang in the air. A small stage sat in the corner; a well weathered testament to just how many performers the small club has seen. A terribly thin black man sat in a simple folding chair playing the guitar. Autographed photos of performers lined the entry way. Luke guided them to a small, round table in the corner.

He and Jasmine spent several hours in the club listening to the music and dancing. They seemed to take turns drawing each other in. One moment, Jasmine could feel Luke pressing his body to hers; the next moment, Jasmine would tighten her own arms, drawing Luke to her.

They would whisper into each other's ears while slowly swaying to the music. Their feet seem to float above the floor as they moved in harmony across the hardwood. With each dance, Luke and Jasmine seemed to draw closer together until they could get no closer.

The scent of her hair and feel of her warm breath on his exposed flesh had every part of Luke's body alive and screaming for more. He looked deeply into her eyes and smiled as his hand pulled Jasmine's head to his chest.

"Would you like to go somewhere more private?" Luke whispered to Jasmine.

"Yes," was her simple, and to the point, response as her eyes lifted to meet his deep pools of blue.

"Let's go back to my home," he replied with a tremble in his voice.

"We can sit and talk in private."

"Is your kingdom safe my knight?" Jasmine asked with a chuckle.

"It is, my lady. Nothing would dare enter the walls of my kingdom," Luke replied with a smile.

Hand-in-hand, the couple returned to the parking lot. Luke opened the car door, and Jasmine gracefully slipped into the seat. Again, they were on the road.

All the Way?

The speed of the car gradually increased as they drew closer to their destination. Luke's palms were becoming sweaty, as his excitement built. Turning recklessly into the subdivision, the two looked more like Bonny and Clyde running from the police than a couple returning home from a date. Jasmine clutched the seat, holding on for dear life.

"Luke!" Jasmine screeched, "Perhaps a little slower would be better! I'd like to be alive when we get there!"

Luke glanced at Jasmine and realized that he was driving a little too fast, but his anticipation was difficult to control. Before he could react, the turn was upon them. Luke hit the brakes, turned the wheel, and like a sprint car driver, slid the car sideways into his driveway, coming to an abrupt stop.

Taking a deep breath, he turned the key, and silence enveloped them. Sheepishly, Luke looked over at Jasmine. A wide eyed woman looked back with a "what the hell were you thinking" look. He tried to defuse the situation as he leaned over the console and kissed her softly as if to say, I'm sorry.

Luke got out of the car and came to her door. Jasmine's eyes found his and a smile formed as she quickly set aside her fear. He extended his hand and lifted her from the car. The simple act of taking Luke's hand had become a special thing for Jasmine. Each time he did it, she felt more special.

They had played out this scene many times during their late night chats, but this, was reality. A turn of his key and the door swung open. Luke reached for his precious Jasmine and guided her across the threshold of his home. Each seemed to be frozen in time. Luke could feel Jasmine's hand trembling in his own as neither was sure where they were going. It had been many years for them both. Each were struggling with what could or should come next.

The door slowly swung closed behind them, and with a loud click, trapped them in their moment. There they stood, together in the darkness, like two adolescents afraid of being caught by their parents.

Luke struck a match and lit a small candle on the coffee table. It's warm glow provided just enough light to bring out the beauty he had been enjoying the entire evening. The candlelight showed the way as Luke turned to face Jasmine, and, once again, took her into his arms.

The room was silent except for the loud pounding of his heart. *Can she hear that,* he wondered? Luke's heart felt like it might leap from his chest at any moment. He wanted to pinch himself and make sure he wasn't dreaming. *Am I really standing here, with her, in my home,* Luke thought to himself, as he listened carefully to the sound of their labored breathing?

He slipped Jasmine's jacket off of her shoulders. She let it slide effortlessly down her arms. He folded it neatly over the back of the chair and returned his focus to Jasmine.

Luke's body naturally leaned into hers, and their lips touched. Their tongues responded like two talented dancers; their movements choreographed with the passion of the tango. His tongue circled her mouth, moistening Jasmine's lips as her tongue attempted to follow. Her hands trembled as she navigated this long, lost path, struggling to remember the steps to this most passionate of dances.

The warm glow of the flickering candle seemed to soften the scene. Their tongues continued to dance as she felt his hand move up her back, then along her side, until it was gently cradling her left breast.

A soft moan escaped Jasmine's mouth as her body melted into his arms. She had not realized just how much she missed the soft, yet firm, touch of a man's hand. She could scarcely breathe as the fire within her raged.

Jasmine was having trouble with her inner self. She desired this. She had fantasized about what she hoped was coming many a time after one of their steamy chat sessions. The fear of rejection began to creep into her head. A thousand what-ifs flooded her consciousness.

Luke's lips slowly pulled back. She could feel the trembling in his hand as it cradled her breast. His warm breath caressed her cheek, and Jasmine lost all doubt. She wanted to feel more, much more.

Luke's head was spinning as he struggled with his own body and mind. He fought to concentrate on the wonderful feeling of her tongue swirling on his lips, while taking in the softness and heat of her breast. Paying attention to that hard nub that was in his palm, and the feeling of her nibbling on his lower lip, pushed him further towards the edge of his control.

Jasmine drew away to catch her breath, as her heart seemed to beat out of control. Luke stepped away, flicked a switch, and his home illuminated.

Jasmine reached for his hand and in a soft voice said, "Give me the tour."

Luke led her through the house, showing her the dining room, kitchen, and living room. They paused in the doorway of his bedroom as he awaited her reaction. Luke knew what he wanted, but his gentlemanly respect for his precious Jasmine caused him to pause, and wait for her acceptance of what will surely follow if they enter this private space.

Jasmine sensed his concern and took control as she guided Luke to the king-sized bed. Another kiss and their hands continued the adventure, the passion of exploration. Her hands moved to his chest, and he shuddered as her fingers glided over him.

Again, Jasmine's mind wandered, wondering why she had waited so long to touch a man. All those nights alone, nights she could have been experiencing the passion and love of a man. Nights where she punished herself for her failed marriage, rationalizing that Fred's leaving was somehow her fault, and that she needed to perform years of penance for her shortcomings.

Jasmine began to feel pangs of anger, until her fingers touched Luke's erect nipples. She could feel his body tremble as her fingers stroked over their stiffness. The sensitive nubs seemed to strain against the fabric of his shirt, and she enjoyed the feeling of power each time he shuddered.

Her own body was on fire now, tingling everywhere. She could not remember ever being so excited. She had only known Fred in her life, and he NEVER kindled feelings like these. She was now completely out of control, wanting to know just where these new feelings and passions would lead.

Jasmine boldly turned to the bed and pulled the covers back with incredible grace. She looked deep into Luke's soft blue eyes as a smile came to both their faces.

Luke cradled her in his arms and gently lowered her onto the bed. Now she lay before him, looking incredible, with her lovely hair framing her face in the soft light. Jasmine's beautiful femininity emanated as she lay before him. Luke looked deeply into her eyes, as he slowly climbed onto the bed.

The mattress gave in to the power of his body as he moved above and beside her. Being careful not to crush her delicate frame, Luke's left hand slowly curled under Jasmine's head. His right arm lowered him onto her until their moist lips met. As if on cue, their mouths resumed the sensuous dance not having missed a beat.

A soft moan escaped from Jasmine's throat as Luke's manhood pressed against her thigh. The feel of Jasmine's leg as it stroked along his shaft, sent shivers though him. Jasmine's own body strained for details as she pressed into him. Without a thought, Luke's hips began to undulate as his erect manhood demanded attention.

Jasmine's arms encircled his shoulders and pulled him even tighter into her wanton body. Luke could feel Jasmine's soft breasts as they pressed against his chest. He broke their kiss and his lips quickly moved to her neck, then up to her ear, and finally, back down, to Jasmine's shoulder. His lips struggled to visit every bit of wonderfully exposed skin. Luke's lips moved around and under Jasmine's throat, feeling the vibrations as sounds of passion escaped her body.

Jasmine was on fire as she felt him moving over her tingling flesh. She now realized exactly what she had been missing all those years: the heat, the passion, and the pure joy of sharing another person's body for the simple pleasures it could bring her. Her fingers gripped the sheets as her body seemed to explode under his skillful touch. She struggled to hold off her first real orgasm in years. Jasmine bit into her lower lip, trying to avoid making too much noise.

Luke's right hand slid slowly down Jasmine's arm, caressing the goose-bumped skin. His strong fingers moved down further along Jasmine's ribs, desperately searching for the hem of her blouse. His lips returned to Jasmine's and began to softly stroke hers, barely touching them. Only their hot breath joined them together.

Luke could feel the shiver in her body and hear the gasps that encouraged him to continue his probing. Finally, his fingers reached their destination, and Luke's hand dipped beneath her blouse. Spasms rippled through Jasmine from the simple touch of his fingers. Her skin felt incredible. Luke's breathing was now nearly a pant as the simple feel of her warm stomach enhanced his excitement.

Slowly, his hand moved up her torso, taking note of every inch of Jasmine's female form. His trembling hand reached the stiff underwire of her bra as Jasmine arched her back, thrusting her chest upwards, begging for more.

Luke's hand retreated as he slowly began to open the buttons of Jasmine's blouse. He gazed into her lust filled eyes, as the last button yielded. He paused. Jasmine smiled, and he knew exactly what she desired. His hands opened the sheer fabric and revealed more of her sexy body.

Jasmine's mind was racing as conflict within, once again, erupted. She was filled with desire, but she was about to allow a man to see her true form. *Will he find me disgusting? Will he find me sexy?* Just then, she looked up into those soft blue eyes, so loving, so caring. She knew she was not only doing the right thing, but she wanted him. In the worst way, she wanted him.

Jasmine had little time to think as Luke lifted one arm, then the other, to free the blouse. She looked into his deep blue eyes, felt his gentle touch, and knew she was not only beautiful, but sexy.

Jasmine continued to squirm with excitement, her thigh pressing into Luke's manhood. She tentatively worked her hand down to Luke's leg, stroking his muscular thigh. Her hand brushed the obvious bulge in his pants. *Oh my God, should I touch him? Will he think me too forward? I don't care. I want him.* With that, her trembling fingers obeyed her wanton mind and began to trace the outline that she desired.

Tentatively, she began to rub and squeeze his member. Only two layers of fabric separate her fingers from his throbbing excitement. Jasmine tried to rise up, but the weight of Luke's body would not allow it.

He looked into her eyes and saw the lust, the raw desire of a woman. He pushed himself up to a sitting position and gazed into Jasmine's eyes. His hands slid down her body, following the form of her hips, and thighs, down to the nylon covered legs. Jasmine's legs were alive. She couldn't hold them still, even if she wanted to.

Sensuality overcame her. Her legs parted, reacting to his gentle touch. Luke's fingers slid under the hem of Jasmine's skirt and began to stroke with the lightest touch. The heat of her body coupled with the feel of the nylon, pushed Luke's excitement to new heights.

He began to push the hem up towards her waist. His eyes filled with Jasmine's loveliness as more and more of her form came into view. His fingers slid up past the tops of Jasmine's hose.

There was just something about a woman's leg covered by stockings. He couldn't explain it, nor did he want to. He simply wanted to savor the beauty this incredible woman was sharing with him.

A jolt of electricity traveled through his body when he touched the soft flesh of her inner thigh. Jasmine's low moan confirmed she desired this as much as he.

Luke felt her hand close tightly around his shaft. Her mouth opened slightly, and another moan added to the sounds of passion within the room.

Luke's attention shifted for a moment as he noticed the zipper on the side of the skirt. He reached up and slowly lowered the zipper. Trembling fingers tugged at her skirt. Jasmine smiled and raised her bottom as the skirt yielded to the pressure. He guided it down her legs, and with a toss, the skirt floated to the floor. There she lay, exposed before him, clothed only in her bra, panties, and stockings. What a vision of beauty she was.

Luke's own breathing had become labored as his hand approached her panties. Now, the moan came from Luke's mouth as he took in her sexy body lying vulnerable before him. His trembling fingers traced the soft fabric, moving across the top, feeling the skin of Jasmine's stomach, and watching as her body responded to his gentle touch. Fingers followed the soft fabric onto her leg where he could feel Jasmine's muscles tighten and her pelvis rise to meet his touch.

Jasmine felt sexy as she watched him. She was in awe of the way he made her feel both feminine and beautiful. She had made love many times with Fred, but it was nothing like this. There was no rushing or urgency, only the wonderful, gentle attention of desire.

Luke's finger moved down, and then, turned slowly towards the opposite leg. He went slowly, taking note of the soft curls and the outline of her womanhood. The thickness of Jasmine's panties was the only thing separating Luke's finger from her special place.

His finger tips reached the center. The moisture was evident, and Jasmine's body rose to meet his touch. He could feel the subtle indentation of her delicate opening. Luke's finger involuntarily followed the indentation up, up towards Jasmine's most sensitive place.

He paused for a moment, then, went back down, moving lower this time and allowing his palm to rest over her hot womanhood. Luke's long fingers probed down between her now outstretched legs, providing just enough pressure to push Jasmine's pelvis back onto the bed. The wetness and heat caused Luke's breathing to become more difficult as excitement was overcoming him.

Jasmine could not believe the sensations coming from his touch. She had made love hundreds of times in her life, but nothing ever felt like this. It was as if Luke had studied her body and knew exactly how, and where, to touch her. She didn't know how he knew what he knew, she just wanted more.

Luke's gaze returned back to Jasmine's lovely eyes. Volumes of information passed between them without a word being spoken. He slowly moved to the side of the bed and then slid off the edge onto the floor.

Luke turned to face Jasmine. His gaze never strayed from her eyes as he unbuckled his belt, and released the clasp on the waistband of his pants. The quiet silence was broken by the zzzzziiiiipppp of his zipper. Jasmine's eyes slowly dropped, finding the bulge, that only moments before, she had held in her hand. With a look of confidence, he released his grip and let his trousers drop to the floor.

His shorts were stretched tightly across his manhood. She could see his shaft throbbing beneath the thin fabric. Luke hooked his thumbs into the waistband, and with a single motion, released his manhood. He then slipped his shirt over his head, and he stood before her, naked; naked for her pleasure.

Luke climbed back onto the bed. His shaking hands gripped the waistband of her panties. As he looked into her eyes, he slid them down, and off her legs. Where they went, he was not sure, nor did he care. Her lovely womanhood was before him, with its mantle of soft, curly hair.

He ran his hands up her legs, over her thighs, then into the softness of her curly hair. Luke's hands left her curls and began to travel up her stomach. Jasmine smiled a devilish smile at Luke, then reached down, and with a single motion, removed her bra. These lovers could hide nothing from the gaze of the other; nor did they want to.

Luke's hands continued up her body, as Jasmine's began to roam over his. The sensitive skin was alive with goosebumps as her touch sent chills cascading over him. Soon, Luke was lying on top of her, their naked flesh pressing together.

They worked to become one. He could feel her stiff nipples pressing into his chest. His own hard nubs felt the heat of Jasmine's wonderful breasts. Her legs began to wrap around him as his hard shaft pressed against her. Luke felt her pelvis come alive as she ground her hard and sensitive bud into him.

His lips found hers once again. Kissing in that most sensual of ways, her tongue entered his mouth, as she pressed harder against him. Her mouth was open, inviting Luke's tongue in where he could taste the woman he so desperately needed.

Strong arms encircled Jasmine as Luke struggled to support himself on his elbows. Her arms reached out, and her nails raked up and down his back as she lost all control.

Luke gently stroked her cheek, coaxing her back into control. Strong fingers slipped into her hair and drew Jasmine's lips tighter into his. Their heads moved side to side as their mouths continued the lust filled kiss.

The need to breathe finally overcame them, and they separated. Each took a quick breath as urgency seemed to consume them. Luke could feel Jasmine's chest rising and falling in unison with his own. He looked into her eyes and smiled as they rolled onto their sides, facing each other.

A jolt of high voltage electricity rushed through Luke's body, causing every muscle to stiffen uncontrollably and stoking the fire of passion within him. In the next second, his brain finally processed the feeling, and he was wonderfully aware that Jasmine's fingers had tightened around his right nipple. The sensitive nub took the express lane to his manhood as the surge of excitement caused his shaft to pulse.

Her fingers continued to stimulate as his hand was drawn to Jasmine's side. The feel of her rib was incredible, but he wanted to feel more. Luke longed to feel that softness, that incredible sensation that was her breast.

His eyes never wandered from hers. His hand deftly began to trace the gentle outline of the object of his desire. Luke's large hand moved to cover the magical orb as the palm settled over her hardened nipple. A moan escaped her mouth and her lips curve up into a smile.

Jasmine's closed her eyes, as she focused on the sensations. She felt Luke's lips lower to hers. The couple dropped into another passionate kiss; his hand firmly massaging her breast. Jasmine's mind was in chaos as she jumped from the wonderful feel of his strong hand massaging her sensitive breast, to the moistness of his lips on her own. The cornucopia of tingles and feelings just kept washing over her.

Luke savored Jasmine's softness as he slid his hand to Jasmine's side. She could barely breathe as he began to move lower on her body. She watched, behind closed eyes, as his fingers continued past the curve of her waist and around onto her bottom.

Jasmine was never comfortable with the way her backside looked in the mirror. Her eyes squeezed shut as she waited for his reaction.

"I've been imagining holding your naked bottom since that first night in the club. You have a fantastic bottom."

Luke's hands slowly stroked over her backside as he moaned softly in her ear. His fingers traced along one of the garter. Jasmine could feel his fingers as they trembled.

Luke's fingers curled, gripped the soft flesh and pulled her body into his. The power in his hand lifted Jasmine as though she were a rag doll, joining their most intimate places together.

The heat from Jasmine's body was incredible, as the passion of their minds was transformed into the passion of the flesh. Luke and Jasmine were both struggling for oxygen, as their arousal continued to build.

Luke watched Jasmine, as her breasts heaved in passion. She could see the pure desire in his eyes as they settled onto her chest. In Luke's mind, it was as though her breasts were reaching out, then drawing away, like a schoolgirl saying "please, more" then changing her mind and saying "no, stop."

Jasmine's body continued to tease Luke's senses, until he could take no more, and his lips dropped to her chest. His moist lips trailed across her, seeking out the exquisite dark peak that was Jasmine's nipple.

His lips felt the texture change from soft and smooth to tense and rough. He knew he was nearing his goal. Luke could feel the hard nub against his cheek, and with a quick turn of his mouth, he captured the prey. His tongue traced Jasmine's nipple, stroking it. Her chest thrust up, pressing her wonderful breast deeper into his mouth. Jasmine gasped as the intense sensations flood her mind.

"OH-MY-GOD!" Jasmine shouted uncontrollably as the wave of her first orgasm washed over her.

This was nothing like the orgasms she had come to know during those private times. This was so intense, her fingers, toes; even the tip of her nose was tingling out of control. The spasms within her caused her fingers to grip his curly locks as she sought to drive his head into her chest.

Luke froze in position as he witnessed her entire body shaking. For a moment, she actually stopped breathing. He rose up, concerned it she were all right. The look of concern quickly changed to a smile when he realized what was happening. He watched as the look of satisfaction came over her, and her eyes slowly openrd. Jasmine smiled, momentarily, and Luke knew he had been a part of something very special.

He gave her a soft kiss, then returned to her delicate chest. His tongue began circling once again. He gently suckled her hard nipple, drawing it in and out as his tongue stroked over the tip.

A moan rumbled from her causing his hard member to twitch. Luke felt Jasmine's fingers entangle themselves in his curly hair as she pulled him tighter into her chest. Her leg was out of control, as it pressed harder into his steely manhood.

Luke's hand slid down along the supple curves of Jasmine's leg then moved back up her soft inner thigh. Closer and closer, his powerful hand moved towards Jasmine's fiery sex until it gentley cradled her womanhood.

His large hand was soothing yet stimulating. She could feel each of his fingers caressing her special place. Jasmine squirmed desperately, working to apply pressure to where she needed it most.

Luke's mind was lost now; lost in making love to the woman he had desired for so long. He need not think of what to do next, Luke simply sensed what Jasmine desired and took her where she wanted to go. His nervousness was gone, and they continue to make love to one another. Jasmine had surrendered herself to the man she had trusted with her every thought and feeling these past months. Her private desires for him were finally coming true, and she had no time, or need, to contemplate them. She needed only to live them.

Luke's mouth continued to suck and lick her nipple as his finger began to apply pressure on Jasmine's private place, beckoning it to open. Jasmine bit her lip as her body continued to burn in the fire of passion. She had never experienced this before, wanting a man to pleasure her and then having him do exactly that. Her tummy trembled as her body pressed into his penetrating finger. She could scarcely breathe as he seemed to know exactly how to touch her.

Jasmine's body resisted at first. Luke's fingers seemed to know exactly what she needed. His touch was feathery, fingers stroking along each side of her passage. Her mind was flooded with desire, as she tried to follow his fingers in her mind. The wispy touch caused her inner thighs to tremble. A part of her wanted to just grab his finger and push it into her to relieve the pressure building within her.

Luke knew how to pleasure a woman. He knew he had fanned the flames of arousal to the perfect point. His stiff finger began to coax her flower to open. The heat of her body and moist dew on the petals of her flower were indescribable. Luke could feel Jasmine's body stiffen as his finger separated the folds and entered Jasmine's most private place.

Luke's finger gently ventured into her most secret place, bathing in the copious amounts of nectar. Her body began to undulate, driving his finger deeper and deeper into her hot sex.

Luke could no longer hold still, and he thrust his hard member into Jasmine's thigh. The stiffness of his member stroking against her thigh only added to his need for her. The feel of her leg rubbing the soft spongy head of his manhood was driving Luke crazy.

His actions did not go unnoticed by Jasmine. The fire inside her demanded that she reach for what she desired. Jasmine's hand searched, until, finally, it grasped his stiff member, and she begins to stoke.

Luke's body stiffened, and for a moment, these two lovers held each other, their free hands pulling each other. Each was experiencing something totally new. Oh, they had both been in this place before, but never with the passion and desire that was washing over them at this very moment.

Sensations flooded Luke's senses as her hand moved along his shaft. She could feel the thick veins pulsing, as her hand moved slowly up and down. The smooth sponginess of the head as she stroked was magical. It had been so long since Jasmine had held an aroused man in her hand. She struggled to maintain a rhythm.

Luke's fingers stroked her as she stroked him. The passion was building as each fought to maintain control over themselves, while working to give the other as much pleasure as possible. This could not go on for long, and finally, it was

Luke that gave in. He rose up forcing Jasmine to release her grip. He looked deep into her eyes and slowly slid atop her.

Luke's hard shaft seemed to position itself perfectly. Jasmine knew what was to come and prepared herself for him. She wrapped her arms around her man. Jasmine gazed into her lover's eyes, letting him know that what was about to happen, was what she wanted also.

He slid down slightly and the head of his pulsing shaft breached the petals of her flower and began to enter. Jasmine stiffened, and then froze, as she felt Luke's manhood slip past her opening.

Time, seemed to stand still as her mind went into overload. *What am I doing? It's been so long, will this hurt? My God, he is so hot. What if this ruins everything? Will he think I'm a slut? Oh this feels so wonderful! Will he be gone tomorrow? He is what I want; I only hope I'm what he wants!* Jasmine was jerked back into the moment as she felt him inching into her. She looked into his eyes and saw everything she needed to see. *I want him, all of him.*

Luke watched as a tear formed in the corner of Jasmine's eye. She had abandoned her feelings of pleasure long ago. She believed that, never again, could she experience the incredible passion, closeness, or pleasure, of being with a caring man. Not only was she wrong, but Jasmine was feeling things she had never felt before. *Was this real lovemaking?* Luke filled her like she had never been filled before.

Passion seemed to disappear, if only for an instant. Emotion rushed in to consume each of them. There was something more here, much more than the pleasure one person can impart on another. Emotions were running wild within both of these lovers. Tears of joy streamed down Jasmine's face, as she held Luke tightly.

Luke gazed into Jasmine's eyes. He sensed that these were not tears of sadness and leaned down to softly kiss them away. Gentle kisses captured each tear as his warm lips touched Jasmine's eyelids. His lips lingered at one eye, then the other.

"I'm here for you, my lady, here, where I belong. We are one," Luke whispered in his soft loving voice.

The world stopped revolving, and they lay there, motionless, consumed in the feeling of being one. Jasmine smiled.

"This is incredible Luke, please don't stop."

Jasmine took a breath and pressed her lips to his, her hands returned to those curls and desperately pulled him to her. The kiss, with renewed force, passion, and urgency, drove them back into a state of pure passion. Their tongues no longer danced, but rather, fought for dominance, as they sought out what they desired.

Jasmine's hips moved up as Luke pressed down. Luke withdrew slightly and then moved slowly back in; filling her once more with short gentle strokes, as Jasmine's body became accustomed to the fullness.

Gradually, they increased the pace until Luke was driving long, deep strokes into Jasmine's fiery hot flower. Each stroke ended with her body reaching to greet him. Her breasts moved with each thrust and the look of total lust in Jasmine's eyes was driving Luke at a blistering pace toward the precipice.

Oh my God, I'm getting close, Luke thought to himself. *I can't let this end yet. I don't want this to end!*

Jasmine sensed Luke's concern and with some secret, only women know, she rolled them over, so Luke was now on his back looking up at an incredible vision of loveliness. Jasmine took control, rocking her hips a few times before she lifted herself free of Luke.

"Not yet," Jasmine whispered softly.

She moved down Luke's body and settled between his outstretched legs. She reached out, slowly wrapping her fingers around Luke's member. Jasmine stared lustfully at it, as she began to slide her hand up and down, holding his pulsing shaft.

Her touch was soothing to Luke, yet stimulating. Her fingers traveled around the base of his shaft and down, cupping the delicate twins. Fingers slowly stroked and rolled his balls. She worked with great skill to apply just enough pressure to sooth. Luke watched as, ever so slowly, she brought her lips to the sensitive head. They parted and his manhood disappears.

Luke's head began to spin as Jasmine enveloped his stiff manhood. His eyes rolled back, and a low moan echoed in the room. He drifted away into a place that he had never been before. Luke could feel Jasmine's tongue swirling around, up to the tip and back down along the crown. He was not sure how, but she was driving his body wild with incredible stimulation, while allowing his urge for orgasm to subside.

Jasmine smiled as she felt the fruit of her actions. She had done this before, but never had she experienced such pleasure herself. Oral sex had been something she grudgingly performed for Fred. This was different, she actually wanted to feel and taste Luke, all of Luke.

She could not explain it to herself, but she wanted to bring Luke all the way with her mouth. She had her man just where she wanted him; trembling with incredible pleasure, while she swirled her tongue over his throbbing shaft. The tip of her tongue found the drop of salty moisture and captured it, treating her taste buds and mind to something truly special.

Luke continued to be inundated with new sensations. The feeling of her hard nipples on his inner thighs sent shivers though his body. He clutched the sheets in an effort to relieve the pent up pressure. Jasmine's sensuous body undulated causing the stiff buds to drag down his thighs and up again. Her hand continued to stroke Luke as he wildly shook his head from side to side. Jasmine began to twist her hand as she stroked. He could feel the return of her hot, wet mouth pushing him towards the edge of orgasm.

"My God, please let me cum!" Luke begged as he felt her free hand begin to massage the twins again.

"I can't take any more!" Luke cried out and pulled Jasmine up on top of him.

The heat and passion between them was unbearable. Luke's arms wrapped around her, pulling her tightly into him. Their wet mouths continued their dance as Luke's hand slid down Jasmine's back, seeking her lovely round bottom. His fingers gripped the roundness of her buttock and pulled her ever tighter into his manhood. He could feel her pelvis rock, as she ground her throbbing bud into his hard shaft.

Their passionate kiss continued. As Jasmine's fiery sex captured his manhood they were one. Their bodies moved in unison, driven by the passion consuming them. Luke's hot shaft slid effortlessly into her, then out again. The two continued with stroke after stroke until Luke drove deep into her and rolled them over once again.

He pushed himself up onto his arms and gazed down at the woman before him. Her beauty struck awe in him as her lovely hair framed her face. Feelings transitioned and he was almost afraid to admit to himself what he had been feeling as he gazed into Jasmine's eyes.

After a momentary pause and silent exchange, they resumed their rush to the edge, hand in hand, desiring to leap at the exact same moment. Each stroke was more powerful than the last. Her eyes stared deeper into his, trying to gauge the exact moment of release. They continued this as her arms struggled to hold tightly onto him. Suddenly, Jasmine pushed Luke away, and his hard shaft slipped from her fiery petals. She rolled over and thrust her beautiful bottom into the air. Her desire was unmistakable.

Luke positioned himself behind her. His eyes were naturally drawn up her legs to the glistening folds of her engorged womanhood. He frantically guided his pulsing shaft to the opening and which accepted him without effort. Her body welcomed him as the head separated the moist petals and he entered her.

His heavy balls slapped against her as she braced against his power. Jasmine's hot, hungry body sucked him inside, and the grip of her vagina was too much. She let out a loud groan, and Luke heard her scream into the pillow.

"Harder, drive me hard. Now! I need you now!"

Luke's body, dripping with perspiration, sprung into action as he drew his manhood from her body, and then, with a powerful thrust, his shaft slammed back into her. Again and again, he drove, driven by her muffled cries. Faster and faster, they sprinted together towards satisfaction. It was all a blur to them as he grabbed onto her hips to help pull her further onto his shaft.

Jasmine suddenly raised herself up onto her arms, her head swayed side from to side as she repeated, "Oh God, YES! Oh My God, YES!"

Her passion was overflowing. Her body slammed back against Luke with each stroke. Luke wondered for a moment, *am I making love to her, or is she making love to me...* He didn't care, the feeling of him slapping against her bud, the wetness that was covering his swaying balls was testament to their pleasure.

Luke reached forward, gripping her shoulders as they continued to drive harder, faster, and deeper. Jasmine tilted her pelvis and groaned again. They both knew the edge was near. Luke pulled out of Jasmine, and somehow, she knew to turn over.

Luke mounted her, once again, and they stared into one another's eyes. It was time, and Jasmine's vagina began convulsing. Luke couldn't wait another second either.

"I'm Cumming," escaped his lips, as he felt her muscles tighten around his shaft.

One last deep stroke and they froze; Luke holding Jasmine tightly as his manhood swelled and began to pulse. His hot seed gushed into her convulsing womanhood. First one, then two, then a third stream blasted into her trembling body.

"Oh my God, yes!" Jasmine shouted.

A low groan came over her as her body shook uncontrollably. She threw her head back and filled the room with an animal like scream as she continued to shake and spasm. Sweat rolled from Luke's chest and forehead as he desperately tried to cool himself. He noticed that Jasmine's skin was also glistening. He could support himself no longer, collapsing onto her. His hot breath now blasting onto her neck as his body continued to have smaller tremors.

"You are incredible," Luke whispered in a breathy voice

They kissed softly as they looked into one another's eyes. The feelings and emotions pouring from them were almost frightening as each wondered where this was going. Luke kissed Jasmine softly and smiled. They didn't care where this was going; they only knew where it was at this instant in time.

Together they rolled to the side and spooned. His arm reached around her, gently cupping her soft breast, as they lay together. Lust was gone now, replaced by the wonderful peace and closeness lovers share. Jasmine pushed her bottom into Luke as he drew her close and kissed her cheek. Silently, they drifted off to sleep as the candle cast its' soft light onto Jasmine's beautiful face.

The First Day

Wow, what a night, Jasmine thought to herself as the steaming water of the shower cascaded down through her hair and onto the rest of her body. *I feel like I've been given a second chance at life. I haven't slept that well in years; so relaxed; so content. He was wonderful to be with, and those hands, my God, those hands,* Jasmine recalled with a shiver. *Did last night really happen or was it just a wonderful dream?*

Quickly, she answered out loud, "I feel alive again!"

He was so mysterious on the way home about where they were going tomorrow. It's summer, why would he tell me I'd need to dress warm? Warm and casual, I wonder what he has up his sleeve? I just know I can't wait to be with him again. How could it get more special than last night? My God, he made me feel beautiful and sexy, more like a woman than I've ever felt.

Luke not only helped Jasmine to see the person she had been running from for years, but he awakened the sensual part she'd kept suppressed and hidden from the world for so long.

MMMM my body still tingles every time I think of his touch, she thought to herself as she stood under the refreshing shower.

The soapy cloth glided over her body. Jasmine's eyes closed as she relived the electric touch of his hands. The cloth spread the lather over her shoulder. The bubbles tingled and tickled as she imagined the soft touch of his lips on her neck. The warm wet cloth continued to glide the lather over her skin just as his soft hands moved over her last night. Jasmine's mind continued the replay of feelings as though his hands, not hers, washed her tingling body.

Once done, she stood and let the jets of warm water rinse away the lather and gently coax her back to reality. Stepping out of the shower, she reached for the fluffy bath towel, dried, and wrapped her hair in the damp towel. Jasmine took her silk robe from the back of the door and slipped it on, recalling his embrace.

The silk felt cool as it clung to her. She'd always loved the feel of silk, but with her reawakened femininity, it seemed to feel better than it had for years. She allowed her mind to wander back to a time when she welcomed the touch of not only silk, but the touch of a man. Luke had shown her that life was not over. It's out there to be embraced.

Sitting at her dressing table, Jasmine glanced at herself in the mirror and noticed a glow that she hasn't seen for years. Oh yes, and she saw that long absent devilish smile looking back; the look of a confident, attractive woman, anxious to face the world. Jasmine gave that woman in the mirror a wink as she unwrapped her hair and began her ritual: drying her hair, then styling it. Applying her makeup came next. The day awaited, and it somehow seemed like a day of new beginnings.

Dressing quickly, Jasmine went downstairs. But before heading out the door, she stopped in her tracks, rushed into her sewing room, grabbed a short piece of ribbon, and stuffed it into the pocket of her "Jasmine's" smock. It will be a busy day at the salon. Jasmine and Mary had their work cut out for them. Samantha's entire wedding party will be there shortly.

It's not that wedding parties are difficult, it's just that the girls usually get silly and if you get behind, well, let's just say, a bridal party under stress is not a pretty picture.

She slipped the key into the door of the salon just as Mary came up the walk with the cappuccinos in hand. Jasmine's beaming smile told Mary that something was up. Quickly, the two ladies prepared the shop for the day's work and took up their positions behind the chairs. As they had done every day since Jasmine's divorce, the ladies came to attention, and with military precision, they turned to face the picture of Fred on the wall. Mary began to raise her hand towards Fred.

"Stop!" Jasmine shouted.

She stepped forward, pulled a length of black ribbon from the pocket of her smock, draped it across one corner of the photo and took a step back.

"My life is no longer driven by the ugly memory of a man whom I'm working to prove wrong. Today, my life is driven by the feelings of life and what it has to offer someone as lucky as I."

Mary looked at Jasmine as a knowing smile spread across her face. Mary stepped towards Jasmine and wrapped her arms around her dear friend. They silently celebrated Jasmine's new beginning.

"We are going out tonight, Jasmine," Mary giggled.

"I want to hear all about this."

Mary had watched Jasmine struggle after her divorce, and even though Jasmine no longer felt the need to salute Fred, Mary did. She raised her arm and extended her finger in the traditional "Fred Salute".

Saturdays in June were always special at Jasmine's. This was wedding season. Jasmine glanced out the window just as a long black Lincoln® Town Car pulled up. Jasmine knew this car well. Its' long elegant lines and deep black color made it look as though it stretched out forever. The cloth top, wire wheels, chrome trim, and distinctive Lincoln® emblem standing proud at the front, all combined to announce, "I'm here, the party may begin."

It was June making her normal entrance. With her, was Robin. These two ladies were like two peas in a pod. They had known each other for years and actually met in the maternity ward. Robin had moved to the next town over, but the ladies stayed in close contact. They met frequently at Jasmine's to have their hair done and to catch up on the happenings in each other's lives.

June had raised an absolutely stunning daughter, a real girly girl that reflected June's own personality. June was always dressed to perfection. She exuded graceful elegance and all heads turned when she entered a room. Her hair was always perfect and she depended on Jasmine to keep it that way. June and her daughter, Samatha, spent many a day in the salon. When prom came, June and her daughter were a team; combing the malls and specialty shops for the perfect dress and shoes, of course. They would come to the salon to have their hair done. Samatha was June's own personal Barbie doll, and she seemed to love playing the role.

Robin was a bit more earthy. She had raised a handsome son; a boy that would try the patience of a saint. Many a day, she would come to the salon, flop into the chair, and say, "You girls will never, in a million years, guess what my son did this time!" Sometimes, it seemed like the salon was Robin's only break from the reality of motherhood. Robin would seek out the pampering and relaxation that came with having ones hair done, giving her some kind of normalcy to hold onto.

Today was an extra special day for these ladies; their children were about to be married. The kids had met quite on their own several years earlier and had developed a relationship. Today they would tie the knot, and as the mothers of the bride and groom, June and Robin would be first up. The ladies had just settled into the chairs when the long white limousine pulled up to the salon.

"Jasmine, I want to apologize in advance for what is about to happen," June said with a chuckle.

"These girls have been bouncing off the walls for days living and reliving this week. You should see the pictures from the bachelorette party. It was like something out of one of those Girls Gone Wild videos they advertise on TV," she said shaking her head.

"I don't think that even I was that crazy in the 60s! Robin, you better hope your son is up to the task at hand, I have a feeling he is in for a real treat tonight!" she said with a devilish grin.

All four ladies, then, giggled like school girls.

Jasmine looked over at Mary; gave her a wink.

"Don't you worry, June, we will take wonderful care of them, and I'm sure they won't get out of hand…much."

The four ladies laughed loudly together as they had many times over the years. The door of the limousine flung open and out spilled four girls and a photographer. A tidal wave of silliness descended upon Jasmine's. Jasmine looked at Mary and grinned as the girls popped the corks on two bottles of champagne. Another wedding day at the salon began.

Jasmine and Mary worked their magic, and by 2:00, the four young ladies, and the photographer got back into the limousine and sped away. Mary and Jasmine spent more than an hour cleaning up the shop and getting rid of the evidence left behind. Jasmine's shoulders, back, and feet were hurting. She was just plain tired. Jasmine looked over at Mary and saw the fatigue in her eyes. Weddings were always tough days. They basically did a full day's worth of work in half the time and twice the stress.

"Mary, let's get out of here and go somewhere quiet. I'm hungry, my feet hurt, and I just want to sit and relax. If we happen to have an apple martini, or two, or three, that's ok, too," Jasmine said with a laugh.

Jasmine didn't drink often, but when she did, she just loved an apple martini.

"Jasmine, you have got to tell me what happened last night. You've had a glow about you all day today."

"Ok, Mary, but I have to get a shower and changed first. Meet me back here at 7:00. We'll go out for drinks and I'll tell you all about it."

"I'm with you," said Mary.

"You better not leave out one detail when you tell me what's put that smirk on your face all day."

Jasmine locked the door, and the ladies headed out. Jasmine hollered over her shoulder and waved goodbye to her friend.

In no time, they were giggling at the table as they recounted the days antics at the shop. Bridal parties were always entertaining, a lot of work and stress, but always entertaining. Jasmine and Mary had found the wedding night talk particularly fun. Over the years, Mary and Jasmine had encountered every kind of bride. The frightened ones who were terrified about what was going to "happen" to them on their wedding night, brides who talked a good story, but really had no clue, brides that had no business wearing white, and in fact, probably frightened the groom, to the bride on her third marriage who, not only knew what was coming, but, had prepared a "special" treat for her new husband.

"Come on Jasmine, spill it!" Mary prodded.

"What's going on with this Luke? So last night worked out? I've been waiting to hear all of the details. Where did he take you? When did you get home?" Mary fired questions faster than Jasmine could answer.

"Mary, I never knew it could be like this. I wake up in the morning aching for his touch, wondering what he is doing. Just the mere thought of him sends tingles through me. I feel like a teenager again. Oh-my-God, Mary, when I'm with him, I feel so special. He never leaves me alone. No, that's not right, he never lets me feel alone. He seems genuinely interested in everything I say, and he seems to notice everything."

"Sure he does, he's a man. He notices if you forgot to button your blouse all the way or if your skirt is too tight." Mary giggles.

But Mary did notice a real passion in her friend's voice. A tone she hasn't heard for a very long time. In fact, she couldn't remember ever hearing Jasmine sound like this.

"Mary, I never knew I could feel this way about a man. Just thinking of him gives me butterflies in my stomach. When we talk on the phone, I spend nearly the entire time with goose bumps. Mary, I'm having dreams about him nearly every night, and when he pops into my head during the day, things within me spring to attention. I've had to switch to wearing my thick bras just to avoid being embarrassed. I'm telling you Mary, I feel like a high school girl again."

Mary reached out to her friend and took her hand.

"I'm so happy for you, Jasmine. But Jasmine, take it slow; you've really only just met this man. Guard your heart for awhile until you are sure about him."

"Mary, I've known Luke for more than six months. We've spent more time "together" than I ever thought about spending with Fred. We talk, and talk, and then talk some more. I haven't spent a single day in the last six months without chatting or talking with Luke for at least two hours.

We either call each other on the phone, chat on-line, and now, we meet face to face. I know everything about him. What was good in his first marriage and how he let it slip through his fingers; eventually letting it die. I've listened to the pride he has for his son, and even his dreams for the future. What turns him on and what makes him laugh. I'm not sure I could know more about him."

"Well you just be careful Jasmine. It's one thing to talk on-line, but it's something else to relate to each other in person. He could still turn out to be one of those internet perverts that take advantage of women."

"Mary, he's been a perfect gentleman every time we've been out. I haven't found one thing that he wasn't truthful about when we talked. I'm not sure why some woman has not snatched him up, but I just know that I want to be his girlfriend and he seems to want me also."

"I'm happy for you Jasmine. You are a wonderful woman and you deserve someone special in your life. I really hope Luke is all you think he is, but he better watch out! If he does you wrong, he will have me to answer to, me and my biker friends!" The girls laughed out loud and picked up their glasses.

Mary made a toast, "To Luke, may he be what he seems to be, and may he retain his balls for the rest of his life!"

"Mary!" Jasmine said with a laugh. "You are simply terrible."

The girls enjoyed their drinks and continued their conversation well into the night, laughing, giggling, and just relaxing.

Up Up and Away

The alarm jerked Jasmine from her dream just as she was about to ride off with the handsome knight. Suddenly, she realized she would see him in a short while and her body snapped bolt up in bed. Jasmine kicked the warm comforter away as she scurried to the bathroom. A quick twist of the shower knob and the water began to flow. The sense of urgency was unmistakable, as she began her morning routine.

5:30AM, how is a lady supposed to look beautiful at 5:30AM?

A quick rinse and spit then into the now steaming shower. The water hit the top of Jasmine's head. Tiny fingers of water massaged her scalp then ran down her body. She stood there with eyes closed as a battle waged inside her mind.

Sleep, I can just relax and perhaps return to my wonderful knight… no, I must get ready he will be here soon!

Her hands flew through her hair as the shampoo lathered. Conditioner soaked as Jasmine quickly washed her body, then came the rinsing from head to toe. She stepped out of the steamy shower and a blast of cold air hit her. Goosebumps erupt everywhere as the chill swept over her. Quickly Jasmine grabbed the towel and dried off. Her silk robe came off the hook and she glanced into the mirror.

Oh my God, I cannot go out looking like this! What was I thinking agreeing to meet him at 6:30 in the morning? What was he thinking asking me to meet him at 6:30 in the morning?

Jasmine shook her head and then the thoughts of being with him came over her. A smile began to cross her face. She knew she wanted to see him. *Who cares what time it is, I'll get to be with him.*

Come on Jasmine, you are a professional, work your magic, knock his socks off, she thought to herself as she let out a chuckle.

Jasmine's hands reached for her makeup and before she even realized it, foundation was on and mascara was skillfully applied to one eye.

Oh my God it's not even six and I'm putting on makeup, I must be nuts! A smile came to her face once again. *Nuts over him that is* and her skillful hands continued. A little lip gloss and Jasmine's shiny, kissable lips only needed something to kiss.

Over to her dresser, she selected a nice pair of white lacey panties and matching bra. Jasmine was pleasantly aware of her sensitive nipples as she positioned each breast in its cup. The tingle traveled instantly to all the right places as her mind rewound to Friday night.

What a night she recalled. Jasmine walked over to her closet. She paused, *casual yet warm. Jeans? Denim skirt? Sweats, I think not, I may just burn those sweats* Jasmine laughed. *My embroidered jeans and this nice v-neck sweater, this will look good together.* Jasmine slipped on the jeans then critiqued herself in the mirror. *MMMM just enough, snug but not too tight.* Jasmine slipped the sweater over her head and pulled it into place. *I normally wear something under this, but not today.* Jasmine gave the hotty in the mirror a wink. A few dabs of perfume, strategic places, and she was ready.

Just in time as she heard the bell ring. Jasmine opened the door and her heart dropped. It wasn't him.

Politely she asks "May I help you?" straining to cover her disappointment.

"Miss, your car is here. There is no rush. I just wanted you to know that whenever you are ready we can leave."

Jasmine looked over his shoulder and there, at the curb, was a white limousine. Her heart raced as she struggled not to act like a dumb hick.

She took a breath, and replied, "let me get my jacket and I will be right out."

Closing the door Jasmine pressed her eye to the peephole and watched as the driver returned to the car, stationing himself at the rear door. Jasmine grabbed her phone and beep, beep, beep as she punched the buttons.

"Mary, you will never guess what is in front of my house."

"Jasmine!" Mary scolds in a groggy voice.

"Is everything OK? Do you have any idea what time it is?"

"A limo" Jasmine screeched with excitement. "He sent a limo for me. How cool is that? Mary, what should I do?" Jasmine asked her dearest friend.

She already knew but needed Mary to confirm it was okay to enjoy what she was experiencing.

"Go! Go experience life, the life you've been hiding from for years" her friend replied.

"Just wait until the sun is up next time to call me. I have strict rules about early morning calls."

Jasmine heard Mary chuckling into the phone.

"Sounds like you found a real gentleman."

"I'm out of the closet Mary. I cannot believe what I've been missing all these years. I feel like a princess, and my knight has sent a carriage for me. Mary, I have to go. I'll tell you everything when I get back. Don't wait up" Jasmine said in her most sarcastic of voices.

"Have a terrific time," Mary replied and hung up the phone.

Jasmine went to the closet for her spring jacket, slipped her lipstick, ID, and a twenty into the pocket and out the door she went. It was early, but the beautiful blue sky greeted her as she looked around. *It's got to be 75 degrees out here. What could I possibly need this jacket for?* Click, click, click her heels sounded on the sidewalk as she approached the limo. She took a quick look up and down the street to see if any of the neighbors were out.

She had a bit of a bounce in her step and sway in her walk as she approached the limo. On cue, the driver swung the door open and like the stars she had seen on television, she gracefully slid into the limo. The door closed behind her and silence filled the space. A moment later her carriage started to roll as her adventure began.

Jasmine was trying to take it all in when she noticed an envelope on the seat with her name on it. She picked it up and held it momentarily. She slipped the flap open and pulled out the card from inside:

> **"My lady, Friday night was wonderful. I want this feeling to last forever. Please relax and have a glass of champagne as the driver brings you to me. I hope you've dressed warm and brought a jacket as I asked. You are in for a real treat. For now just lean back and enjoy the 30-minute ride. I have a passionate kiss and hug waiting for your arrival.**
>
> **Luke"**

Her mind was on overload as she looked around. The rich smell and the soft feel of leather of the leather excited her as she stroked her hand over the seat. Jasmine saw the champagne wrapped in a white towel, chilling in a bucket. A subtle mist rose like smoke from the bottle. She reached for a crystal flute and poured. She always loved the light tickle on her nose that drinking champagne brought. She sipped slowly from the flute. Jasmine noticed a television, a DVD, and even a computer neatly built into this office on wheels.

The tinted windows protected Jasmine from the curious eyes of passersby, but afford her a look at the town as the limo snaked through the narrow streets of her neighborhood and escaped into the openness of the countryside. The rolling farmlands, beautiful forest, and quaint little towns passed by and helped relax Jasmine as her adventure continued. Pouring another glass of champagne, she relaxed and sat back, enjoying the luxury as the limo continued its journey.

Time passed as her mind wandered into her fantasy world. A bump jerked her back in to reality as the limo turned off of the road and into what seemed to be a field. Her carriage seemed to bounced a bit on the rough path but soon slowed to a stop. The window that separated her from the driver began to lower as she struggled to get her bearings.

"We have arrived ma'am." The divider rose and Jasmine wondered what was to come.

Suddenly the door swung open. Luke stood as a pillar of power before her with his hand extended. She presented her hand to him. He gently took her long slender fingers into his hand and lifted Jasmine from her seat.

"Hope you had a nice ride."

Luke guided her out of the limo and into his waiting arms. He pulled Jasmine tight to him as he gave her the promised hug and passionate kiss. He didn't stop with one. His soft lips pressed to hers and the two lovers become lost in each other, until Jasmine remember they are not alone; the driver. *Where is the driver?* She broke their kiss, looked around, and saw the driver is still in the car.

Jasmine's eyes pan taking in the wonders of the countryside. She stopped when she noticed only 100 feet away, stood a hot air balloon, majestically filling the soft blue morning sky. Her head tilted skyward as she took in the teardrop shape, colorful panels, and large wicker basket. Jasmine noticed the heavy rope wrapped around a large wooden spike. Its mushroomed head bearing witness to the hammering needed to drive it deep into the ground. The rope was pulled taut holding the balloon firmly to the ground. The teardrop swayed ever so slightly in the wisps of the morning breeze.

"Oh-my-God, is that yours?"

"Yes, my lady. I'm going to take you for the most wonderful ride you could ever imagine."

"You are going to do what!" she exclaimed with near hysteria. "Do you know how to fly that thing?" I've never been in an airplane, much less a balloon!"

Luke smiled, reached for her hand, and gave it a gentle squeeze while looking deeply into her eyes.

"I said you will always be safe with me and I meant it. Trust is all I ask. Give me a chance and I will show you things you've never imagined."

For some reason, her fears were gone. Is it his voice, his confidence, or simply the trust he instills in her? It doesn't matter. Jasmine's feelings of anxiety seemed to switch instantaneously to excitement as he led her to the balloon and the basket waiting there to take them away.

Luke jumped up into the basket. He turned to guide Jasmine to the stool he had placed on the ground. Tentatively, she stepped up onto the stool. Perhaps excitement was not the proper feeling? She put pressure onto the basket's rolled top edge. The basket creaked out a welcome, flexed slightly, and returned the firm support she needed to steady herself as her legs trembled. Jasmine turned to rest her backside onto the edge of the basket.

Slowly, she transferred all of her weight to the basket. The basket didn't complain, but rather welcomed her. First one leg, then the other, and suddenly she felt the basket's edge nudge her in. It was like a hand on her backside saying "come on already, I want to get going." The sudden push knocked Jasmine off balance causing her to stumble into Luke's arms. The strong arms she craved, circled around her, drawing her in for a passionate kiss that left her light headed. She was his to do with as he wished.

"Are you ready for an adventure?" he whispered into her ear.

Luke's moist lips moved to her neck.

Jasmine gasped as his kisses found that special place on her neck. Her fingers sought out his hair, becoming entwined, and encouraged him to continue the attention she instantly craved.

"Here we go," he whispered as he reached past her to release the rope.

She did not even notice the heavy braided rope fall away as the basket began to rise. His arms released her and he looked up. Luke's large hand grasped some sort of pull chain. Jasmine could not take her eyes off of him as she studied his every move. Luke glanced down at a small cluster of dials, then back upwards. She watched in amazement as he shifted from the sexy passionate man, to someone of absolute authority; the captain.

His focus was intense as he studied the mechanism above their heads. Luke pulled the chain. A loud "ROAR" came from nowhere. Jasmine was startled and jumped into Luke for safety. She looked up and was greeted by Luke's warm smile. Above their heads the two large burners came to life. The balloon rose and she hugged him, demanding he protect her from the unknown. The balloon continued to rise, leaving the earth behind. Slowly they rose above the trees. She watched as the limo became a toy and drifted from sight.

The silence was incredible. Still holding onto Luke's strong body she allowed herself to look down at the earth. It was incredible. Everywhere she looked she saw beauty and serenity.

The earth appeared as a wonderful painting laid out for her eyes to consume. Once again he pulled on the handle, and the burners roared to life. He took a step towards the edge of the basket, holding Jasmine tightly against him. Together they looked out at the sheer beauty below.

"This is incredible," she whispered, fearing to disturb the wonderful silence.

Jasmine tentatively placed one hand onto the top edge of the basket. She carefully leaned forward and gazed down at the countryside.

"Look at the deer" she whispered, "and that beautiful woodland."

Jasmine had never seen something so wonderful. Her fears drifted away as she took in the sights. The basket swayed gracefully in the soft breeze. Each time she shifted her weight the basket seemed to speak in a low, almost soothing, tone: "Creak, swish, creak," as if to say, "Welcome to my world, please enjoy the ride. I'm here and will keep you safe." Looking up she saw the beautiful bold colors of the balloon silhouetted against the soft blue of the morning sky. The white puffy clouds were smiling back their, welcome. Jasmine's mind was on overload attempting to greedily capture all of the new sights and sounds so she could revisit them later.

She was consumed by the beauty laid out before her while the balloon silently drifted through the air. Her inner self remained cautious and she could feel her fingertips grip into the basket as she struggled to put her fears behind her. Jasmine leaned into the basket's edge as she attempted to see everything. The soft blue of the sky with its graceful puffs of clouds seem to sooth her deepest tensions and Jasmine could feel herself relaxing.

The small farmhouse below reminded her of the dollhouse she had as a young girl. Her father had built it from a kit. He worked for days while she sat next to him watching as he skillfully cut each piece. He then lovingly glued it in place. Her father had taken her to the hardware store so she could pick out the paint for each room. He never complained once, as she picked color after color in order to make each room perfect. *Dad I really miss you.*

Jasmine would sit for hours and imagine herself in the perfect life with the perfect man. Well, life didn't take her there and she had a few bumps and bruises to prove it. She no longer wore the wedding ring, and the memories of her son still brought her a mix of joy and terrible sadness. She still misses him but long ago came to grips with his passing. Now it's her turn to rediscover herself and her inner woman. Thank God Mary convinced her to explore the world again. Jasmine could still be sitting in that house, alone, while life passed her by.

Thank you, Mary, she muttered to herself.

A bright bean of light from the rising sun caught her eye and brought her back to the present. Jasmine turned and looked into the eyes of this man. The man who had awakened things within her she never thought she would feel again.

"ROAR" breaks the silence once again as the capable pilot guides his balloon through the air. Luke reached for Jasmine's hand and pulled her close.

"We are the only ones in the world right now. It's just you and me together up here." Luke whispered.

He held Jasmine tightly in his arms. She loved the feelings of him holding her. She returned the embrace while he began to nuzzle and kiss her supple neck.

"Oh my God that feels incredible."

Her hands came up and moved through his curly locks. Jasmine's head tilted to the side, giving him more access to those special places. His moist lips moved up higher on her neck. Luke's hot breath on her ear caused her to gasp. Boldly her other hand went to his chest, feeling the muscles she enjoyed stroking and yes those hard nubs that strained against the smooth fabric of his shirt.

Jasmine's fingers stoked across one nipple then the other as she felt him shiver. A grin came to her as she began to realize just how sensitive these nubs were. It almost seemed as though he derived the same pleasure when his nipples were touched as she did when her own received attention.

Jasmine let her hands explore, feeling his ribs as she pulled him closer. She felt Luke's trembling hand moving up her body.

A jolt of electricity shot through her as his finger slipped past the hem of her sweater, touching the bare flesh of her stomach. Jasmine could barely breathe as his fingers moved slowly upward. Her chest heaved in anticipation of his touch.

Why did I wear a bra? Jasmine asked herself as her body craved his large hands.

He broke the embrace, reached into the air and once again released the roar of the burners fired. Jasmine felt the subtle results as the balloon gently rose.

Luke and Jasmine moved to the edge of the basket. He wrapped his strong arms around her body as he placed another fiery kiss on her shoulder causing a shudder to travel through her. His hands were just below her breasts and she welcomed the feel of him pressing into her. There was no mistaking the wanton feelings she had for Luke.

Her mind wandered to the passion and lovemaking they had already shared. She knew she was alive again. Luke made her feel beautiful, sexy, and desirable. Her arousal seemed to gush from within her. Jasmine was like a teenager, out of control in the arms of her first lover. The unmistakable feel of his swollen manhood against her bottom caused her to push back desiring to feel more.

Luke inched Jasmine's sweater up exposing the soft flesh of her back and the bra strap that divided it. Deftly his fingers touch the clasp and it fell open. The sudden release of pressure and sense of freedom served to heighten her senses.

His big hands moved around her sides and up Jasmine's torso cradling each breast. Her knuckles whitened as her fingers gripped the top of the basket. She could feel her body scream as what she hoped was the first of many orgasms swept over her.

Jasmine pushed back even harder against him. He continued to lavish those wonderfully moist kisses on her neck. Luke's lips moved up capturing her earlobe. She could feel her nipples hardening as they seemed to separate his fingers with their power. Jasmine heard an animal-like groan escape her lips as his tongue began to probe her ear. She turned her head towards him and she was met with a passionate wet kiss.

Jasmine held tightly onto the rail. She could feel his powerful hand release her left breast. For a moment his moist lips vanished. The reason was quickly realized as a "ROAR" again pierced the silence. Like the fire burning within Jasmine the heat of the burner caused the balloon to rise. His lips returned, this time kissing Jasmine's bare back. She felt his moist lips moving over her. The cool sensations as the air hit the trail left by his soft kisses was electrifying. Goosebumps erupt from her arms and legs as the sensations traveled through her. His hands moved down her torso and reached the waist band of her jeans.

My God, here; he cannot be serious. Not here... His power is undeniable; Jasmine's excitement was too far along to stop now. Passion quickly pushed aside sensibility.

"Yes, yes" Jasmine heard herself say as those strong hands release the button on her jeans.

She could hear the pounding of her heart as the silence was broken by the song of the zipper sliding down. *Oh my God, what am I doing Jasmine said to herself?* She felt his hand move beneath the waistband of her panties. Her hips rotated, involuntarily, towards his hand as she struggled to guide it where she craved it to be. She gasped as his finger touched the small patch of neatly trimmed hair. His lips were once again on her neck. Jasmine's head was spinning as the fire within her body raged out of control.

Does she push back against his throbbing shaft or does she press more firmly against the fingers that have now begun to enter her secret place.

Jasmine felt his hot breath on her ear as he whispered, "I want you. I crave you now my lady. Make love with me."

"Yes, my God, yes I need you" was the nearly frantic reply.

She tried to turn around, but the weight of his body, the stiffness of his manhood, and his strong fingers kept her pressed to the rail.

"The beauty of the earth can only be matched by your own" Luke whispered.

Jasmine felt herself pressed back against his arousal. Suddenly he backed away, but only for a moment. Luke began to nudge Jasmine's pants over her hips. The chill of the early morning air wisped across her naked backside. Seconds later her panties and jeans were on the floor of the basket. He continued as she felt her clothes slip over her shoes. Another wisp of cool air stroked her naked bottom. A shudder rocked her body as goose bumps covered her soft skin. Luke's hot breath now caressed her backside.

"OH-MY-GOD!" Jasmine cried out as she felt his warm tongue touch her.

As if with a mind of their own, her legs parted and her pelvis tilted, attempting to guide his tongue to her most sensitive of places. She leaned down and her nipples now drug across the rough surface of the basket's edge. Fire shot from Jasmine's nipples to her pulsing womanhood. She leaned into the basket. In return, the basket began to caress her sensitive nipples.

Luke's tongue continued its probing. His attention caused Jasmine's body to respond with copious amounts of nectar. She had never felt so wet. The two lovers were completely out of control now. Jasmine's rational side made one final attempt to bring her back to reality. *Act your age*, popped into her consciousness. The attempt was weak at best and her passionate side quickly overwhelmed her rational thoughts.

"Please!" Jasmine pleaded "I need you, I need to feel you now!"

Jasmine felt him draw away and the mood was momentarily broken as the burners burst to life. Once again the balloon rose.

ZZZZZZIIIIIIPPPP she heard above the silence and anticipation took over. Her hands tightened onto the basket bracing for what was to come.

"Take me! I need you now!" echoed across the countryside.

Jasmine could barely breathe as she felt him begin to enter. Her moist petals opened as his member entered her. She could feel the heat and fullness within her as inch by incredible inch they became one. Jasmine relaxed her knees slightly, squatting a bit, in order to take him deeper. Luke leaned forward placing his hands onto her shoulders. He pulled her into him as she pressed back straining to have all he offered.

Jasmine was completely out of control now as she rocked her hips side to side. The sounds of lovemaking echoed through the countryside as the two surrendered to each other.

Luke's fingers slip into Jasmine's hair. She felt his grip tighten and draw her head back. She braced herself against the basket's edge as Luke slowly withdrew from her. Jasmine's head continued to spin while sensations and emotions poured over her. The feel of Luke pressing into her was incredible. Her fingers dug into the weave of the basket. Luke was in complete control of her now as he drew her head back by her hair. Every muscle in her body strained to participate in what was to come. She could feel his strong fingers as his free hand roamed over her back side. The fullness she felt was like nothing she could describe.

Jasmine's body finally yielded as he pressed deeper and deeper into her until she felt his heavy balls against her sensitive bud. With a great shutter, she exploded in orgasm. Her body trembling around his stiff member as the wave of pleasure washed over her. He leaned forward, wrapping his arms around her and cupping each breast. She could feel his embrace tighten as he shared in her release.

"Just us my lady; just you and me here in the silence as we make love."

A soft moan came from within Jasmine as she pushed back against him. She was consumed by the feeling of his shaft filling her entire body. Her hips seemed to circle on their own as she became accustom to his manhood cradled within her.

The pace of their pleasure quickened as these lovers strove to give their all. Soon the sounds of slapping flesh, the creeks of the basket, and their guttural, almost animalistic groans filled the air.

Luke released Jasmine's hair, but her head remained thrown back as she attempted to catch a glimpse of her lover. Luke's powerful hands gripped her hips as his thrusts continued. The pace increased. Jasmine could feel the beads of sweat slowly moving along her breasts as they jerked violently from the force of his passion. Faster and faster they moved. Luke sought the deepest penetration, while Jasmine pushed back harder. Both halves of this whole desired the same thing.

His rhythm continued as she felt him slide in, then out, then in, and out. Her body responded meeting his every thrust with a push back. In perfect unison they rushed together towards the light, the light of orgasm.

Jasmine could feel her breasts shake with every thrust. *Is he going deeper now* she wondered? Then she felt it. Deep within her body the wave began to build once again. Jasmine could feel the sweat pouring from his chest onto her back as he continued to piston into her.

He rose up now, with one hand clutching each hip. He began to pull her back onto his shaft as he worked frantically to control his release. She felt his thrusts getting more powerful and more purposeful as he began to lift her from the floor of the basket. She was wonderfully aware each time his heavy balls brush against her. Faster and faster he thrust.

"Now my love! Now is the time!" Jasmine pleads as the wave begins to overtake her. Her release was imminent as her body shuddered with convulsions, sweet wonderful convulsions.

Luke groaned a deep animalistic groan. One last powerful thrust drove deep and then just stopped. Every muscle in his body tightened as he held her up on her toes suspended by his manhood. Jasmine could feel the wonder of his pulsing shaft deep inside of her as it exploded, depositing his hot seed into her. Jasmine's own body convulsed as her stomach tightened and she felt herself trembling out of control.

Another single stroke and again she felt his shaft swell within her. A scorching hot flow of his seed gushed into her as she quivered around him. Jasmine trembled as a second wave washed over her. Her entire body was alive with tingling feelings, and goose bumps as she bathed in the wonder of the orgasm. One more time he withdrew and drove back into her body. He stiffened as a third rush of hot seed flooded into her.

Jasmine collapsed, supporting both of them on the side of the basket. Her chest rose and fell as she gasped for air, her lover clung to her. Both remain there, quietly enjoying the moment. Luke's chest heaved as she felt his breath on her shoulder.

"You are incredible my lady, simply incredible" escaped breathlessly from his mouth.

"No, my love, you are the one who has awakened this in me. You are the one that makes me want to give myself to you."

His powerful arms held fast, pulling her tightly into him as Jasmine's legs began to tremble. She felt that tightness in her stomach. The feeling of another orgasm as his softening shaft slipped from her body.

The basket let out a loud creak, saying, "don't forget me, I need attention too." Gently he kissed her cheek as he raised himself up. Her eyes returned their attention to the beauty of the countryside.

"ROAR," she heard as the balloon once again rises. Jasmine turned and looked into the eyes of this wonderful man. A single step towards Luke and her arms naturally encircled him. A passionate kiss followed. He released the handle and gently wrapped his strong arms around her. They stood there together and enjoyed the view, and serenity of their world. It seemed as though it was a world of two as they basked in the glow of each other.

"ROAR," the burners screamed as he continued to fly the graceful balloon.

"Perhaps we better get dressed. You seem to be getting chilled."

Jasmine just loved the sound of his voice. A voice that was so calming yet had a definite tone of being in charge.

"You have goose bumps everywhere my lady."

Little did he know he was causing the goose bumps not the chill of the morning air. "ROAR" and another blast of heat erupted from the powerful burners. They both took a moment to dress, hug, and kiss. Then they simply stood together, drifting on the soft currents of air, enjoying nature's beauty as it spread out before them.

Jasmine looked at her watch and could not believe they had been in the air for more than 3 hours. The sun had climbed high in the sky and she noticed her pilot becoming more active. He reached down and opened a small box on the floor of the basket removing a radio.

"Landing team, come in."

"Landing team here" came blasting out of the radio.

"We are five miles north of Pleasantville and I anticipate touchdown in about 15 minutes, copy."

"Ten four" is the response.

"I'll see you in the north pasture of Frank's farm."

"Ten four" again came from the radio.

"I'll just stand over here and watch if you don't mind? I would not want to be in the way."

"Jasmien, you are never in the way. Come over here and land this thing with me."

"Oh, I could never do that. We would crash for sure."

"No, I'll help you. Just come here, and I'll talk you through the whole thing.

Oh-my-God, Jasmine thought to herself as she stepped to the center of the balloon.

"See the smoke from the chimneys down there?"

Jasmine looked down and noticed the smoke rising nearly straight up from the chimney of the small cabin below.

"The winds are nearly calm, so this will be much easier. Now grab this cord and pull it down for a moment or two. That will open a flap in the top of the balloon and let some of the hot air out, allowing us to descend."

"Are you out of your mind?" Jasmine screeched. "Let the air out! You want me to let the air out of the balloon? What if I let out too much?"

"Relax, I'm here. I told you before, I will always keep you safe. Now just pull the cord and get a feel for the balloon's reaction."

His hand on hers instilled the confidence she needed to embrace the unknown. He had an almost magical way with her. When he spoke she felt safe, beautiful, sexy, and capable of doing anything. Jasmine didn't understand what was happening, but she liked it. Her knuckles turned white as she maintained a death grip on the cord.

Jasmine took a deep breath and gave the cord the first tentative pull. The balloon began to descend slowly. The basket creaked out its approval. Luke leaned over and gave Jasmine a kiss on the cheek.

"See that field off in the distance? That is where we will land."

Jasmine laughed as she noticed the white limo moving down the country road heading in the direction of the field.

"He better hurry or we will beat him there" she chuckled.

Another pull on the cord, and the descent continued. The rate of descent began to increase.

"Not so fast my lady. Give it a little burner to slow our descent."

Jasmine, with more confidence now, pulled the other cord and awakened the burners. Their descent slowed and Jasmine began to feel a bit confident in what she was doing.

"Excellent, you're a natural pilot."

Jasmine continued to juggle the two cords until she was near the field and VERY close to the ground. She could look straight out into the tree tops.

"You take it from here, please," Jasmine pleaded.

"No you can do this, just keep doing what you've been doing."

Oh-my-God, I'm going to kill us both, she thought to herself.

"A little more burner Jasmine, you are doing fine."

"ROAR" and the balloon's descent nearly stopped as the huge balloon simply hung motionless in the still air. Jasmine looked over the edge of the basket. They are only a few feet off the ground.

"A little more now" her pilot commanded.

Her hand pulled the now familiar cord and the basket slowly descended. "CREAK" the basket moaned. She felt a slight jolt as the basket hit the ground.

"I told you, you could do it. Great landing my lady I could not have done better myself."

Jumping up and down with excitement Jasmine hugged Luke and kissed her man.

Two men raced over from a van. They each grabbed a side of the basket and one dropped a stool onto the ground. Luke took Jasmine's hand in his own. The basket creaked its goodbye as first one, then her other leg swung over the edge of the basket and onto the stool. Luke's firm grip and strong arm steadied her as she exited the basket, stepping down off the stool and onto firm ground once again.

Luke jumped from the basket, saying something to the two men, before walking Jasmine to the waiting limo.

"Who are those men?" she asked.

"They are my ground crew. One is my brother, and the other is a long time friend. My friend is also a pilot and we share the balloon. Sometimes he flies and I chase. Other times I fly and he chases. Today was my turn to fly."

"How long does it take to get your license?" Jasmine inquired.

"About a year," Luke replied, "unless you can fly every weekend. Normally we can only fly about once a month due to availability and weather."

"What will you do next?" Jasmine asked.

"We need to deflate the balloon, let it cool, fold it up, and pack it back into the van in preparation for the next flight."

"Oh, how long will you be?"

"About an hour, but I have some things I need to attend to today so I won't be able to chat tonight. I hope you understand. You ride home in the limo and I'll see you on-line tomorrow." Disappointment came over Jasmine as she realized the day together had come to an end.

When they arrived at the limo Jasmine turned and wrapped her arms around Luke's neck.

"I had a terrific time" she whispered.

She then gave him a deep passionate kiss with a wink.

"It was something truly special for me also Jasmine."

Jasmine smiled and slid into the limo. Luke shut the door and the limo began its bumpy ride through the field back to the road. Reaching for a glass and the champagne, Jasmine poured herself a drink, and leaned back into the soft leather seat. With a few sips of the champagne, and a deep breath, she closed her eyes, reliving the entire day as the limousine whisked her home.

The limousine pulled up and stopped in front of Jasmine's house. The door swung open and a hand reached in to help her out. She looked at the driver and after a polite "thank you" she walked up the sidewalk to the door.

At the door she turned and watched as the limo disappeared down the block. A quick turn of the key and she was home. Tossing her coat onto the sofa, she reached for the phone, and dialed.

"Hello" came over the phone.

Jasmine spent the next hour relaying to her friend the incredible adventure from which she just returned.

Return to Reality

Jasmine rolled out of bed, the day somehow seemed different, brighter, and more joyous. She grabbed her robe and rushed downstairs to her computer, pushed the ON button, and noticed her reflection in the monitor. She shook her head and laughed. *Now that's a look!*

To describe it as "bed head" would just not do. Somehow her hair was defying gravity, but today she didn't care. Her heart was filled with joy, excitement, and anticipation as she waited for her computer to boot. It's agony as she impatiently watches the screens go by.

Can this thing be any slower? I have got to get a new computer, one of those really fast ones that boot up in the blink of an eye. Another click and Messenger is open. Her heart raced as she saw a message from Luke. Quickly she clicked on it and waited as the computer did whatever a computer does. Finally the message opened:

> My dearest Jasmine,
> I've never had a flight so wonderfully peaceful nor so deeply moving. I feel badly that we had to part so abruptly after landing. Let me make it up to you. I'd like to take you for a drive in the country today if you are not busy. I'll see you soon.
> Hugs and kisses

What? No more she questioned as she quickly typed a response:

> Luke, I had a great time also and yes, I would love to go for a drive. What time were you thinking? How about 2:00 pm? I'll be ready.

Jasmine watched her screen, waiting for a response but nothing came. *Guess he stepped away from his computer* she thought to herself. She decided to get busy on the few things she needed to get done. Jasmine didn't want to worry about trifles when it was time to meet Luke again.

She quickly moved into her normal routine, but somehow this day did not seem normal. She placed her robe onto the hook behind the door and quickly slipped into her "cleaning" housedress, and turned on the stereo. She placed her favorite "cleaning" CD into the slot and turned the volume up.

There was a bounce in her step and music in her heart as she went about doing the laundry and cleaning the house. The music on the stereo filled the house with a fun beat. Even dusting, something she usually dreaded seemed fun as she danced around the bedroom like Donna Reed.

Jasmine spotted the pair of black heels she had worn on their first date.

Looking around as if to make sure no one was watching, she picked up the heels and slipped them onto her feet. She laughed to herself, as she stepped up onto them. That once familiar squeeze on her toes did not seem so bad this morning. Remembering when she and Fred would go out dancing, she began to dance around the room imagining Luke, not Fred, guiding her across the floor.

The nights would always start with her in heels. She loved the way they made her feel. Heels added height, confidence, and sexiness. She knew that even her posture was better in heels. It had to be or she would fall.

Shoulders back giving her a much curvier shape that drew the attention of every man in the place. She felt beautiful. The discomfort was not only worth it, but barely noticed for most of the night. She knew she looked fabulous in them and that's what mattered.

Jasmine continued her dusting in the heels, up on her toes, twirling about, envisioning herself on the dance floor; her dress flowing outward as she twirled, extending her hand to the man she loved just as she had watched so many times in old movies.

Soon she recalled just how all of those nights ended as the discomfort of the heels overcame the joy of wearing them and she would kick the heels off and dance in her stockings.

Jasmine's mind jumped back again to thoughts of Luke.

Will Luke take me dancing one day? she asked herself as she continued to dance around the house.

He is nice and tall, his grip firm. I would love to feel him take control of me, moving us around the dance floor. Maybe he pulls me tightly to him as we dance a slow dance, two people moving as one in perfect harmony with not only the music but each other.

The sound of the doorbell jerked Jasmine back to reality as she continued her dance towards the door. She stepped up onto one foot as she pirouetted and reached for the doorknob. Lost in herself she flung the door open to see who was there.

"Luke!" she shrieked and slammed the door shut.

Oh my God, look at me! I can't let him see me like this! Oh my God, my hair! I must smell like Lemon Pledge®!

Jasmine's practical side broke into her thoughts. *I can't just leave him standing out there. He must think I've lost my mind.*

With an unsteady hand she opened the door and there was Luke, smiling sweetly but looking a bit puzzled. He was holding a bouquet of white daisies looking handsome as ever.

"I wasn't expecting you until 2:00" Jasmine stammered trying to push her hair into some sort of order.

"Sorry Jasmine, I wanted to catch the morning light and the cool of the day. Guess I should have been more specific about the time" Luke said sensing her obvious discomfort with her appearance. Luke felt embarrassed about his miscalculation.

"Shall I come back later Jasmine?"

"No, no need to be sorry, just let me grab my purse and I'm ready to go" she said with a chuckle trying to make light of her appearance. Her crimson face gave away her true feelings though.

"You look ravishing to me, the outfit works," Luke said with a smile as he handed Jasmine flowers, then wrapped her in his arms. Luke starred into Jasmine's eyes as they inched closer together until their lips touched ever so softly.

Jasmine looked at the wonderful flowers, set them onto the table then returned to Luke and the deep blue eyes she loved to get lost in.

Luke took her hand and extended it; the dancing began as he led her around the house, moving in perfect time with the music. Jasmine melted into his arms and thoughts of bad hair, old house dress, even hurting feet, disappeared from her mind as she was swept away in his arms, lost in the music and the deep pools of blue that were his eyes.

The dancing continued for who knows how long as the two enjoyed each other. On the third time around the house Jasmine stopped them at the steps, kissed Luke passionately and took him by the hand leading him up the stairs.

Jasmine had not had a man in her bedroom since her divorce and her heart was beating with such force she thought it was trying to explode from her chest. Her stomach did flip flops with each step. They reached the door, Jasmine turned and took Luke into her arms and kissed him.

Her passion was overflowing and her desire was clearly visible to Luke. She looked deep into his eyes and with a sexy smile on her face, reached behind her, turned the brass doorknob, and pushed the door open. Luke stood there for a moment as he gazed into those eyes knowing what was about happen.

"I hope you don't mind, I didn't make my bed this morning" Jasmine said with a devilish grin.

She knew what she wanted and wasted little time as she led him to her bed, a sturdy four poster that her grandmother had left her. The heavy linen quilt lay atop the tall bed. Pillows were everywhere as she loved being surrounded by them, feeling the pressure as she slept. This morning she wanted a much different kind of pressure and she would not be denied.

Jasmine turned to Luke and pressed her lips to his, stroking her hands along his face. He knew to let her lead as he attempted to hold still for her. She stared into his eyes as her long fingers moved slowly down his neck and onto his chest. Her fingers spread wide as she stroked over his firm chest, then back up to the buttons of his shirt.

Still lost in his eyes, her fingers began to open the buttons of his shirt. One by one she released them exposing the curls of his sparse chest hair. She allowed her fingers to slip through the soft curls as she stroked his wonderful chest, feeling every muscle flex as she teased him with a feather light touch. Jasmine's hands explored, but her eyes stayed awash in his. These two individuals were craving to be one.

His body shuddered as her fingertips stroked across his stiff nipples. She loved the reaction and smiled as she mounted her assault. Jasmine continued to play until he could take no more. She pushed his shirt from his shoulders and cast it aside.

Her lips quickly found her new toys; his entire body shook as she drew the stiff nipple into her mouth. Her tongue circled, stroked, and then flicked its stiffness as he squirmed under her attention. He reached for her to take control but she would not have it. Her small frame exerted considerable force; letting him know just who was in charge.

Jasmine continued to undress Luke, working slowly but efficiently until he stood before her just the way she wanted him, naked and very aroused. She pressed herself into him, guiding him back against the bed until he got the idea. Luke pushed a few pillows aside and slipped down onto the soft mattress.

Jasmine let her hands slide tenderly down his arms until she held his strong hands in hers. She leaned down, kissed each one softly and then released them. Her eyes were glued to his as she began to slowly open each of the buttons on the front of her tattered house dress. A devilish grin came to her face as she allowed the dress to open only wide enough to give him a glimpse of her feminine wears.

For years she had watched men attempt to look down her blouse or steal glimpses of her curvy body and she knew exactly what men wanted. Luke was no exception as his eyes focused on her long fingers and the supple flesh that she wanted him to see.

When Jasmine's fingers reached her soft belly, each hand then began to slide up the open dress. Somehow, the old tattered dress had become a beautiful gown, and as her fingers slid up the worn fabric, Luke's eyes followed.

She allowed her fingers to linger as her hands hovered over her breasts then up until she slipped the house dress off and allowed it to fall into a puddle at her feet. Jasmine watched as Luke scanned up and down her naked form. She helped guide his eyes as her hands stroked sensuously over her aroused flesh. His eyes followed as her slender fingers slipped over her chest, around her breasts and down her supple belly and back up again.

She moved onto the bed, climbing up to straddle Luke. Her knees on either side of his torso, she leaned forward and kissed him passionately. Luke reached for her but she intercepted his hands and pressed them into the pillows as she pushed herself up. She allowed her hands to slowly wander down his chest until his hard nipples were in her palms once again.

Jasmine's hips began to gyrate, side to side then forward and back, until she had his stiff manhood just where she wanted it. She rocked her hips and he began to enter. Luke's eyes widen as he was overcome with excitement. The two lovers were soon one and Jasmine grinned as she enjoyed the feel of being the aggressor.

She began to slowly guide them towards the edge. Her body rocked as she controlled the experience. She was taking Luke where she wanted him to go, not alone, but with him as her partner.

Faster and faster she rocked watching and feeling Luke's every move. Soon his eyes widen and she squeezed him tightly. Her own arousal began to peak and she knew the edge was near. Panting and passion overwhelmed the two lovers. She knew his release was at hand and time seemed to stop as they stepped off the edge together.

He stiffened and groaned a deep primal sound, as Jasmine's own release began to build in her stomach. His powerful body lifted them from the mattress as he reached and pulled her to him seeking the safety and comfort of the woman he loved as he lost himself within her.

The couple did spend the day on a beautiful drive as Luke had suggested, they just never left the room. Jasmine had never taken the lead in matters of lovemaking, but her need to please Luke was overpowering.

She wanted to show this wonderful man what it was like to have your sexuality reawakened after years of denying yourself the simple pleasures of a loving relationship. When the day finally came to an end she walked him to the door and they kissed. A tear began to form in Jasmine's eye. Luke, sensing her fear, reached up and kissed it away.

"We can never be apart my wonderful Jasmine," Luke whispered. "I love you."

His heart struggled with leaving her as their fingers stretched to maintain contact. Finally their hands separated. Jasmine watched as Luke walked down the sidewalk looking over his shoulder, obviously in no hurry. With a look of longing on his face, he got into his car and slowly drove away. She could feel his love as he disappeared into the darkness. Jasmine closed the door and reached for the phone. She needed to share this with someone and Mary was always there for her.

A Bump in the Road

The alarm sounded and Jasmine awoke; well, perhaps part of her awoke. She reached for the snooze button to silence the intrusion into her slumber. Closing her eyes, she rolled over and lay there thinking, *how wonderful is life?* Her arms stretched across her queen bed to clutch one of her firm pillows, drawing it into her chest. Like a little girl, she hugged it close imagining what it would be like to awaken every morning in his arms. His scent still remained on the pillow as her mind continued its visit to the wonderful time she had yesterday.

It had been so long since she allowed herself to imagine that feeling. The pain of Fred leaving, the months of tears, self-doubt, and loneliness had killed every hint of happiness a man could bring her. She had spent months huddled in this very same bed wanting God to just take her and end her misery. Somehow she survived.

Many a time finding the courage to keep going in the anger she felt when Fred said "You can't do it on your own. I'll see you crawl one day." There can be no denying the anger and ugliness divorce can bring out in a person, especially this divorce. Ten years have passed but the memories of that pain were still fresh.

Jasmine knew she was capable of doing anything, well almost anything. Boldly she pondered, *Can I ever be a loving wife again? Wake up woman* she screamed to herself. *My God it's only been a couple of dates. Let's not rush to call the minister!*

But there was something special about this man, something that allowed her to put the past behind her and focus on the future. At least for now, the feelings were wonderful. The alarm sounded once again, and Jasmine was forced to release the pillow and shut it off.

I wonder what he is doing right now? Wasting no time, her hand thrashed about until she captured her cell phone. With the flick of her wrist, the cell phone was open and she was greeted with the familiar "Good morning Jasmine." Luke had been sending her a good morning text message every day since they met on-line. Her heart always skipped a beat as she realized he was thinking of her.

This is a drive-by hug and kiss from someone who is longing to be with you. See you soon. Hugs and kisses

Jasmine's heart melted as she read the simple message. Her fingers quickly pounded out a return message, and now, her day could begin.

Work was somehow more joyous as Jasmine began to live her life with Luke in it. The customers came in and out as she and Mary perform their magic for customer after customer. Jasmine kept checking her phone for more "drive-bys" but the phone was uncharacteristically quiet. She couldn't take it any longer and constructed her own message to the man she can't get out of her mind.

Hi Luke, I've been thinking of you and your beautiful tushie (lol) all day. I hope you enjoyed yesterday as much as I did. You made me feel like a beautiful woman and I hope you knew that yesterday was all about you--exactly like I wanted it to be…Love always

The shop was quiet for a moment and Jasmine and Mary took the opportunity to flop into the salon chairs and take a well-deserved break. They sat there allowing the stresses of the day to flow from their tired bodies.

"Jasmine do you remember my neighbor I was telling you about earlier this week?"

"Do you mean the woman who wanted you to shave her head?" Jasmine replied.

"Yes, her name is Antoinette, but she goes by Toni, and she lives just a couple of doors down from me. I saw her at the mailbox, and she seemed to be quite upset. I invited her back to my apartment and we talked for hours. She is divorced and lives alone. About a month ago she discovered a lump in her left breast. She found out she has breast cancer."

"That's terrible," replied Jasmine in a very concerned voice.

"My mother died of breast cancer about 14 years ago. It was terrible to watch her fade away to nothing. It wasn't like it is now. They knew almost nothing about it and the treatments were horrible."

"Well, she is starting her chemo and said she just couldn't take watching her hair fall out one clump at a time." Mary replied in a somber tone.

"Oh, I can't imagine going through that alone," Jasmine replied.

"I was with my mom the whole time, and it was still horrible for her. The throwing-up, weakness, mouth sores, she even lost all sensation in one hand from the radiation. There were days she could not even use the bathroom herself! I just can't imagine going through it alone. Doesn't she have anyone who could help her?"

"She said that her parents had passed and she is an only child. She and her husband never had any children and she has had little contact with him since the divorce. She truly is alone."

"Maybe she could talk to her ex-husband and see if he will help her, at least until she gets through the chemo," Jasmine suggested.

"Already did that," Mary said. "It took some talking and many tears, but she finally agreed that she would call him. I sat and held her hand while she called. It nearly broke my heart to listen to them. He seemed as devastated as she was and was very sympathetic. I think he will help her for awhile, at least. I guess, unlike Fred, all ex-husbands are not a-holes," Mary said with a chuckle as she turned and saluted Fred.

"Jasmine, if you don't mind, I think I'll leave a little early today. I want to drop in on Toni just to see how she is doing. Her first chemo treatment was today."

"Sure, Mary, take off. I'll close up" Jasmine replied.

Jasmine swept up and put things away. She removed the cash drawer and headed back to the office to balance the drawer and make the deposit for the day's receipts.

While in the office, she popped open her computer to see what her message from Luke would say. She looked forward to his messages. They just lifted her spirits.

The computer came out of its slumber, but no message was there. This was the first time since they had begun chatting that he had not sent her a message during the day. Her fingers began to fly over the keyboard creating another drive-by message to her Luke.

> I was just closing up the salon and the thought of your warm hand in mine as we walked down the park path, and it warmed my heart. Our hands swinging in unison as the setting sun colors the evening sky. Pausing, you pull me tightly into your arms, look into my eyes, and our lips meet... Just a thought, my Luke

Jasmine packed up and headed for home. She was not concerned, but it was still unusual that Luke had not left her a note of some sort. They had invented the drive-bys many months ago when they started to send "secret" short messages to each other. They were usually only one or two lines and meant to make one another smile. His made her pause a hectic day to take a few moments to enjoy him, if only in her mind.

Jasmine fixed herself supper and did some light cleaning. Once she finished her routine, she logged on to the computer and looked for Luke. He was nowhere to be found. Jasmine began to worry a bit. She really had no reason to suspect anything, after all, he had not told her he would meet her on-line. She answered her e-mails and checked for him once again before she turned the computer off and settled in to watch a movie she had rented.

Jasmine had special ordered an old romantic movie about a knight and a princess. She loved movies about medieval times when chivalry was king. Since she was a child, Jasmine would dream of being a princess waiting for her handsome knight. Old movies helped her visualize this as she thrust herself into each one. She enjoyed the movie as always. A tear trickled down her cheek at the end when the knight swept the fair maiden away to his castle and they lived happily ever after.

The movie's credits began to roll by and she found herself with a need to be with her own knight. Jasmine could not help but see Luke whenever she dreamed of her own knight. After the wonderful movie, she could clearly see Luke atop his stallion. She was seated behind him, her arms pulling them tightly together as they rode off into the sunset.

She opened her computer again, but no messages! Now, she was becoming concerned.

Jasmine decided to take a bath and try to head off the building tension caused by Luke's unexplained absence. She started filling the tub, while she lit her favorite lavender scented candle. She grabbed her fluffy bath sheet, and headed for the dryer. She tossed it in, set the dryer for maximum heat, and swung the door shut.

A bath for Jasmine was not a way to get clean. As a matter of fact, soap never played into bath time for Jasmine. She left the bath sheet tumbling as she poured herself a glass of wine. The glass with its long stem was placed on the table next to the tub. Jasmine dipped her finger tips into the water to check its temperature.

Satisfied, she left the water running as she headed to the dryer and recovered her now hot bath sheet. She was nearly ready. The bath pillow was next. She placed it under the stream of steaming water to warm it, then she positioned it carefully at the end of the tub.

Jasmine looked around and checked her preparations. Satisfied, she let her robe slide off her shoulders and hung it on the hook. Stepping gracefully into the steaming water, she slowly slipped beneath the soothing water.

"Aaaahhhhh," escaped from her lips as the water soothed her tense muscles, dissolving the stresses of the day. Jasmine lay there, sipping her wine, and enjoying the wonderful scent of the candle.

Her mind began to wander. *Where is Luke? Something is wrong! Why is he so quiet? Maybe he was in a car accident and is lying in a hospital bed calling for me!*

Jasmine jerked up out of the water. *Oh my God, I wonder if he was intimidated by last night. Perhaps I should have held back more. Did I come on too strong? That must be it, I've embarrassed him. I've driven away the best thing that's ever happened to me.*

Jasmine gulped down her wine in an attempt to calm her nerves. Her hands were visibly shaking now. The candle was flickering as she realized that the water was now cold.

She quickly stood up and reached for the warm towel. After cursory pat down, she wrapped the huge towel around herself. She rushed out of the bathroom, and headed for the computer, droplets of water falling from her shivering body as she moved through the house.

The leather of the computer chair groaned as her wet skin attempted to slide across the seat. Fingers pounded the keys with a sense of desperation as she struggled to open her e-mail. "Incorrect password," the computer barked back. Frustrated, she made a second, more careful attempt and her computer finally yielded.

It must be there. It has to be there. The computer screen finally came up. Jasmine's heart was in her throat as she saw "no new messages" flash across the screen. She didn't know what to do. Jasmine looked around and spotted the phone. *Mary will know what to do!* Frantically, her fingers punch out the numbers and the phone began to ring. *Mary will know what to do.* Jasmine listened as the phone rang, and rang, and rang...

It's All In Your Head; Isn't It?

Jasmine arrived at the shop early, pacing, as she waited anxiously for Mary. She had barely slept the night before, and desperately needed to talk. Luke's silence had continued into this morning, only stoking the fires of doubt that now raged within Jasmine.

Mary's car pulled up outside the salon. Jasmine ran to the door to meet her. Mary was puzzled as she looked at Jasmine holding the shop door open. Jasmine definitely looked upset and Mary wondered what was up with her friend.

"What's up Jasmine?" Mary shouted as she grabbed her purse and headed for the shop.

"I've done it now; I know I've done it!" Jasmine shouted, her voice trembling.

The ladies embraced at the door and Mary knew something was quite wrong. Jasmine held onto her friend with overt desperation. Mary was not sure what to do next; she sensed that her friend was on the verge of tears as she returned the hug.

"You've done what?" asked Mary as her friend continued to hold tightly.

"Let's go inside, Jasmine. We can sit down, and I'll make you some tea."

The ladies released their embrace, and headed into the shop. Mary walked to the coffee station and grabbed two mugs. She poured herself black coffee, and dropped the herbal teabag into the second mug for Jasmine. The steaming water filled Jasmine's mug, while Mary fondly recalled the prior night's events that kept her out until well after midnight. Now was not the time to discuss her wonderful night

Mary turned back and took a quick look at the schedule. No clients until 10:00. They have plenty of time to talk about whatever it was that had Jasmine so riled up. Mary took the cups back to Jasmine, who was pacing around her styling chair.

"Jasmine. Sit down, and tell me what the hell is going on with you."

Jasmine reached for her tea and sat down in the chair. She looked down at her cup as her trembling hand gripped the spoon. She started to stir her tea, but then looked up at Mary with a tear in her eye.

"Mary, I think I've scared Luke away. I haven't heard from him for two days. Mary, I let him see my wild side, and now he's gone."

"Wild side? Your wild side? We are talking about you, aren't we?" Mary questioned, desperately struggling to hold back her laughter.

Jasmine rolled her eyes and headed for the office in disgust.

"I thought you were my friend Mary." Jasmine tossed back over her shoulder as she stomped into her office and slammed the door.

Mary knew she had crossed the line with her friend and quickly followed her into the office.

"Jasmine, I'm sorry." Mary said as she placed her hands on her friend's shoulders.

She turned her around in the desk chair and saw the tears flowing down her cheeks. Mary knew she had made a big mistake not taking Jasmine's statement more seriously. She pulled a chair up and held Jasmine's hands in hers, looked into her tear-filled eyes and said "Now tell me what is going on."

"Mary, Luke stopped by yesterday morning and we had a great day together. I was feeling very confident and I made love to HIM."

"OHHHH" replied Mary who found herself uncommonly speechless. "AND…"

"I haven't heard from him since. No texting, no e-mail, no phone calls, nothing but silence. Luke is a very old fashioned man. He loves chivalry, and I don't think he was ready for a woman to take charge, especially in bed."

"Well Jasmine, just let me say this: EVERY man I'VE ever made love to, and that's no small number, have always wanted more not less. Perhaps, you've misjudged Luke here. How did he react?"

"Mary, do you mean, did I leave him a panting puddle of goo? The answer is yes, his eyes were wide and he was panting when we were done"

"Just how kinky did you get, Jasmine? I mean, you didn't do any whips or chains, did you? Tell me you didn't tie him up on your first time."

"No Mary, nothing like that. I just took the lead, and didn't release it the entire time."

"Jasmine, you held onto his thing the entire night? That can make a man very uncomfortable, unless you do it just right you know. You have to be very careful how you hold it; and the twins, did you watch out for the twins? That can kill an evening in a heartbeat."

"Mary, be serious. I just made love to him rather than letting him make love to me. It seemed to go very well, and he seemed satisfied afterwards. We lay together and cuddled like we usually do. It felt beautiful, but Mary, he hasn't called me. He always calls, texts, or e-mails me before either of us goes to bed. I've heard nothing from him, not a sound. He's disgusted with my boldness. He's told me many times he loves his women to be ladies, and what I did last night was not lady-like. I was more like an Amazon than a lady. He probably felt like an object, a toy to be used, not a man to be loved. Mary, he had the strangest look on his face as I sat atop him rocking to my rhythm not his."

"Jasmine, I've seen that look many times. Men just don't understand how good it can feel when they let go and just enjoy rather than having to wonder if they're doing it right. They love it when we take charge once in awhile. I think you're reading this all wrong. From what you've told me of Luke, he wants a woman to be herself, not pretend to be something she's not. Men seldom get to see a woman being a woman, one that has wants and desires. Most men only get to see the woman that we're taught to be, sexually passive, lady-like, and pure. When we're confident enough in ourselves to let down the wall and take a chance, it's my experience that they're amazed, not afraid. I'm sure you're reading this all wrong, Jasmine."

"But he hasn't called! Not a word. This is the first morning since we started dating that he hasn't sent me a good morning e-mail. Something is wrong, very wrong, I'm sure of it or he would have sent me a message."

"Maybe his computer broke, ever think of that? Maybe he just had something he had to do at work and it screwed up his schedule. Jasmine, there could be a million reasons and I seriously doubt that one of them is that you made love to him last night. Get a grip, girl!"

Jasmine felt better, if only slightly. She still had this unmistakable feeling that something was wrong. She wasn't sure what it was, but she just knew something was not right.

"Jasmine, remember my neighbor Toni? You will not believe what happened last night. It was about 10pm when I got back to the apartment from one of my late night grocery runs. I found a note on my door asking me to come to Toni's apartment. For some strange reason the note said to come right over, knock, and walk right in.

I put my groceries away, made a pot coffee, and took it with me to Toni's. I figured that after her first chemo appointment she might need a cup. When I got to her apartment, I knocked, walked in and there was an eerie silence as I looked around. I thought maybe she had changed her mind and went out. Then I heard a noise coming from the bedroom so I called her name and headed that way."

Mary's voice was becoming more excited now.

"I went down the hallway and turned into her room. The noise was coming from her master bathroom. I took a few more steps into the room and there stood a man! I was ready to kick his ass. I'd left my purse at my house so I didn't have my pistol, but I figured I could take him. He had his hands around her neck and was trying to stuff her head into the toilet!"

Jasmine leaned forward as Mary spun the story.

"Oh-my-God, Mary, what did you do?"

"Not while I'm here, you're not going to hurt my friend," I screamed at him, "Leave her alone!" and began to run towards him. Just then I heard Toni groan and begin throwing up. He turned back to Toni and said, "You'll be ok Toni, I'm here for you." I stopped dead in my tracks."

As usual, Mary's story was taking an unexpected twist.

"He was actually holding her hair, and taking care of her as she got sick. Boy was I glad I didn't have my pistol. I know I would've shot him, and then asked questions!"

"Mary!" Jasmine screeched. "You are such a hot head. I told you that gun would get you into trouble some day. What happened next?"

"That's not the half of it Jasmine." Mary said. The guy turned out to be her ex-husband and he was so nice. After we all caught our breath and calmed down we laughed until we cried. He said that he had been through a lot but had never been shot and really didn't ever want to be." Mary giggled as she recounted.

"So what happened next? How is Toni?" asked Jasmine in her normal, concerned way.

"Well, Toni is having a very, very difficult time with the chemo. She was violently sick and could barely walk around her apartment. John, her ex-husband, had been there all evening taking care of her. I suggested he go lie down and take a nap since he looked drained after taking care of Toni all evening. He just looked emotionally and physically exhausted. Besides, I think he needed to wash out his shorts after what I did to him. He sacked out on the sofa for a couple of hours while Toni and I drank coffee and chatted. I just tried to keep her mind off of what was happening to her. John woke up about 2am and went home.

Once he was gone, Toni and I could finally talk girl to girl.

"She said she was desperate when she realized she couldn't do anything. Frightened and nowhere to turn she figured "what the heck" and called John to see if perhaps he could help her. Their divorce was not ugly, but they hadn't seen or even talked to each other for years. She got his number from a mutual friend and called him."

"Awe... now that is a truly wonderful man. To come to her aid after so long, he must have really loved her. I cannot imagine what it would take for me to call Fred and ask for help. Is there anything else we can do to help her?"

"No, with John there now, she said she's fine. He said he would come over each day and help her and he would even take her to her chemo appointments so she doesn't have to take a taxi. He seems so sweet." Mary replied with a slight tear in her eye.

"Well what does our schedule look like today?" Jasmine asked.

"Not bad, my first should be here any minute. Your first is open today."

"Ok, then I'll stay here and get some paperwork done," replied Jasmine.

Jasmine reached over and booted up the computer. She anxiously awaited the message that she just knew would be there. The computer blinked and winked at her as the screens flashed by. Ending in an eerie silence, Jasmine's heart dropped as she realized that there was nothing, not a word from her Luke. No e-mail, text message, or IM; not a word.

Jasmine tearfully wondered, *perhaps Luke is not her long-awaited knight in shining armor after all? Had she moved too quickly to give herself to him? She gave him the milk and now he's not interested in the...*

Jasmine tried to shake off her disappointment and threw herself into the day-to-day paperwork of running her business. She placed orders for supplies, paid the bills, and the other things that had to be done to keep Jasmine's running. Every few minutes, though, she glanced down at the lower right corner of her screen, hoping to see her e-mail icon flashing but alas nothing. She could find no excuse to sit in her office and stare at the computer screen, so she reluctantly returned to the salon floor and threw herself back into the comfort of her customers.

Mary could sense the sadness within her friend. She tried to distract her with small talk, but nothing seemed to work. The atmosphere in the salon was noticeably down without Jasmine's upbeat spirit. The ladies worked through their morning appointments but the clock seemed to simply drag.

Madge burst through the door in her usual manner. Her loud voice and funny comments seemed to raise the mood in the salon instantly.

"What the hell is everyone so down about?" Madge bellowed.

"If I wanted to go somewhere depressing I'd have gone to my granddaughter's house and listened to her bitch about that monster she's raising."

Mary walked over to Madge and whispered "Luke is missing in action. She hasn't heard from him for two days."

"Is that all?" Madge bellowed.

"Let me guess, you gave it up to him didn't you, and now he took the milk and ran like hell! Didn't I tell you, all men are pigs? Just about the time you learn to live without a man, one of those son-of-a-bitches gets under your skin and then breaks your heart. What happened Jasmine, spill it!" Madge commanded.

"Madge, I just don't want to talk about it, OK?" Jasmine replied in a stern voice.

"Aw Jasmine, just spill it. Tell us all the juicy details."

"Madge, sit your butt in this chair and let's get your hair washed."

Madge grumbled and leaned back in the chair placing her head into the washbasin. Jasmine turned on the water, got the temperature just right, and then began to spray down Madge's hair.

"Mary, can you get me that fresh bottle of shampoo I left on my desk, please?"

"Sure." Mary replied.

Jasmine continued rinsing Madge's hair while waiting for the shampoo.

"Jasmine, this guy really hurt you didn't he?" Madge spoke with an uncharacteristic softness.

"I thought he was the one" Jasmine replied in a nearly tearful tone.

"Jasmine! Jasmine!" Mary screamed as she came running back waving the shampoo bottle.

"YOU'VE GOT MAIL!"

Jasmine looked up as the words seem to sink into her brain.

"Mail?" she questioned, and then realized what Mary was saying.

Jasmine let go of the sprayer and ran back to the office. Madge began coughing as the water sprayed her face. The sprayer then proceeded to fly freely about the area, like a snake, hissing and shooting water everywhere as it jerked about the sink. Mary struggled to capture the serpent, but could not until it had thoroughly washed Madge, Mary, and covered the mirror with water.

"She has completely lost her mind!" Madge cackled as she wiped the water from her face and clothes.

Mary and Madge looked at each other and began to laugh uncontrollably.

"Shoot, I just peed myself! Damn, it's tough to get old." Madge announced

Mary was laughing so hard, she could barely stand. Finally, she threw a towel towards Madge.

"For God sakes, Madge, that's more information than we needed."

Meanwhile, back in the office, Jasmine struggled to open her e-mail, having mistyped the password twice.

If I do this one more time, they will lock me out and I'll have to get tech support to get me back in. Steady girl, steady, she thought to herself. Jasmine took a deep breath, slowly and deliberately; she typed each letter of her

password. The computer relented, and the mail burst onto the
screen.

> Hi Jasmine, what a night I had. I went home and
> just flopped onto the bed and died. We need to talk.
> Can I take you to lunch? I'll pick you up at 12:15 at
> the shop, be ready.
>
> Luke

Jasmine's heart sank as she read the mail again. *WE
NEED TO TALK!* she thought to herself. *I've heard that from
the girls in the salon and I know what comes next. We need to
see other people, we're moving too fast, I'm in a different
place in my life...* Jasmine burst into tears. She stared in
disbelief at the computer screen.

"Are you ok?" came from down the hall as Mary
approached. Her friend saw the heartbreak in her eyes and
the two friends embraced.

"He said he needs to talk to me, Mary. There's only one
way to take a statement like that." The two ladies embraced
as they struggle to keep from crying.

Jasmine looked up and saw the clock, 12:15.

"He'll be here any moment, I've got to pull myself
together, Mary."

Jasmine heard the bell on the salon door ring, and went
running to the front in a desperate attempt to leave the salon
before the ladies figured out what was going on. The last
thing she wanted was a scene in front of her customers.

Luke smiled as he saw Jasmine approaching and reached
out to greet her. She brushed by so fast that she nearly
knocked him over. *Not even a hello, or kiss, or anything*, he
thought to himself. *It must be a tough day at work.* Luke
turned and followed Jasmine down the walk. He had to break
into a trot in order to catch up to her before she got to the car.
This was definitely not the Jasmine he was used to and when
he opened her door and leaned in for a kiss, she simply
slipped into the seat and briskly pulled the seat belt across

her body. Her eyes were red and he could tell she had been crying. This was a new look for Jasmine; he had never been with her when she was upset.

"What's going on Mary?" a confused and wet Madge asked.

Mary took a towel and quickly dried Madge off all the while trying to see what was going on in front of the salon.

"I'll be right back, Madge."

Mary did not want to alert the customers to her concern but she did walk as quickly as she could to the front of the salon. Mary watched from the front window of the shop as the car drove off. She hoped that her friend would find the answers she was looking for, but Mary sensed that this would not be a good lunch for Luke or her friend and Mary's heart ached for her Jasmine. She fought back the tear that was welling up in the corner of her eye knowing she had a room full of customers. She was not prepared to discuss this with them. Mary took a deep cleansing breath, put on her best smile, and mentally returned to her customers.

A Much Needed Distraction

Mary returned to the styling chair and her customers. Her mind was still racing as she wondered what was happening with Jasmine and Luke. She knew how much her friend thought of Luke and a few times she thought that she detected signs that Jasmine was falling in love with him. Jasmine was definitely smitten with him. *He will find out what my pistol is for if he hurts her.* Mary knew she needed to quickly get her mind back into her work or she would be in trouble. There were still ladies expecting to get their hair done.

They had scheduled for two and now Jasmine was gone. Mary was a professional and she knew she could handle this. What she needed was a distraction, something that would take the ladies minds off the clock as Mary worked her magic. A smile came to her face as she thought: *A story, yes a story that's what I need.*

"Joanne, I drove past that farm on Old Hickory road yesterday and there was a lone cow in the pasture. It made the hair on the back of my neck standup as it reminded me of a ride I took on my bike last summer," Mary said with a chuckle in her voice.

"A cow reminded you of last summer? You must have one boring life" Joanne snapped back.

Joanne was one of the more uppity clients that Jasmine had. Her husband was the District Attorney and she had led a particularly charmed life. She had her nails done every week, hair touched up every other week, and her housekeeper ensured that she did not understand any of the issues the other clients at Jasmine's had to deal with on a daily basis. Years ago, she was desperate to get her hair fixed after being caught in a downpour and Jasmine's was the only salon open. She forced herself to drive from uptown out to the "less desirable" part of town to Jasmine's. Jasmine kept the salon open to take care of her and Joanne had been a loyal yet aloof customer ever since.

"Yes, a cow reminded me of my trip," Mary returned, with a touch of sarcasm in her voice.

"I'll bite," Madge said.

Tina, another regular, moved to a chair closer to Mary. "If this is like your other stories Mary, I want to make sure I can hear," Tina said with a laugh.

Mary looked over the top of Joanne's head; grinned, and winked at Madge and Tina then began her story.

"I was on one of my weekend rides to take in the beauty of the spring colors. The trees, with their fresh leaves seemed particularly green. The wild raspberries were in bloom along the roadsides and the farmers' fields had a tint of green as the winter wheat reached for the warming sun. I weaved my way through the countryside, the wind in my face and the steady rumble of the Harley between my legs."

"Rumble between your legs?" Madge questioned. "Gotta get me one of those!"

"Oh Madge, just be quiet," Tina shouted.

"I felt the sense of freedom that keeps me riding. I stopped along the roadside and there before me, was the most beautiful and peaceful meadow I'd ever seen. Green grass coated the gently rolling hills. A wonderful clear stream meandered; its gentle current pushing along with such ease and grace that I could feel the tension flowing from my body. What a great place to stop for lunch, I thought to myself."

Mary noted the look on her audience's faces and knew she had them. She continued to work on Joanne's hair.

"I grabbed my saddlebags and headed out across the field looking for just the right place to settle in and relax. I walked a short time and there it was, the perfect spot, up on a slight knoll overlooking a bend in the stream. Off in the distance a tree, having long ago given its life, stood almost majestically. Its bare branches reached for the sky."

"That sounds beautiful" Tina sighed.

"While I was eating, a doe and her fawn emerged silently from the brush and joined me. They were cautious at first, but when they realized I was not a threat, they proceeded to graze on the tender young grass. The fawn was quite young and had a bit of trouble controlling its long spindly legs."

"It was like a postcard. I only wished that I had a camera. Relaxing for nearly two hours I let the warm rays of the sun sink deep into my tired muscles. I just sat there enjoying the day and relaxing. The sun moved across the sky and I realized it was time to get going in order to be home before sundown."

"I took one last look in an effort to remember this special place forever. I gathered my things and headed back towards the bike. Walking across the field I noticed a hawk perched in the top of a tree. I kept walking while watching, his head turning from side to side as he scanned the field for his own lunch."

"Suddenly, he spread his wings and began to take flight. Just then it happened. My foot flew out from under me. I found myself in the air and knew this was not going to end well. The bag with what was left of my lunch went one way, my saddle bag went the other and I slammed to the ground. My bottom hit first with a distinct splat. My left hand tried to cushion my fall but to no avail."

"The feel of something squeezing between my fingers made me think that this would not have a happy ending. I was not wrong! When I came to rest flat on my back, eyes shut tightly, I first took note that everything seemed to still work properly."

"My mind was racing as I put the clues together. Farmer's field, slippery, squishing between my fingers, the smell (yes, suddenly, I realized there was a less than pleasant smell surrounding me), and my eyes flew open."

"I looked over at my hand; it was covered in a greenish brown goo that I was certain was the source of the awful smell. Now what do I do, I thought to myself? Do I roll left? Do I roll right? Do I simply levitate to a standing position? Well, I rolled left then pressed myself up onto my feet, only to see the extent of what had happened."

"My butt, the legs of my jeans, the left sleeve of my shirt, and God only knew how much of my back was covered with the greenish brown slime. There was so much of it that I was sure a cow had recently shit itself to death on that very spot then managed to crawl away and hide out of sight."

Mary looked over at her audience as she continued to cut Joanne's hair. Madge was cackling with tears streaming down her face. Tina was thrashing in the chair as she attempted to catch her breath. Even stuffy Joanne was fighting to hold back a laugh. She had them right where she wanted them, so she continued. Mary looked over at the two and continued her story.

"I shook my hand, and droplets of greenish brown slime flew through the air, but I knew this would not help. Looking around, I determined that I was indeed alone. The stream was my only hope. I walked over to the edge of the stream, my eyes scanning the ground taking care not to step into any other surprises."

"The water was shallow, clear, and as I put my hand into it, extremely cold. I washed the slime from my left hand so I could at least touch things without further contamination. I surveyed the damages and realized that there was no hope for my shirt or my jeans. They would both have to come off in order to return myself to civilization."

"I opened my saddle bag and pulled out the only other clothes I had brought along, my thin plastic rain coat. It was black, as all Harley garments are, but consisted of thin lightweight plastic whose only purpose was to keep the rain from soaking you to the bone if you were ever caught in a storm."

"It would have to do. I laid it on the creek bank. Next, I slipped off my tall leather boots and the only thing that had escaped the incident, my tall socks. I just laid them onto the bank and continued."

"The boots weren't too bad. A couple of swishes in the current and they were clean. I set them aside while I tended to the more challenging clothing. I took another look around to make sure I was still alone and took off my shirt. The greenish brown slime was all over the left sleeve and covered the back. It had soaked through so much that I was sure my bra had fallen victim to the goo."

"Crouching low along the stream bank, I slipped off my bra. Yes, there it was; my white bra had a swath of color that covered the clasp and most of the strap. I couldn't just leave it on and expect to smell somewhat acceptable. I turned and tossed it onto the stream bank."

"I crouched even lower, my knees against my chest and washed the soiled shirt in the creek. My mind flashed back to all of those television specials I had watched over the years, African woman, standing in the river, boobs swaying in the breeze, slapping their clothes on a rock. At least they had a rock."

"Once I had most of the poo rinsed from the bra and shirt, I tossed the bra onto the bank. I took the shirt, rung it out, then flopped it over my back and pulled it side to side like a bath towel, hoping to clean most of the awful goo from my back. Based on the color of the shirt, I continued to wash and rinse until my back was clean."

"I reached behind me and discovered chunks; yes chunks, in the waistband of my pants. Cow shit in the waistband of my pants! Could this get grosser?"

Joanne turned her head and looked up at Mary with her mouth agape, furrowed brow, and eyes so wide they seemed like they could drop onto the floor with the slightest jar. Tina was leaning towards Mary hanging on her every word, nose scrunched up and eyes squinting as her mind processed the picture Mary had so skillfully painted for the group. Madge, having grown up so many years ago on a farm, simply laughed at what her friend was saying.

"Oh, get over it ladies!" Madge said with a chuckle, "it's only manure."

"Well, it may be manure Madge, but it was in my pants!" Mary said in a stern voice then laughed.

"What the hell do you do when you have fresh gooey cow poop in your pants? Well there I was, crouched over the stream, topless, with a handful of wet brown chunks. I quickly rinsed my hand in the water and pondered my choices."

"I could keep scooping in hopes of getting it all but that seemed unlikely to result in anything other than a stinky hand and soiled pants. I could stand up, drop my drawers, and quickly slip on my rain coat. I could slip the pants off, sit my butt into the freezing water, and try to wash up without the help of soap. And what about my soiled panties?"

"As I crouched there over the stream, contemplating my options, I noticed the Hawk had once again taken up its perch, and he seemed to be staring down on me. I looked around again and hoped that the hawk was the only thing watching this crazy, half-naked woman splashing in the stream. Finally I decided I only had one option: strip the soiled pants off and use my wet shirt to wash up, then slip on my rain coat and get the hell out of this place."

"I hadn't been naked in a field since Timmy Olson and I went skinny dipping and let me tell you, there was a lot less of me at 15 then there is at 55."

"I carefully peeled off the pants, though I'm not sure why I was careful, after all what was going to happen? I would get poo on my legs. What was a little more poo when you were already covered in it?"

"You cannot imagine how cold it was as I lowered myself into the shallow water. I went to my knees first, trying to ease myself in. Do you have any idea how slippery river rocks are? Well, as I was carefully lowering myself into the icy water, it happened! Kaploosh, and suddenly, there I was, bathing in the icy water, flailing about like a beached whale. By the time I was done, I had indeed taken the coldest bath of my life, but at least I was clean."

"I was never so thankful to have picked up that rain coat at the Harley store. It may be thin, but at least it was clean and dry. I swear my entire body was shivering, desperate for something warm. Well let me tell you girls there is nothing warm about a plastic rain coat."

"I slipped my frozen toes into my boot. I then gathered up my "wash" and stuffed them into my saddlebags. I was about to walk off when I spotted my socks lying on the bank. I grabbed them, stuffed them into the pocket of my rain coat, and headed for my bike."

"I didn't remember my boobs being so alive when I was 15. Somehow, the years had turned my jiggle into a definite sway, and at one point, I considered locking each one under an arm to keep them stable."

Finally, I made it to the bike, threw the saddlebag into place, and started to mount the bike." "Oops, you can't straddle a bike wearing a raincoat. Oh, shit, what now. I looked and started unbuttoning the raincoat from the bottom."

I just needed enough room to spread my legs across the bike. That wasn't too much to ask was it? I finally got enough give to swing my leg over the bike seat. When I looked there it was, my who-ha was staring up as if to say you have got to be kidding! First pooh and now this?"

Joanne looked up at Mary in horror.

"Oh my God, you didn't! Tell me you didn't ride your Harley without anything covering your... oh my God, you did!"

"I wasn't sure what to do but I knew this would not work for a two hour trip home. I thought for a moment then remembered my socks. That could work I thought. I got off the bike and took out the socks. They were nice and long, those really great tube socks. I laid one across the seat where my butt would go and took the other one and laid it the long way on the horn of the seat."

"The bike seat looked like a happy face with its tongue stuck out! It would just have to do because I wasn't putting any of those cold, stinky, wet clothes back on. I swung my foot over the seat and took a moment to do some final positioning of the socks."

"I looked down and while my who-ha was now resting on a sock, it was still in clear view. I lifted slightly and pulled the sock forward and up until my who-ha was covered. I took the end of the sock and pulled it through the raincoat just above the bottom snap. It held. The raincoat held the sock in place and my who-ha was covered. I was feeling pretty good about myself by this time."

"With a quick sweep of my foot, the kickstand disappeared. With a turn of the key and the press of the start button my faithful bike roared to life. I knew I could depend on her to get me the hell out of there and bring this nightmare to an end."

"One last look at the field of shit and I was on my way. I had no more gotten onto the road and there he was, the farmer, sitting up on his John Deer, a broad smile from ear to ear as he waved to me. What could I do? I looked him straight in the eye, bowed my head, and swept my arm toward him as if I were the star in a Broadway play, then hit the throttle and was gone."

"Well, Joanne, you're done. Tina you're next," Mary said in her most professional voice. Meanwhile the ladies were struggling to breathe, Madge was laughing so hard, she immediately excused herself to the ladies room.

Tina grabbed a tissue from the box on the small table between the chairs in the waiting room and tried to dry her eyes and catch her breath as she moved to the styling chair.

"Mary, I just love your stories," Tina said as she continued to chuckle.

"So he was there watching the entire time?"

"Well, I wish that was the end."

Mary continued as she began washing Tina's hair.

"Wait!" exclaimed Tina.

"You can't continue until I can hear. Hurry up and get my hair washed, and then continue."

Mary quickly washed Tina's hair, sat her up, and was ready to begin her cut.

"There I was, naked, except for a raincoat, riding like the wind. All I wanted to do was get home, get a real shower, and put on some clean clothes. A kind God would have let me get home without incident. Unfortunately, I'm not a big church person so he decided to screw with me."

"I was doing about 50 when a semi passed me by. The wind was fierce as we passed each other. Suddenly, the bottom snap tore free and my who-ha sock went flying. I was concerned, but what could I do? I squeezed my legs together, but, let me tell you, with a Harley between your legs it's no use. A fifty mile per hour wind suddenly buffeted my who-ha. I don't care how warm it is, a fifty mile per hour wind chill is damned cold!"

"Yeah, I had a man rub my winki with an ice cube once. That was damned cold," Madge said.

"Yes, I've had that, too, Madge, this was one hundred times colder, and at least when a man does it, there is some pleasure involved!" Mary replied with a chuckle.

"That wasn't the worst thing though. Once the bottom snap let go, in very quick succession, all of the snaps let go! There I was, like some Hells Angel riding along with my black coat flapping in the breeze, only I was naked! Let me tell you, I'm not sure how I got home without getting arrested or killed by one of the people going the other direction on the road, but I did."

"I've never gone for a ride since, without making sure I have a change of clothes in my saddle bag."

The day continued as Mary performed magic for each and every customer. The last customer left Jasmine's, and Mary flopped back into her styling chair, feet aching and hands sore from the day's activities. Mary slipped off one shoe, then the other, to let her sore feet breathe. Her mind kept returning to her friend and hoped that she and Luke were able to work out whatever it was that had caused Jasmine's disappointment with him. The night would be a long one. She would be checking in on Toni, since today was another chemo day, and then sitting close to the phone awaiting Jasmine's account of the evening with Luke.

Suddenly, the door swung open. Mary turned her chair towards the door expecting to tell the would-be customer, "Sorry, but we're closed," only to see Jasmine racing in and back to the office. The smile on her face told Mary that Jasmine and Luke had worked out their differences and all was right in the world.

"Well, what was up with Luke, Jasmine?" Mary asked as she stood up from her chair, her sore feet enjoying the cool tile floor as she walked towards Jasmine.

"Mary, it was all a big misunderstanding," Jasmine replied as she flitted about the office gathering her things. "He had simply gotten busy with a friend, that's all," She explained. "I just got nervous and insecure, but everything is wonderful again. I really must hurry, Mary; he's picking me up in two hours so we can go out dancing tonight."

"Jasmine, it's the middle of the week! Where are you going to find music tonight?"

"I don't know, and I don't care, that's his problem and he is picking me up at 7:30. I need to get home, shower, shave my legs, do my hair and makeup, and find a dress, all in 2 hours. It will take some doing, but I know I can do it."

"Jasmine," Mary insisted," a misunderstanding? What kind of crap is that? I've been worried about you and misunderstanding is all you can say?"

"Mary, I'll tell you all about it tomorrow. I just don't have time right now, I have to get going. Can you lockup? Thanks, you're a doll. Tomorrow, I promise. I'll tell you everything tomorrow." With that, Jasmine was out the door and off into the dimming light of evening.

Mary sat for a moment, slipped her shoes on and left Jasmine's; heading for home. At least her friend was happy once again, but Mary was beginning to wonder about this Luke guy. He seemed as though he was bringing Jasmine unlimited pleasure, and he definitely put a glow on her face and a bounce in her step. That's when Mary suddenly realized that she had never actually met Luke. It seemed that every time he came to the salon, either she was in the back, or Jasmine was rushing out to greet him and the two left for whatever adventure they had planned. Her friend never even bothered to introduce them.

What's up with that? Mary thought to herself. She got into her car and headed home. She was looking forward to a quick bite to eat and then a little conversation with Toni; maybe even a good chick flick. Today had been Toni's second treatment, and based on the last treatment, she knew her new friend would need some encouragement, support, and someone to be with.

I'll pop some popcorn for me, a little orange sherbet for Toni, and we can have a girl's night out, Mary thought to herself.

Mary finished her dinner, popped the popcorn, grabbed the orange sherbet, and headed down the hall to Toni's. As she approached, she saw John pulling Toni's door shut.

"Hi, John," Mary said. "How is she doing?"

"Ok, I guess. I brought her some split pea soup to help keep her strength up and a box of fudgesicles for her sweet tooth. She doesn't seem sick yet, but last time it wasn't until the day after that the nausea hit her. She is having trouble with her scalp hurting and itching. I guess it's from the chemo. I offered to put some lotion on her head, but she said no. She likes talking about the past and remembering the fun times she had before she got sick. We talked about what it was like in college and our fun, silly dates. We used to do the oddest things together. Neither of us had any money, so we had to find things to do that didn't cost anything. We used to drive out to the airport and get as close as we could to the runway. We had a blanket we would spread out, then just lie there together, and watch the planes come in."

John's eyes were welling up as he spoke. Mary could tell he was struggling to maintain the strong facade he presented to the world.

"I'm glad you're here, Mary. I think she needs company tonight, and I can't stay."

Mary patted John on the shoulder as he turned and left.

She knocked on the door, twisted the doorknob, and walked in. Toni was sitting in her over-stuffed chair; a steaming bowl of soup beside her on the end table. A smile spread quickly across her face, as Mary entered the room. Mary could tell she had been crying, but chose to ignore it, not wanting to risk taking her back to where ever she was that had caused the tears.

"OK, here it is, <u>First Wives Club</u>, Orange sherbet for you and your sore mouth, and popcorn for me. How does that sound?" Mary said in her cheery voice.

Mary looked over at the bowl of soup, then back to Toni.

"Hum" said Mary.

"Hot soup for a lady with sores in her mouth?"

"He means well," Toni replied with a smirk and a chuckle.

"He stopped at the deli on the corner. It's my favorite," she said as she gingerly lifted the bowl from the table, and gazed almost lustfully into it.

The whole peas broke the surface like tiny turtle shells among a sea of green. Toni slowly lifted the bowl to her nose, inhaling deeply as she drew in the wonderful aroma. A smile spread across her face, and a soft "mmm" escaped her lips. It was almost a religious experience for her.

"If only I could eat it, Mary, if only I could eat it. I'm sure the sores from my treatment will make it nearly impossible. The inside of my mouth is so raw, all I want is something cold, but this smells so good," Toni moaned.

"Maybe just a taste, a taste couldn't hurt that much could it, Mary?"

She slowly and cautiously extended her tongue. The tip strained to reach the green liquid. When it finally made contact, she was overwhelmed with delight as the smooth liquid spread across her tongue. Suddenly, she pulled away, and the experience was over. She could not control the path of the soup, and once it struck one of her open sores, the magic was broken as she quickly grabbed the glass of water. Tears came to Toni's eye as she set the bowl back onto the table.

"I've only begun, Mary! I've only begun, and already, I miss my life. I'll never take the simple things for granted again, Mary! Never!" Toni said with anger and frustration in her voice.

"Toni, look what I've brought you." Mary said trying to bring her friend back from her bout of self pity.

"Orange sherbet and First Wives Club. Let me get you some sherbet while you put on the movie."

The two friends settled in for a quiet evening.

How Could I Think That?

Jasmine was riding high now as she prepared to meet Luke. The silence had been torture wondering what happened to him. The roller coaster ride from fear to anxiety, then to anger, had taken a lot out of her both mentally and physically.

She had become moody as time dragged on. Sleep eluded her and when it did come, it was more like passing out than restful sleep. Her mind had raced, questioning everything in her life. Was she wasting her time with Luke? It had been so long since she opened her heart to someone. Fred had not only killed her desires for a man, but also severely damaged her sense of self worth and self-confidence.

Jasmine was in her 50's now, and in her mind, her prime was long past. No longer could she compete with the 30 and 40 something women that frequented the shop. Oh, she smiled and laughed with them, but what man would want her? No matter how much lotion she applied, her skin was no longer supple; her hands had developed those ugly brown age spots; it would take a spatula, not a make-up brush, to fill the creases in her face. Oh, and let's not even get started on the once firm breasts, or the cottage cheese thighs. Yes, Jasmine knew what she looked like; after all, she had spent many a day in front of the mirror arguing with the old woman that stared back at her.

Then Luke came into her life. He made her feel not only beautiful again, but sexy and desirable. The odd thing was that he did it with such ease. Was it all just a line? Was he just a silver tongued, man-pig that knew just what to say to get what he wanted? At this point, Jasmine didn't care. She loved the way she felt with Luke, and she didn't want it to end. As long as he wanted her, Jasmine would be there for him. However, she was going to have to work on her thoughts; thoughts that could only be described as jealousy, jealousy towards whatever it was that distracted him from her. She didn't want to spoil this by getting too clingy or too demanding, but she didn't like the secrecy. He said he had something to do that required his full attention, and he was sorry he hadn't let her know he was all right. "Confidentiality" did not permit him to tell her more, he said. *Confidentiality my ass,* she thought.

The touch of his hand and the deep pools of blue in his eyes had melted away all the anger and doubt she felt. That was before, and this is now. Somehow, it didn't really matter once he was back. What did matter was that he wanted her in his life. She could deal with anything as long he was there for her. The soft voice in her head which told her something was just not right here could no longer be heard. It had been replaced by the voice of a giddy young woman who had been silent for so long. Now that she was back, she refused to be silenced any longer. Jasmine would not let suspicion ruin the best thing that had come into her life in years.

Jasmine emerged from the shower, quickly wrapped herself in a towel, and rushed to get herself together. Hair, makeup, she even took the time to pluck a wayward hair from her chin. The outfit was next. She wanted it to be casual, but pretty, after all, how formal could you get on a Thursday night? She flipped wildly through her closet, searching for just the right look.

Pants, she wondered? *No that would never do*, she liked looking feminine for Luke. *Perhaps a skirt? Yes, a skirt would look nice, with a nice sleeveless blouse.* As she continued flipping though the hangers, she paused at a sun dress. It had been purchased for a day out with the girls that never materialized. Its thin spaghetti straps and bright colors made her smile.

Jasmine pulled the dress from her closet, and tucked the hanger under her chin as she gripped the fabric, pulling it tightly across her mid section. She turned and looked into the full length mirror. The dreaded mirror; it could be cruel, but this night, it was very kind and a smile spread across Jasmine's face. *Looks like it still fits* she told herself. *It'll be close* she thought, as she turned left, then right, imagining the colorful fabric lying seductively across her curves.

Jasmine let her towel fall to the floor and took the delicate straps from the hanger. She carefully pulled the dress over her head so as not to muss her hair and gradually wiggled into the dress. The *top was fine but now for the moment of truth* she thought as she began to pull the dress over her hips. *I should have been eating yogurt for breakfast all these weeks rather than those McDonalds® bagels. Oh but those bagels are so good.*

She wiggled her hips while she tugged on the delicate sun dress. Finally the dress fell free. Jasmine adjusted it noticing how light the dress felt. It was almost as if it weren't there. She scooped up one breast and positioned it properly in the top, then repeated the ritual with the other. She chuckled to herself as she recalled the 60's, when it was the dress that got adjusted not the breasts.

A couple more wiggles and tugs and the dress was on. It felt good, a little snug in the hips but certainly wearable. She looked at herself in the mirror and saw a younger woman looking back. She had a smile on her face as she nodded her head in approval; thank goodness she had shaved her legs yesterday. Into the bottom of the closet now, that tangled mess of footwear, looking for those perfect sandals she knew she had. The hunt continued until the wilderness that was the bottom of her closet, yielded its treasure. She smiled triumphantly, as she slipped them on; strappy with a slight heel, perfect.

Jasmine had no more than let that thought escape her mind when the doorbell rang. It was Luke for sure and she ran down the steps to greet him. The door swung open, and his eyes lit up as they always did when he saw her.

"You look beautiful, Jasmine," he said with a smile, reaching out to wrap his arms around her.

Jasmine relished in the feel of Luke's strong arms pulling her tightly to him. She just loved the way he could make her feel wanted and safe with his powerful hugs. Sometimes she wondered if it was his hugs, those soft lips, or just his presence that made her feel better. There was really no need to wonder since they all came together. Soon her eyes were closed and head tilted slightly back as his soft lips pressed to hers. Her entire body was alive as his hand moved up her back and onto her bare shoulders. *This is perfect* she thought to herself as her own arms, hands, and lips returned the fiery passion. She leaned in to feel every inch of his embrace, and sighed; deeply content to be in his arms once again.

When the lovers finally broke their embrace, Luke began to drag her out the door. She reached for her purse, and was barely able to catch the doorknob, pulling it shut behind her.

"I've got something special for you tonight, my lady."

"I hope you'll like it. The idea came to me on the way home. I think we have just enough time to make it all work."

Luke seemed particularly excited as he spoke. He opened the car door for her and helped her into the seat. Jasmine's eyes widened as she slid across the leather seat. She could feel way too much of the seat, as she adjusted the dress. Luke slammed the door, jumped into the car and thrust the gear shifter into drive. The tires squealed a bit as they sped away from the curb.

"If we hurry, I think we will have time," he said again as he raced through the neighborhood and onto the country road.

Jasmine was paralyzed as she realized what she had done. She stared straight ahead wondering what to do next. Never before had she left the house without panties. Her mind raced as she considered her options: ask to return home, because she had forgotten something, maybe stop at a convenience store and hope they had some there, or say nothing, and get through the night.

Maybe he won't even notice, she thought to herself. Jasmine fidgeted in the seat as the leather clung to her flesh. *Oh my God,* she thought to herself, slightly panicked, *now my butt is starting to sweat. I'll be stuck to the seat by the time we get to wherever we're going.*

"Luke, where are we going in such a hurry?" Jasmine asked.

"I don't want to spoil it. You'll just have to wait my love. It's a place I went to as often as I could in my younger days. I saw it a few weeks ago on one of my balloon flights. I couldn't believe the place was still there, untouched."

The car wound through the countryside at break neck speed. Had it not been for the seatbelt and the extra adhesive provided by her sweating bottom, Jasmine was sure she would be sliding back and forth on the seat. Luke took the turns at ever increasing speed. Jasmine normally would have been frightened, but Luke had demonstrated his driving skills on many occasions and he definitely knew how to control his car. Besides if they had an accident what would her mother say at the emergency room?

"Jasmine, where are your underpants!"

She watched as Luke and the car became one. His soft touch on the steering wheel, the way his thigh muscles tightened as he pushed his partner. Faster, one minute then slower the next. He knew exactly what was right for her.

Jasmine imagined she was the steering wheel. Luke's strong hands gripping her. Her imagination was about to take her over the edge, when suddenly, he jerked the car around the corner. She could feel his forceful touch release as he guided them through the corner and into the straightaway. She was becoming aroused as if she were watching two people making love. Jasmine could feel the subtle vibrations from the road coming though the seat.

The fabric of the dress moved over her sensitive nipples as the car's momentum caused her breasts to sway side to side. The tingles in her nipples pushed her imagination further as she pictured his powerful hand moving along her bare thigh. Jasmine longed for him to drive her, not the car, as they continued to race through the countryside. Suddenly, he slowed and began to look along the edge of the road.

"What are you looking for?" Jasmine asked.

"It's an old, overgrown road. I could see it from the air, and it should be along here somewhere. It's gravel, so it may be difficult to spot."

Jasmine scanned the side of the road looking for anything out of place, a break in the brush, a sign of gravel where there should be none, maybe tire ruts, but she saw nothing.

"It has to be here," Luke said insistently. "I know it's here."

"What's that?" Jasmine asked pointing at a small break in the brush.

Vines covered a long forgotten, and almost unreadable, For Sale sign. Trees stood on either side of a barely discernible pathway hinting of an old road lost in time. The shape of the bushes seemed to form a tunnel.

"Could a car fit between there?" she asked.

"Let's find out," Luke said as he turned off the road.

"Hold on, this could get a little bumpy," he said with a chuckle.

And bumpy it got. It had definitely been a long time since this road had seen wheels. The bushes stood as sentries along the road, discouraging intruders from entering this place. Each time a bush scraped against the side of the car making awful sounds, she wondered what could possibly be worth scratching your car to see.

"Guess I should have brought my truck," Luke said with a smile.

"But, I know once we get past these few bushes, things will be fine. You'll see. I just hope we are not too late."

"Too late for what?" Jasmine asked.

"Patience, my lady, patience," was all that Luke would say.

Suddenly, they emerged from the thick brush. There, before them, was the most beautiful scene. A lush meadow of green grass flowed over small rolling hills. The green was like a carpe leading towards a small lake, its water shimmering in the evening sun. Trees dotted the hillside as if some master painter had placed them exactly where they would add the most impact to the painting.

To the right, a small stream meandered along towards the lake, and willow trees bowed down like a veil along the far side of the stream. A footbridge had fallen into the water after years of neglect. Vines of wild honeysuckle embraced the fallen bridge as if to memorialize its service. To the right was a small marsh, its cattails standing proud around the edge while lily pads spread across the open area, their brilliant white flowers standing in stark contrast to the deep green of the pads. A duck with her ducklings swam lazily along in the evening sun.

The remnants of an old house were perched on one of the knolls overlooking the shimmering waters of the lake. All that remained was an old stone fireplace reaching steadfast towards the sky like a soldier refusing to give up the lost war. The walls, which had given their lives defending the little house from the elements, lie strewn in an outline hinting at what once was. A small tree had taken root in what must have been the main room of the house as if to say, "nature will always reclaim what man has built." The peaceful serenity was undeniable.

Luke stopped the car and looked at Jasmine; a smile on his face.

"Was it worth the fifteen minute ride?"

"Oh my God, Luke, how do you find these places? This is the most beautiful place I've ever seen."

Luke smiled back and leaned over for a kiss, knowing he had hit a home run. He got out of the car and began to move towards Jasmine's door. She used that time to wiggle her thighs free from the seat so as not to make what she knew would be a disgusting noise as she peeled herself from the leather.

He opened the door and reached out for her. Hand-in-hand, he lifted her gracefully from the car, looked deep into her eyes, and kissed her. Not just any kiss, but a long, passionate, sensuous kiss. The kind of kiss that takes a woman's breath away. Luke slowly pulled away, and as she opened her eyes, there were those wonderful blue pools. Their lips seemed to resist ending the kiss as they held on until the very end. Both were struggling to catch their breath, as they stared into each other's eyes.

"Oh Luke, I've never seen anything as beautiful as this." Jasmine whispered.

Luke reached up and gently stroked her cheek.

"For years I thought the same thing."

He leaned in, softly pressing his lips to hers, and then whispered, "but, I was wrong, my lady."

The two continued to hold each other as they stared off into the countryside. For the first time in her life, Jasmine felt complete as she stood there in the arms of the man she loved. All of the struggles she had endured seemed to be a path to here. If she hadn't met Fred, she wouldn't have opened Jasmine's. If she hadn't opened Jasmine's, she would not have met Mary. If she hadn't met Mary, she wouldn't have placed the posting that brought this wonderful man to her. Everything happens for a reason in life, and Jasmine was thankful that everything had happened to her. This is where she belonged. She was happy.

"Wait until you see the sunset from here. You are in for a real treat," Luke whispered.

He broke the embrace and went back to the car. Opening the trunk, he retrieved a large heavy blanket and a picnic basket. Jasmine chuckled as she recalled the last time they attempted a picnic together. With the blanket and basket in one arm, he reached for Jasmine with the other and began to guide her further down the road until they came to a clearing. This, at one time had been the front yard. Jasmine could almost see the manicured area; the rose bushes that had once been proud and well maintained, had gone wild, and resembled bramble bushes. The tangled vines could not hide the beautiful blooms that were its heritage. The crumbled walls were strewn in a disorganized line reflecting what time had done to the once loved home. Luke spread the blanket out, and brought the basket close. Reaching inside, he pulled out plates, napkins, utensils, wine glasses, cheese, meat, and even some fresh strawberries. As Luke worked to arrange the meal, Jasmine watched his every move. So deliberate, so precise, he had really thought this out. When he pulled the baguette from the basket, she could no longer contain herself.

"Sir Luke, are you expecting that ferocious beast again, or will we have sandwiches this time?" Jasmine said with a laugh, barely able to keep a straight face.

Luke responded with a puzzled look as his mind processed the unusual question. Once her meaning sank in, he gave her a mock frown, and then joined her in a silly laugh.

"Could that have been a bigger disaster?"

"I'll remember it always Luke. You were so gallant defending me from that monster."

The two sat down and enjoyed a quiet meal as the sun sank lower and lower in the sky. Cheek to cheek they cuddled as the sky revealed its brilliant hues of red, orange, and purple. Somehow the sunset was even more beautiful as they shared it together. Once the show was over and they found themselves in the twilight, the soft wisps of steam began to form over the lake and the frogs started to croak. The sound of a loon could be heard in the distance and the two lovers moved even closer together.

"I promised you dancing Jasmine." Luke said in an almost surprised voice.

"Its fine Luke, I love this even more than dancing."

"No, you were promised dancing and dancing you shall have."

Luke went to the car and soon music was floating across the valley. He returned to Jasmine, stretched out his hand and said "May I have this dance my lovely lady?"

Jasmine smiled and placed her hand in his. The couple walked hand-in-hand through the remnants of the old door. Luke turned to face his lady and stepped in so close she could feel the heat of his body. He slowly leaned in as he raised her hand into position. Their fingers gently entwined while he placed his other hand on her waist. Looking into her eyes, their lips barely touched and Luke began to lead them around the room. Music wafted across the countryside somehow in sync with the croaking frogs. The dirt floor seemed as smooth at the most expensive hardwood as Jasmine's feet moved in perfect unison with his. They whirled and turned moving effortlessly around the small tree that stood as a centerpiece in the room.

Jasmine wondered how she could ever have doubted this man. This is what she wanted in her life, someone that could make her feel like the world was hers. For so many years she had longed to feel special. Having given up, she had spent even more years hiding from the world, not wanting to chance the pain that failure and rejection could bring.

In his arms she was complete. Her fingers could feel the firm muscles of his shoulder, flexing as he controlled her every movement. Whenever Luke took her into his arms and danced, she couldn't be sure her feet were even touching the ground.

This is surely it, she thought to herself. God would not inject someone so wonderful into her life, if he didn't have a plan.

Being with a man who made her feel so complete, now this, was a fairy tale come true. *Luke*, she thought to herself, *had to be the Prince Charming she had dreamed of so many times as a little girl.* She couldn't deny it any longer… she loved him.

The two danced, as the evening sun slowly disappeared beneath the horizon. A continuous flow of wondrous sensations filled her body as he danced her around the room. She didn't even think about the dancing, she simply relaxed and let the music flow through her. One song blended into the next. Jasmine let her head fall back as she looked up at the stars, and inhaled the fresh country air. She could smell the wildflowers, and hear the crickets as they called out in the darkness. Close to the ground, the fireflies began to brightly flash their love signals. Croaking loudly, the frogs joined the love chorus. The night air was filled with the sounds of love, and Jasmine knew she had surrendered herself to him, and wanted nothing more than to be right where she was.

The tempo of the music suddenly changed, and Luke changed with it. The solid pounding beat of tango filled the night air. Luke snapped her to him, spun her around, and snapped her tightly to him again. Their bodies seemed to merge in the dance, and Jasmine could feel her skin come alive. He suddenly stopped. As his body was pressed tightly to her back, his arm crossed her chest, and drew her to him. The roughness of his late day beard brushed against her cheek. His hand reached down low on her leg and slowly drew up tracing every sensual curve of her body. She leaned back against him searching for a kiss, when suddenly, he spun her again with solid quick steps as he moved them across the dirt floor. The brightness of the full moon shined upon them like the spotlight of a stage. His powerful arms flipped her to and fro as if she were a rag doll. He was in complete control, and Jasmine only craved more.

Luke's hand slid under her hair as he gripped her neck. He leaned her back as his powerful arm curled around, supporting her. There she was suspended in mid air. Jasmine had never been dipped before. Luke looked at her, gave her a passionate, forceful kiss, and then jerked her back to a standing position. Jasmine's head was reeling with pure excitement. He continued to step deliberately as they, continued to move around the room. Suddenly she found herself draped over his knee as his lustful eyes penetrated deep into hers.

Luke's hand, on her naked thigh, began to slide up, inch by inch as his chest heaved. She could feel the fabric of her dress pushing up as more and more of her body became exposed. *Was it the cool night air or the excitement of the moment that raised the goose bumps on her exposed thigh? Would he discover her secret? Would he care? What would he think of her?* These were the things that raced through her mind as his hand continued to move up her now trembling thigh. Suddenly as fast as he had put her down, he raised her up and they were moving once again to the beat of the music. He turned her around, then back again, each movement snapped with the passion of the dance. They turned, cheek to cheek and stepped across the floor. She could feel his heart pounding against her chest as they moved as one; out the door to the blanket. He dipped her again, holding her by the back of the neck as his lips pressed to hers. The fire and passion consumed them. Neither was sure if the music was still playing. They were in their own world now, two lovers consumed with each other as they made wonderful love beneath the stars.

It was well past midnight when the couple returned to Jasmine's. Luke walked her to the door, gave her a soft good night kiss.

"Thank you for sharing that with me," Luke whispered.

"Stay with me Luke," was Jasmine's simple reply.

Their lovemaking continued long into the night, and when they were both totally spent, she rolled away from him, scooted her behind in, and waited for the spooning she so loved. He knew what she wanted and he was more than happy to oblige, as his strong arm wrapped around her, drawing her to him as they spooned the night away. His head on the nape of her neck, she could feel his warm breath as he slept. Luke's large hand cradled her soft breast and provided her the security she needed and desired, as she too, slipped off into a deep sleep.

The sounds of singing birds gently awoke Jasmine from her slumber. She paused, and enjoyed the feel of awakening in Luke's arms; his warmth on her back and strong arm around her. She hated to break the spell but felt the need to rise and begin her day. She quietly slid out of bed, slipped her robe on, and moved into the kitchen, leaving Luke sound asleep, or so she thought.

Luke quietly followed her into the kitchen. The small window above the sink allowed the beams of morning sun to illuminate her hair. He crept up behind her wrapping his arms around her. Soft kisses on her neck brought her hands from the soapy water. The wonderful scent of her hair filled his head as he molded himself to her.

Luke could feel her press back into him as their arousal grew. She placed her hands on the sink for leverage then pressed her round bottom back into his swollen manhood. Jasmine threw her head back seeking the attention of his soft lips. Luke did not disappoint her and his lips moved slowly up and down along her supple neck. His hands slipped beneath the robe and began to caress her soft stomach. He could see the outline of her erect nipples as he pressed himself into her.

She continued to lean back against him and sighed happily. She dried her hands on her now open robe. Jasmine brought his large hand to her lips and kissed it. It was warm, and welcomed on any and every part he wished to explore.

He was glad they were alone in the house as their lovemaking continued.

"I thought you might need some help in here," he said in his best low sexy tone.

His briefs did nothing to hide his excitement. Her body seemed to telegraph her own desires. For a moment, her sensible side protested.

Not here in the kitchen, she thought, but just then the tip of his tongue touched the inside of her ear.

The small orgasm silenced her sensible side. She shuddered & moaned as his tongue assaulted her ear. Slowly, his long, powerful fingers moved up her body. Eyes closed and head flung back, she craved his touch; everywhere, and he did not disappoint her. Along the back of her legs she felt his briefs drop to the floor. The heat of his manhood against her caused a moan to escape her now open mouth. Arms pressed hard against the sink as she ground herself into the object of her desire. She was completely out of control now.

Jasmine cried out for her soul mate to make them one as the animal within them both took over. She instinctively spread her legs and arched her back as he crouched down slightly and slipped the throbbing head into position. Together they worked, and with a single, slow, steady movement, they were joined. Flesh in flesh. He wrapped her tightly in his loving arms.

She felt the fullness she desired. The velvet touch of her most private of places was overwhelming to his senses. They paused momentarily to enjoy the feeling of oneness. She squeezed his shaft and he knew what they both wanted. Lust took control as they began their walk, then run to the edge. Arms extended and locked, she braced herself as each thrust became more powerful than the last.

She glanced up momentarily, as she checked the long driveway making sure they would not be surprised. A powerful thrust, lifting her to her toes, brought her back to what was truly important. He, too, could not help but notice the view out the window, but his fiery lover, and excitement of spontaneity jerked him back.

He did not disappoint her as the two lovers gave themselves to each other. The heat and passion was incredible as the edge approached. The kitchen was filled with the sounds and scents of lovemaking as the two threw caution to the wind in favor of the sheer pleasure they could bring each other. They both sensed the edge approaching. He slowed his pace, paused at the peak of arousal, leaned forward and whispered, "now my love," and then proceeded to slip the tip of his tongue deep into her ear as his arms tightened around her.

He slowly withdrew from her and then a powerful thrust drove even deeper into her. He lifted her onto the tips of her toes as they both called out to each other in the language of lovemaking. Her arms began to tremble as wave after wave swept over her. She could feel each wonderful eruption inside of her. Again and again his hot essence blasted into her. Each time he held her tighter than the last, until finally, he collapsed onto her back. Her arms had given way and they both found themselves panting, supported by the counter, having given everything to each other.

He Said WHAT!

Mary arrived at work early the next morning. Even a visit to her friend, Toni, could not get those words out of her head. *A misunderstanding! How could Jasmine be so upset one minute, leave and return with: "a misunderstanding?" There has to be more, there just has to be.* Mary paced impatiently staring out the window watching for Jasmine. She wasn't sure if she should be happy for her, upset that her best friend cut her off, or worried that she was being deceived by a pig. She was leaning towards pig though.

Jasmine finally pulled in, parked, and came up the walk towards the shop. Mary took note of the bounce in her step and the slight strain in her stride. The telltale signs she and Luke had a VERY good night. Mary knew that walk well and recognized it in her friend. She reconsidered her strategy, but she was still worried about her friend and this pig she knew had invaded her life.

Mary was much more experienced with the wildlife that walked the jungle of the internet. She had dated the 45-year-old man who sent a photo of himself, then somehow magically aged 20 years when they met. She had gone out with "pizza guy," a man that was so cheap; he would only let her have one topping on her pizza. There was lipstick man who brought his own lipstick and insisted on applying it to places lipstick was not intended to be applied. Mary had even dated a wonderful man for nearly a year before she discovered he was married. Then there was the worst kind, the ones that would sweet talk a lady, moving slowly towards the physical and once she offered him her precious fruit, he would disappear into the darkness of the jungle, never to be heard from again. There were many dangerous animals in the internet jungle, but Mary also knew there were a few sweet men who simply had trouble meeting women. These were the gems, the treasures that could be found if one had patience and moved cautiously through the jungle.

"Jasmine, tell me you didn't sleep with him AGAIN!" Mary said in her most judgmental voice.

She was fearful that her best friend was being blinded by his devilish charm. She was suspicious of his vague answers and mysterious ways. Jasmine found him to be exciting and spontaneous, while Mary found him sneaky and secretive. Who was Luke, really? Mary wanted her friend to take a long look at the facts and make sure she was seeing the real Luke and not some snake oil salesman working hard to sell her a bill of goods.

"Mary, what we did last night was not sleeping together. I swear the earth actually did move."

"Jasmine, you let him sweet talk you into bed and you refuse to even consider what he is actually doing or saying. You are so caught up in his charm that you throw good sense to the wind. I'm telling you Jasmine, something is wrong here. No man is THAT good."

"Aw Mary, you will never believe what he was doing," she said as Mary's eyes rolled to the back of her head.

"He has a long time friend in crisis, and his friend asked him to respect their privacy and not talk about it to others. He has promised to reveal all when his friend is comfortable with the situation. Mary he has such integrity and honor that he will never break a trust."

"Integrity my ass! I'm telling you Jasmine, there is much more here than you're allowing yourself to see."

Jasmine's eyes began to well up in tears.

"Mary, why can't you just be happy for me? You're my best friend, and I need you right now. I don't need some jealous pessimist trying to rain on the best thing that's ever come into my life!"

"Jealous my ass! Jealous of what? A deceitful, lying pig who screws your brains out then disappears without a trace only to return with some lame excuse! And worse yet, there you are, legs spread, with a love sick look on your face, waiting for him to toss you his scraps of time when he chooses to toss them. I am your friend, and I can't sit here and watch you swallow this shit without being concerned. If you wanted some no brain, yes woman, you wouldn't want me as a friend. I will always speak my mind, good or bad, Jasmine. If you don't know that by now, maybe our friendship is not what I thought it was!"

"Maybe you're right then, Mary. If you can't support me in the best thing that's come into my life, EVER, then fuck you! When it comes to Luke, you just keep your thoughts to yourself. I'm happy! I'm going to stay happy, and there is not one GOD DAMN thing you can do about it."

"FINE, Jasmine, if that's the way you want it, then don't come crying to me when the pig finally shows his real colors and breaks your heart. There is something fishy here and don't come to me later and say, Mary, you were right, Luke is a pig. You know, Jasmine, I'm your best friend and you haven't even bothered to introduce me to Luke. What does that say about our so called friendship? What am I to you, just a loyal employee? No, not even a loyal employee, an employee would have gotten an introduction. What are you afraid of Jasmine, that I'll steal him away from you or something? He's a pig. I'm telling you, he's a pig."

"Shut the hell up, Mary, just shut the hell up or leave! He's mine, and I love him no matter what you say, I love him. Mary, I'm going to the office now. When I get back you better have a better attitude because I'm done with this!"

Jasmine turned, flung her purse into the empty chair, and stomped into the back. The slamming of the office door punctuated her mood.

Mary, left standing alone in the silence of the shop, looked up at the picture of Fred, and said to herself: *move over Fred you will soon have company on that wall.* Mary realized that she could do nothing more but watch as her friend disappeared down the dark path leading into the internet jungle. She felt like a mother who was watching from across the room as her child slowly reached for the hot stove. She could do nothing but watch and try to deal with the horrible thing that was about to happen.

The first customer of the day soon came through the door. It was Jan for her perm. Mary managed to muster a smile and welcomed her to the shop. She pointed at the dressing room and Jan went to change into her "perm shirt". Mary went back to the office, knocked on the door, and called to Jasmine in a gruff tone.

"Your 9:00 is here."

There was no answer only the sound of rustling papers.

"Did you hear me Jasmine?" Mary shouted a bit louder.

The door flung open and Jasmine pushed past Mary and huffed down the hallway.

"I heard you the first time!" was her harsh response.

The day continued in this tone. Customers, who were used to seeing Mary and Jasmine work in perfect harmony, did not know how to act as the two women made no effort to conceal the state of their relationship. The tension was almost unbearable for the customers. Around noon, Madge stopped in, making her usual flamboyant and loud entry.

"I was in the neighborhood, and thought I'd stop in for some of your free coffee, Jasmine."

As she walked across the salon towards the coffee pot, she smiled at Jasmine.

"So how is that Luke guy doing? When do we get to meet him? I bet he has one of those firm tight butts, doesn't he, Jasmine?"

Jasmine and Mary both stopped what they were doing and stared at Madge. There was silence in the salon, and Madge, not one to hold things back, said, "What the hell is going on with you two? This place seems like it's about explode! If I wanted fighting, I would have stayed home with my husband."

With that, Madge turned and left Jasmine's.

Jasmine Meets John

The thought of an evening spent with Luke was something Jasmine not only welcomed, but craved. Luke had purchased the ballet tickets weeks ago, and the performance was the night. Dinner, Swan Lake (Jasmine's favorite), and more importantly, an entire evening with her Luke. She had found the black dress weeks ago. The soft fabric clung perfectly to her curves. The hem struck her just above her knee. She felt feminine and classy when she tried it on that day. The strappy heels placed below the dress had been found quite by accident. Jasmine spotted them one day during her evening mall walk. She stood back and looked at her outfit and knew tonight would be a particularly wonderful night.

She even had a black thong that allowed the dress to cling tightly to her behind without panty lines. Jasmine chuckled to herself because she knew what would happen when Luke's hand gently grazed her bottom as it always did. He had teased her many times about how sexy a thong was. Tonight would be a very special night, and she knew she would drive him insane as he sat next to her and fidgeted during the play. Jasmine's attitudes had definitely changed over these months with Luke. For the first time in her life, she felt truly desirable and totally sexy. The feeling always made her grin. She looked up at herself in the mirror and winked.

Just being with Luke made Jasmine feel complete. She knew in her heart that this was the man she was destined to spend her life with. They had known each other for barely a year now; only a few months since they first met, yet she had never felt such a strong connection to anyone, much less a man. Not even the early good days with Fred compared to this. It seemed as though Luke was inside her, and could sense her every need even before she knew it. Jasmine recalled how she worked to understand Fred, to observe him, and tried to be what he needed her to be. It was so different with Luke. Everything came naturally. Everything from pausing as he opened the door, to the feathery touches across his chest during lovemaking, all came without thought. Jasmine knew, this was the man God had created for her; her soul mate.

Jasmine flopped back onto the bed and watched the fan blades slowly turn as she thought of previous dates with Luke: that first night at the dance club, that first passion-filled kiss. The picnic at the lake where she watched her gallant knight defend her from the monster. The balloon ride-oh, the balloon ride. Never had she experienced such passion. The list went on and on in her mind. The simple act of being together gave her such peace and contentment. Luke was better than any drug the world could produce.

Oh-my-God, and the passion. Never had she felt so much like a woman. Sex was not something you do, like it was with Fred. It occurred to her that sex didn't even exist with Luke. It was lovemaking not sex. The simple act of touching her arm would cause her to tingle in all the right places. She thought she knew what lovemaking was after she married Fred. For years she had been with Fred happily performing her wifely duties, making sure her man was satisfied and, occasionally, even enjoying it herself.

Lovemaking with Luke was something totally different. If she had to compare the two, how could she do it? A glass of water compared to a gallon of water maybe. Jasmine laughed and corrected herself. A glass of water compared to the Pacific Ocean maybe! Jasmine could not contain her laughter as she rolled on the bed, feeling just like a school girl. Luke had opened her eyes to what it meant to truly make love to another person. Something meant to take hours, maybe even days, not minutes. She had to admit to herself, that, as wonderful and powerful as her orgasms were, it was the time they spent lying in each other's arms, having given everything to each other, which was the most satisfying part of making love with Luke. Every part of her life was Luke, and that was exactly the way she wanted her life to be.

Jasmine rolled again, and was now staring at the photo of Luke on her nightstand. His smile, the softness in his eyes, even the way his curly hair seemed wild, yet tamed at the same time, everything about Luke was perfect. She reached for the small frame, brought it to her lips, closed her eyes, and kissed him softly. Jasmine stared into those wonderful blue eyes and brought the picture to her heart as a tear formed in the corner of her eye. It was a happy tear. She hugged the frame to her chest, closed her eyes, and enjoyed the thoughts her Luke brought.

The ring of the phone brought Jasmine out of her dream world and back to reality. It was Luke and he seemed rather excited.

"Jasmine, I have some bad news, and hope you will understand," Luke said with a tremble in his voice.

"What is it Luke? Are you OK?" Jasmine asked.

"I'm fine, Jasmine, but my friend is not. I have to go help right now. It sounds serious, and I need to go right away. I'm so sorry about the ballet, perhaps we can go tomorrow? I just know from the call, that I have to get over there immediately. Please tell me you understand. I wouldn't go if I didn't feel it was absolutely necessary. Will you forgive me Jasmine?" Luke pleaded.

Jasmine could not hide the disappointment in her heart as she took a deep breath and said, "Honey, it will be ok. You go do what you need to do, I'll be OK tonight."

She smiled at the phone, but the pangs of jealousy were working their way into her heart. She had waited for months for the Swan Lake performance. Who was this person that could interfere with her plans so easily? Jasmine drew the picture tighter into her chest. Luke had proven long ago to be trustworthy, kind, and extremely loyal. She knew this was not easy for him. She reached deep inside of herself and managed to reassure Luke that it was indeed OK. A friend in need cannot be ignored.

"Go, hon, get going. I'll be fine, just call and let me know you are OK."

With that Jasmine set the phone back into its cradle. She walked over to the dress hanging on her closet door. Jasmine had been saving this dress for a special night. Struggling to understand, she reached up and took it from the door. With a tear in her eye, she held it up to herself and looked into the mirror. She would have been stunning tonight. She hung the dress back in the closet, and slipped her thong off, kicking it into the laundry basket. She knew she was being selfish, but damn it, she was disappointed.

She reached for the phone and Mary's words rang loud in her head; "Don't call me…" and Jasmine slammed the phone back down. The wounds from their fight were still fresh and she was not willing to make the first move. Mary was the one being ridiculous and Jasmine wanted an apology. She couldn't help it as doubt crept into her mind. *What if Mary is right?* Jasmine was truly alone and that wasn't what she wanted to be right now as she began to cry.

Jasmine moped around the house as she thought of Luke. She wandered into the kitchen and went straight to the silverware drawer, rummaged for the large dipping spoon, then turned towards the refrigerator. She opened the door, then into the freezer, and out came her special treat. She pulled the top off of the chocolate chocolate chip ice cream. It had formed a crust of ice crystals, a testament of just how long it had been since the last time she needed her chocolate fix. She scraped away the top layer of crystals, dropping them into the sink. She then plunged the spoon deep into the brown speckled mixture, scooping out a spoonful. Before Luke, she had spent many a day with her spoon in the ultimate comfort food.

Jasmine sat eating her ice cream, and slowly got control of herself. *What can I do tonight that would be fun? I need to get out of here,* she thought to herself, *but where? A movie, shopping, maybe I'll go to the salon and work on that order I need to place.* Nothing felt right. *Toni! That's it, I'll go over and see what Toni is doing. She loves to have company. Maybe we'll just do each other's nails and watch a movie, a real girl's night out.*

Jasmine ran upstairs, and threw on her jeans and a t-shirt. She grabbed a bag, tossed in her manicure equipment, and several colors of nail polish, then headed back down stairs. She snatched her copy of "Mamma Mia," and out the door she went.

Sure, this will be fun. A smile returned to Jasmine's face as she drove across town. It had been a few weeks since she had seen Toni in the shop. Jasmine's heart went out to her as she tried to empathize with her. Breast cancer is such an awful disease, and Jasmine was thankful that none of her own family had been touched by it. She had several survivors that were customers, and a few pictures on the bulletin board of dear friends that had succumb to this awful disease, and were missed. Toni was special, because she was so alone. Only her ex-husband, Mary, and Jasmine were there to support her, and Jasmine really hadn't done much more than talk with her when she came to the shop. She had gone to visit several times with Mary and usually ended up crying all the way home. Jasmine could be like Toni if something happened to her, and it frightened Jasmine. *Who would take care of me if I couldn't take care of myself?* It was on those trips home from Toni's that she felt the most alone. *There, but for the grace of God, go I,* she would think to herself.

Perhaps tonight they could make each other feel better. Jasmine pulled the car into visitor parking of the complex, grabbed her bag, and out she went. The apartment complex was older, certainly not a bad neighborhood, but definitely an "affordable" place. The metal steps made a strange ting sound with each step. She noticed the roughness of the hand rail caused by too many years, and too many hands since the last time it was painted. The roughness scraped under her hand as she ascended the steps. The apartments were arranged more like a motel than an apartment house. The concrete balcony stretched out before her as she counted down the apartment numbers until she was in front of Toni's.

Jasmine knocked on the door, and waited. No answer, so she tried again, this time adding, "Toni, its Jasmine. Are you in there?"

A weak voice answered back, "sure come in please".

Jasmine opened the door, and saw Toni sitting in her overstuffed chair; pale, and definitely weak. The chemo had taken a lot out of her. She had lost more weight, and her eyes were beginning to sink into her head, adding years to her appearance. Her housedress was mussed, and looked like she had spent too many days in it. She was quite pale, a testament to just how little she was able to get out into the sun.

"Welcome, come in and sit for awhile," was her greeting. There was happiness in her voice, if not on her face. Jasmine came in and sat down.

"I wondered if you would like to watch a movie, and maybe do our nails, if you are up for it?"

Toni chuckled and raised her hands for Jasmine to see. Chemo had taken her nails. Jasmine was horrified at her insensitivity. As Toni's hands hung in the air, Jasmine could see that each finger nail was gone leaving her with only a pink nail bed.

"I'm not sure how long it will last, but what do you think you can do with these? Several of the girls at the hospital have their fingers painted so they can feel more normal. John is here for awhile, though. Maybe we should wait until he leaves, OK?"

"That's fine, Toni, whatever you want. I've heard so many wonderful things about John from both you and Mary, that I almost feel like I know him. He seems like such an angel on earth. Toni, I'd love to meet him," Jasmine said as she looked over her shoulder towards the rest of the apartment.

"Where is he?"

"Oh, he's in the kitchen making me some soup and crackers. Today was a particularly bad reaction day from my last chemo treatment. I couldn't keep anything down. Jasmine, I'm not sure what I would do without him. He's all I have. On days like this, where I desperately need someone to help me, all I have to do is call and he will drop everything. I'm not sure how he does it, but he seems to be able to rearrange his schedule so he can take care of me."

"You are a lucky woman, Toni."

"Can I tell you a secret, Jasmine?

"Sure, anything."

"He's the one who's given me the strength to fight this cancer. There are some days where the dream of getting him back is all that keeps me alive."

"Have you talked to him about your dream, Toni?"

"Oh-my-God, no, Jasmine!" Toni said.

"Speak of the devil. Come here, John, I want you to meet someone. Jasmine I'd like you to meet my husband, sorry, ex-husband, John."

Jasmine rose, turned towards the kitchen, and froze. There stood Luke holding a tray of food wearing nothing but a woman's robe and his socks. Jasmine didn't know what to say. Hundreds of things ran through her head, none of them good, as she stood there frozen in time. Jasmine could hear her heart breaking as she realized that Luke's friend was Toni. *All this time he had been lying to me while he was off carrying on with his WIFE! HIS WIFE!* Jasmine couldn't tell if it was her chest or her head that was going to explode, and her face showed it.

"Do you two know each other?" Toni asked.

Jasmine turned and stormed out of the apartment feeling like she had been played for a fool all this time. She ran down the steps, into her car, and sped away; tears streaming down her face. Jasmine's fingers dug into the steering wheel as she struggled to control the speeding car. She could barely breathe, as the road became a blur. Finally, she swerved to the shoulder and came to a screeching halt. She covered her face with her hands and slumped into the seat as she lost complete control, and began to sob loudly. Her whole body was shaking uncontrollably as she cried out loud. Her heart was pounding so hard in her chest that she thought she might die.

Luke Meets Mary

Jasmine wasn't sure how long she had been on the side of the road. She realized that she was still alive and hated the feeling. Her life and dreams had come crashing down upon her and she knew she could not go on. The pain in her heart was only rivaled by the urge to throw up. Jasmine looked up from her hands, and tried to see but it was only a blur. She struggled to breathe, her heart pounding so loud that it drown out the noise of the passing cars. Her hands just shook as she stared into the emptiness that was her life. The sounds of her sobs echoed around the car as if a chorus was in the back seat crying in three-part harmony. She knew she needed help. She knew she needed Mary. Mary would understand. Mary would forgive the stupid things that she had said. Mary would love her.

Jasmine's hand dug into her purse searching for the lifeline that was her cell phone.

She recalled how Mary had taken her new phone and announced, "I'll be number one in your phone, and quickly entered her own number into the autodial.

"Most people put the police as number one, but what the hell could they do for you that I can't?" was her comment.

Jasmine had never used the auto dialer, but this was different. She stared at the keypad, struggling to see the numbers through her tears. The keypad looked like one blurry block of light. Jasmine brought her shirt sleeve to her eye and wiped. For an instant, the keypad came into focus, and the illuminated key was quickly pressed. She held it in as the curtain, once again, closed over her eyes, and she began to sob. Jasmine's chest heaved uncontrollably as the phone began to ring.

"Hello," came over the phone.

Jasmine's mouth moved but the only sound that escaped was a trembling sob with the random and sudden gasps that come with a complete loss of control.

"Hello?," came across once again.

Jasmine drew in a deep breath, and struggled to speak.

"Mary, Mary you were right!"

She lost complete control again. Cries filled the car as Jasmine's heart continued to break. She dropped the phone back into her purse, and sobbed into her hands.

"Jasmine? Jasmine is that you?"

Mary struggled to hear, but the phone was filled with the painful sobs of her best friend.

"Jasmine, honey, where are you? Jasmine, please answer me."

Mary was frantic as she listened for her friend's voice. Mary's own voice began to tremble now as she struggled to control herself. She knew her friend was in trouble and she fought to keep her fertile imagination from running away with her. She wasn't sure what had happened; but knew her friend needed her. Mary took a deep breath, and composed herself. She knew that Jasmine didn't need a hysterical person right now so she reached deep within herself, and spoke in a softer, more understanding, tone.

"Honey, I'm here for you. Take a few deep breaths, and try to calm yourself. I'm here for you. I love you, Jasmine, please talk to me, please."

Mary tried to keep her voice soft, low, and reassuring. She listened intently for a moment, straining to hear anything coming from her friend. She needed to know Jasmine was ok. *Perhaps she was in a car accident, and was hurt? Maybe she dropped the phone and can't reach it! Oh-my-God, what if she passed out!*

"Mary, I'm sorry for what I said. You were right, you were right all along. He's been playing me for a fool. You were so right, Mary. So right."

"Jasmine, where are you?" Mary asked as she held back the tears welling up inside of her.

"I'm on the side of the road. I just ran, Mary! I just couldn't stay there one more second; I just had to get out of there!"

"Get out of where, Jasmine? Where were you? Are you hurt?" asked a very concerned Mary.

"Mary, my life is over; I just can't go through this again. I just can't. It was too painful the first time, and I know I can't do it again."

"Do what, Jasmine? What's happened? Honey, you aren't making any sense! Where are you? Let me come get you."

"No, Mary, I just need to get myself under control so I can drive. I'll be ok." Jasmine said in a very stoic way.

"I'm not far from your apartment. Mind if I drop by?" Jasmine said in a sheepish voice.

"Now why would you ask such a stupid question, Jasmine? You know you are welcome here anytime."

"Well, after the things I said, I wasn't sure."

"I love you, Jasmine, you are my friend; now and forever. Get your ass over here I'm putting the tea kettle on to boil," Mary said with the best chuckle she could manage.

It wasn't long until Mary heard a soft knock on her door. She ran to the door, opened it, and took her friend into her arms. The two ladies held each other tightly as they stood in the open doorway. Mary could feel the desperation in Jasmine's grip, which simply made her hold her friend more tightly. The two women rocked back and forth as the embrace continued, until, finally, they both lost control and each began to sob in the arms of the other. Somehow they moved inside of the apartment, and Mary kicked the door shut, not wanting to loosen the grip on her friend. She gave Jasmine a soft kiss on the cheek, and slowly released her grip. She took Jasmine's hands in her own, and looked deep into the bloodshot eyes of her best friend. Mary knew the look, the emptiness staring back, the trembling hands. She knew the signs of heartbreak, and wrapped her loving arms around her friend again.

"Jasmine, come sit down and have some tea. Tell me what happened," Mary said in her most understanding voice.

She suspected what had happened, but she also knew that her friend needed to get it out, so she waited somewhat impatiently for her friend to tell the story. Mary reached for one of the mugs of tea on the coffee table. Steam rose lazily from the cup as she handed it to her friend. Jasmine's still shaking hands wrapped around the cup, the heat somehow serving to calm her. She brought it to her trembling lips and took her first tentative sip.

Jasmine looked into Mary's eyes, her emotions running high as she began.

"Mary I'm so sorry for what happened today. You were just trying to be my friend and I thanked you by saying Fuck You! Mary, can you ever forgive me?"

Jasmine's eyes dropped to her teacup as a tear moved slowly down her cheek. She was fearful that she had damaged something so precious in her life, and she had done this over a man. *A man,* she thought to herself, *a man.*

Jasmine's lip began to tremble as she continued, "Mary, you are my one true friend, and what you think is so important to me. I guess I was just caught up in the moment. I lashed out when you were just trying to protect me from myself."

Tears were now flowing freely down her cheeks as her hands gripped the cup more tightly.

"Jasmine, I love you. You are my best friend and no one, man or woman, will ever change that."

Mary reached out and softly touched Jasmine's cheek. With a feathery touch, she lifted her head and looked into her friend's tear filled eyes.

"I will always be here for you, no matter what, Jasmine. We are now and will always be, best friends. No matter what life throws at these old broads, we will always be here for each other, good or bad, we will always be here."

With that, Mary slid across the sofa, took the cup from Jasmine's shaking hands, placed it on the table, and gently wrapped her arms around her. Jasmine began to sob as Mary slowly rocked her friend, whispering words of comfort only a best friend would know.

The two ladies continued their embrace, Jasmine feeling the firm, yet, soft grip of her friend as she lay her head on Mary's shoulder. *How could this have happened,* she thought to herself? *How could I have thought such terrible things of someone who loves me?* Jasmine pulled Mary more tightly into her, wanting to somehow return the love her friend was giving her. She felt herself relaxing and falling more deeply into the comforting embrace of Mary. Jasmine was letting go. Letting go of everything and entrusting herself to her friend, the one person she knew she could count on. The trauma of earlier in the evening seemed to fade, if not in importance, perhaps in intensity. Jasmine took a deep, cleansing breath and lifted her head from Mary's shoulder. She wiped the tears from her eyes, and put a smile on her face. She looked deep into Mary's eyes, and began to speak.

"Mary, thank you for being here for me. I love you."

Mary smiled at her friend, leaned forward, and kissed her on the cheek, ever so softly.

"I'm here for you, Jasmine. I'll always be here for you. Here, have some tea"

Mary reached for the two tea cups on the coffee table. The ladies each sat back in the sofa as the tension that was once between them seem to disappear, leaving them wondering what ever cold have caused such a fuss.

Jasmine looked at Mary, took a deep breath, and began to tell her story.

"When I left the salon tonight, I went home and began to get ready for Luke. I had the perfect dress I'd been saving for this kind of a night. Even the shoes were perfect. Remember those heels I found in the mall a few weeks ago, the black ones with cute straps?"

Mary's head nodded as she took another sip of her tea.

"Aw, I was going to look fabulous for him. I was just about to slip the dress on when the phone rang."

"Uh, oh," was Mary's comment.

"Let me guess, SOMETHING came up, didn't it."

"Mary, just let me tell it, OK! He was upset and said he was so sorry, but he couldn't make it. It was his friend again, and he couldn't help it; he had to go. He said he would make it up to me though. He said he would take me tomorrow, but I knew he couldn't get tickets for Swan Lake the day of the performance. It's been sold out for months. We were lucky to get the tickets we did get. I was just so disappointed."

"So what did you do?" asked Mary as she tried to empathize with her friend.

"Well, we had our fight. You told me not to call you. I was my stubborn self, so I couldn't. I moped for awhile, then decided I would just go visit Toni and spend a girl's night out. When I got to Toni's, she said John was there.

"Oh, isn't he just dreamy. He is so attentive and loving," Mary said.

Jasmine slammed her cup down onto the coffee table and jumped to her feet.

"Dreamy my ass!" Jasmine screeched. "He was in her bath robe! What the heck was he doing wearing her bath robe?"

An extremely agitated Jasmine began to pace back and forth.

"Oh-my-God! I bet that was a sight," and Mary began to chuckle.

"She called him John, Mary! She called him John!"

"Well, that is his name, after all," Mary added.

"Mary! It was Luke!" and Jasmine lost control again. She ran into the bathroom sobbing, and slammed the door.

Mary just stared at the bathroom door as she let Jasmine's ranting sink in.

Wait a minute, Mary thought to herself. *John and Luke are the same? Oh-my-God! John and Luke are the same! I knew it! I knew something wasn't right with that snake! I'll take care of this right now!* Mary dumped her purse onto the coffee table, grabbed her pistol and headed out.

Jasmine got herself under control and opened the bathroom door.

"Mary, you must think I'm some kind of lunatic. Mary? Mary, where did you go?"

Jasmine was confused, and searched for her friend. Then she spotted the debris on the table and Mary's empty purse tossed onto the floor. *What the heck happened,* she asked herself. She looked up and noticed the front door standing open. *Oh my God, the pistol. Her pistol is gone!*

Jasmine ran out of the apartment just in time to see Mary arrive at Toni's door. There she stood like a bad episode of Cagney and Lacey, pistol drawn and leg cocked. Then, with all the force she could muster, she dealt the door a viscous blow. The sound of her powerful heel impacting the door echoed throughout the complex. Unfortunately, Toni's door was not a TV door. Mary stood there frozen in time until the door retaliated.

Jasmine thought she was watching a morning cartoon as Mary began to slowly fall backwards to the cement balcony. The pain could be seen on her face, but Mary's determination was greater than any pain the door could inflict. She picked herself up, reset her position, and thrust her shoulder into the door. The door seamed to yield without as much as a sound, and Mary was swallowed up by it.

The seconds ticked away as Jasmine continued to rush toward Toni's. A shot rang out, and Jasmine's heart skipped a beat. She stopped dead in her tracks as a feeling of horror came over her. *What had Mary done,* she thought to herself. Jasmine's mind composed the picture; Luke lying in a pool of blood on the floor, Toni pleading for her life as Mary's shaking hand pointed the pistol at her chest. Jasmine had to stop her. She ran as fast as she could to Toni's open door.

When she got there Luke was standing wide eyed, his hand still on the door knob, as he looked across the room. It seems that just as Mary was about to strike the door, John chose that very moment to see who was knocking. Mary flew, uncontrollably, through the open door, disappearing into Toni's apartment. She was head first into Toni's sofa and the gun was nowhere to be seen.

"Mary, what the hell have you done! Are you OK?"

Jasmine flew to her side. Mary looked like something from a roadrunner cartoon, her head buried into the sofa, feet flailing above her, arms spread wide and her legs splayed like the wishbone from a Thanksgiving turkey. It seemed to be snowing in the room; white snowflakes hanging in the air. Apparently, Mary's gun had gone off, the bullet struck a fatal blow to one of Toni's embroidered sofa pillows. Jasmine reached up, pulled Mary's twisted body from the sofa, then hugged her friend.

"Have you lost your mind, Mary!" was all a tearful Jasmine could muster.

"I just wanted to kill that snake, John, I mean, Luke; I mean... well you know who I mean," Mary said as her bloodshot eyes cast daggers in Luke's direction. The site of Luke standing at the door infuriated Jasmine.

"Kill me?" a thoroughly confused Luke questioned.

Jasmine turned, now confident her friend was OK, got up and began to stride towards Luke. Like a woman possessed, her finger extended and hand shaking.

"I trusted you! And now I find you've been playing me for a fool all this time. I defended you when my friends tried to warn me, I stood by you. I loved you. Well, not anymore, I'm out of here. I never want to see you again."

"Why would you want to kill me?" Luke pleaded.

Jasmine stopped in front of him, her nose only an inch from his. A smile came to his face as he reached out to kiss her.

A viscous slap caught Luke totally by surprise. The sound it made echoed through the apartment as Jasmine's bloodshot eyes stared into the once comforting blue pools. This time, however, all Jasmine could see was emptiness. With that she turned, her eyes filling with tears. She could not tell if they were tears of anger or tears for pain, as she felt her heart breaking one more time. Jasmine began to run to her car just wanting to get away, away to anywhere but here.

Luke's voice pleaded with her, but she could not, nor did she want to hear what he was saying. He had lied to her, and she could not bare to hear his voice. Her hands covered her ears as she ran towards the stairs. The sound of her shoes on the old steps seemed to scream, I told you so, I told you so, as she became more frantic to reach her car.

Finally, she was in and quickly snapped the locks. Her fingers fumbled with the keys. Suddenly, there he was, at the window. He kept shouting something that she could not hear over her own crying. He kept knocking on the window as she shook her head, and struggled to get the key in the ignition. Her fingers just wouldn't work, and she could barely see through the tears that streamed down her face.

Unbeknownst to Jasmine, someone had heard the gunshot and called the police, reporting a domestic disturbance and a man, dressed in woman's clothes, chasing a woman. Squad cars filled the parking lot. A large officer, his gun drawn, shouted something. Luke's hands shot into the air. The burly officer grabbed Luke and smashed him onto the hood of Jasmine's car. She quickly wiped her eyes, and as she did, the scene came into focus. There was Luke, still wearing Toni's bathrobe, the officer's forearm pressing his head into the car's hood. Luke's arm was being held forcefully behind his back. His face was distorted by the metal as the officer pinned him to the car. He then swiftly applied the handcuffs while keeping him pinned to the hood. A tap on her window startled her and there stood a second officer.

"Are you alright, ma'am?" he asked.

"Yes, I'm fine, just a bit shaken," Jasmine said.

"Well, he can't hurt you anymore," the officer said trying to calm her down.

Jasmine just stared at Luke as the officer patted him down. His blue eyes did not seem so deep, nor soothing. She watched as his face continued to be distorted by the hard metal of the car. Jasmine only wished that it was her forearm inflicting the pain. She had trusted him, given him a part of her that she had protected for years. Whatever happened to him would not be enough to make up for what he had done to her. She looked at him, humiliated, wearing his lover's robe, as she thought to herself, *he deserves this after what he did to me*, and a grin, be it an evil grin, spread across her face.

"Will he go to jail?" Jasmine asked the officer at her window.

"Yes, ma'am," was his reply.

"I'll bet they will enjoy him dressed like that," Jasmine said with a chuckle.

She watched as the officer twisting his arm asked Luke something. Luke seamed to plead with him. He simply laughed and shook his head. He then reached into the pocket of the robe and tossed something onto the hood. It was a small box, about 1 ½ inches on each side. The kind of box every woman recognizes. It tumbled along in slow motion, coming to rest on its top only inches from the windshield. Jasmine looked at the box, then Luke, then the box again. What did this mean? Before she could think, the officer grabbed the box, spun Luke around, stuffed him into the backseat of a squad car, and whisked him away. She could see him staring at her, his eyes pleading, as he disappeared into traffic.

Jasmine shot from the car and up the steps once again. She needed to return to her friend. Fear was now gone and she just needed to be with Mary. She ran towards Toni's door not knowing exactly what she would find. Jasmine passed an officer holding Mary's pistol and shaking his head.

"Is everything OK?" she asked

"Ya, she was just cleaning it and the gun accidentally discharged. Those crazy women are lucky no one got hurt!" the officer said.

"What will happen now?" asked Jasmine.

"Well, she asked me to take the gun into protective custody," the officer snickered.

"Thank you, officer."

When Jasmine got to the door, she ran in and clutched Mary. The embrace was tight and the ladies began to sob.

"I was so frightened, Mary, you just don't know what was going through my head when I heard that shot!"

Mary pulled away and began to chuckle.

"Oh, Jasmine, I've known you for years, and I know that your fertile mind dreamed up a doozy."

Toni came over and hugged the two women. Jasmine was not sure what was happening.

"Where is John?" Toni asked. "His clothes must be dry by now. Well, after Mary's performance, I may need to launder his shorts." Toni's chuckle turned into a loud, though labored, laugh as she struggled for strength.

"He's probably down at the ice machine getting something for his cheek. Man, Jasmine, that was some left hook you threw. I need to get you a bike" Mary said with satisfaction in her voice.

"Jasmine, did you know Luke's real name is John Luke?" Mary asked. "I met him weeks ago and just never knew it. Hell, I almost killed him," Mary said with a laugh.

Jasmine was confused now. *Why would her friend take so lightly to the idea of her boyfriend cheating on her? Why are Toni and Mary laughing?* Jasmine took a step back from the two not knowing what to do.

"Jasmine, you need to sit down for this." Mary said.

"Can I pour you some tea?" asked Toni.

"I think not." replied an indignant Jasmine. "I fail to see the humor in anything I've been through tonight. I lost someone very special tonight, my best friend nearly killed someone, I was chased by a cheating SOB, and you guys think I should sit and have tea! Have you all lost your mind? I just need to get the hell out of here! You guys enjoy your tea!"

Jasmine turned for the door. Mary ran and grabbed her by the arm.

"Wait! Don't go, Jasmine! You really have to hear this. Please come back and sit down," Mary pleaded.

Jasmine paused, looked Mary in the eye and said, "OK, but don't expect me to laugh. I just don't think I have a laugh in me tonight."

A Jasmine Moment

Jasmine returned to the sofa, wiped some errant feathers from the cushion, and proceeded to sit down. She wondered just how much Toni knew about her relationship with Luke. *Was Toni innocent in all of this, simply an unsuspecting ex-wife who knew nothing of Luke's adventures? Perhaps she was a conniving bitch that found out about her and Luke, then set out to break them up so she could have him to herself?* Jasmine needed to know and she would tolerate this little "tea party" just long enough to find out the truth.

Toni sat in her chair, looking weak, fidgeting a bit as her eyes kept returning to the front door. She poured each of the ladies a cup of tea. Jasmine looked at the whole scene and could not imagine, after all that had happened, how her friend and now ex friend could still be interested in tea. It seemed much more like a brandy straight-up evening. This was the night that Jasmine caught the love of her life with another woman, witnessed her best friend commit attempted murder, was nearly accosted in her car, and, oh, ya, watched her former boyfriend hauled off to jail. Not really a tea party kind of night.

"Jasmine, you are not going to believe what happened tonight," Mary started.

Just then a noise sounded from the other room. Toni attempted to rise and tend to the buzzer, but her legs just would not lift her from the chair. Between the chemo and the evening's excitement, her strength was simply drained.

Frustrated, she looked to Mary and said "Could you get those for me, hon?"

"Sure," Mary replied, and she headed down the hallway. She was gone for only a few moments and returned with an arm load of clothes, setting them on the foot stool in front of Toni.

"Thanks, Mary. I guess when my body decides it's done for the night, there is no changing its mind."

"What do you mean?" asked a bewildered Jasmine all the time thinking, *this pathetic bitch better watch herself or I might just rip the stubbles of hair from her balding chemo head!*

"Well I had a particularly bad reaction to yesterday's chemo treatment. It usually takes a day or two before it really hits me, but yesterday's treatment was a doozy. I started throwing up about 3:00, and by the time John got here around 4:30, I was lying across the toilet like a drunken prom queen. I mean my brain would insist that my legs and arms move, but they simply refused. It was as though my arms and legs were teenagers lounging in front of the TV. I insisted that they do something and they simply ignored the noise coming from my mouth. I just could not move to save my soul."

Jasmine just rolled her eyes and thought, *sure, sure you couldn't. I can see right through this weakness bull. You just got him over here and then the two of you did the nasty. You slut bitch!*

Toni continued, "John kept pounding on the door, but I just couldn't get up to let him in. Finally, he used his key, and let himself in."

Oh My God, he's got a key! Jasmine's blood was beginning to boil now.

"He came in and began calling out to me. I'm telling you, I just could not find the energy to call back to him. I could hear him, as he went from room to room calling out. Finally he opened the door to the bathroom. I could barely turn my head to acknowledge him. It must have been quite a sight for him to see. There I was, my legs folded beneath me on the floor, my house dress barely keeping me decent. My limp arms draped on either side of the toilet bowl, the lid resting against the top of my head as my throbbing forehead lay against the cool porcelain."

Jasmine refused to have any sympathy for Toni. She tuned out the story, and focused on the facial movements as she considered what Toni would look like after things got physical. Basically, what Jasmine was hearing was blah blah

blah blah blah. *I just cannot believe this slut has the nerve to sit here and tell me this crap.* Jasmine glanced over at Mary who was hanging on Toni's every word. A tear was trickling down her cheek. Jasmine just wanted to puke!

Toni continued.

"John was so gallant. He rushed to my side and asked if I was ok. I told him I didn't think I could feel any worse, and then he reached out and brushed the hair from my face. His soft hand felt wonderful and oh so soothing. He gently lifted my head from the porcelain and scooped me into his strong arms. My own arms fell limp along his sides as my lifeless legs draped across his other arm. He held me to him, my head against his chest. I could hear his heart beating as his powerful muscles lifted me into the air."

He held her to him! Jasmine was not sure how much more of this she could take. She could finish the story; she had lived it on more than one occasion. She had experienced those wonderful powerful arms lifting her into the air. Jasmine knew what it was like to feel them bulge and flex. How wet it had made her when he held her to his chest. She knew what would happen next. He lifts her into the air and carries her off to bed placing her gently onto the soft mattress as he stared deeply into her eyes… SLUT, was all that came to Jasmine's mind.

Toni coughed and wheezed a bit.

"Can I get you some more tea Toni? Are you ok?" asked a concerned Mary.

I hope the bitch chokes to death on her own phlegm, thought Jasmine.

"He held me so tightly," Toni continued. "I felt safe in his arms. He carried me away from the bathroom, and I began to feel so warm as he held me to his chest."

"I'm not sure how much of this I can take," Jasmine mumbled in Mary's direction.

Mary did not seem to hear Jasmine's comment as she continued to focus on Toni.

"As he carried me down the hallway towards my bedroom, my head began to spin. It was like nothing I'd ever felt before. He held me so tightly; I just wanted to nuzzle into him further. My breathing became more of a pant as my head continued to spin, and I felt things happening inside of me I had never felt before. It was like I didn't have control of my own body. It was like I was in some sort of ever tightening spiral. I had goose bumps on my arms and legs, beads of sweat began to form on my forehead!"

Jasmine slid over next to Mary and whispered. "I cannot take another word, Mary. I have to get out of here!"

"I couldn't help myself, Mary. It just happened. One second I was in control, and the next second."

"Ya, we get it, Toni, we get it. One second you were in control and the next second you were overcome with the greatest orgasm of your life. We get it!" Jasmine screeched in her most indignant tone.

"I started to throw up! And then diarrhea, uncontrollable diarrhea filled my house dress! I was horrified, simply horrified! He held me even tighter, the vomit forming a pool where our bodies came together; the stench of feces filled the hallway. I didn't know what to do, what to say. "

"Wait a minute. You threw up? All over him; you threw up all over him?" Jasmine asked in disbelief.

"Orgasm? What the hell are you talking about Jasmine?" Mary looked at Jasmine like she had two heads.

Toni began to cry. "I just don't know how it happened. I lost complete control of my body. I just kept spewing from both ends. I've never even farted in front of a man, and here I was, in the arms of John Luke, the most wonderful man I've ever known, and what do I do? I vomit and poop my pants!"

"What did you do?" asked Mary. "What did John do?"

"You threw up?" Jasmine repeated still confused.

The room fell silent as the three women tried to regroup and figure out just what was happening. Jasmine was in one story, Toni in another, and Mary, well Mary wasn't sure what the hell was going on. Jasmine slumped back into the sofa.

The look on her face was one of total confusion. It was as if the teacher called on her and she had been gazing out the window. She sat for a moment as she reviewed all she thought she had heard.

Mary got up and moved towards Toni, moving the pile of clothes from the foot stool to the open space on the sofa next to Jasmine. She then sat down on the foot stool and reached her arms out to a now sobbing Toni. As Mary and Toni embraced, Jasmine looked over at the pile. There were dress pants, a man's shirt, and a somewhat tattered house dress. The pile was as tangled as Jasmine's day.

"Wait a minute!" Jasmine shouted. "Who the hell is John Luke?"

"Haven't you been listening Jasmine?" Mary replied.

Toni wiped her eyes and leaned forward.

"John Luke is my ex-husband's name. His grandfather's name was Luke and he loved his grandfather very much. He prefers Luke, but I've called him John as long as I've known him. I guess he tolerated it from me. His mother and I are really the only ones who call him John."

"So let me see if I've got this straight. Luke, I mean John, is your EX-husband. You're the "friend" he's been helping, and the two of you were NOT having sex today? Do I have that right?" asked an extremely confused Jasmine.

Mary and Toni, stopped, looked at each other and then began to laugh; Mary with loud belly laughs, and Toni struggling to breathe as she used the last bits of energy she had to laugh. The laughing was so vigorous, the ladies where not sure who would pee themselves first.

Toni took a deep breath and said "Oh, so that's where that orgasm comment before came from. Let me tell you something Jasmine, sex is the last thing I need right now. I'd trade all the sex I've ever had for control of my bowels. You just don't know what these chemo drugs do to you."

"John knows!" laughed Mary, tears now streaming down her face.

Even Jasmine could not hold back a chuckle at Mary's comment.

Jasmine leaned forward, now listening more carefully as Toni told her story. The thunderstorm in her mind gradually lost strength as Toni's story came into focus. The lightning was no longer shooting from her eyes and the pain in her heart started to change. Jasmine began to question the truths she had built over the last few hours. *Could it be possible that this whole mess was all in my head* she wondered? *Oh, come on now,* she thought to herself. *Toni is just making this up to cover for Luke, I mean John, I mean Luke. She's been WITH him this whole time, the slut.* Jasmine did, however, have to admit to herself that Toni was in no condition to be having sex, at least not today.

Jasmine continued to squirm, but it was becoming exceedingly difficult for her to avoid thoughts that she may have misjudged Luke. *But he did lie about this whole "friend in need" thing. Didn't he,* she thought to herself as she struggled to remember exactly what he had told her. He should have told me that his friend was a woman, his ex-wife! *This isn't my fault, it's his! If he had not lied, then none of this would have happened. He knew it was wrong or he would have told me he was seeing a woman.*

"Where is that John anyway? How long can it take to get ice," asked Toni?

"He's probably looking for his pride, after all, Jasmine did nail him good," Mary laughed.

Jasmine could not help but fidget in the chair. She kept her eyes low for fear her friend would see the truth in them.

"Jasmine," came the call from her friend, "Do you know where John is?" asked Mary?

Jasmine moved her gaze from the floor to the window, but did not utter a sound.

"Jasmine, come on spill it. Where is John" asked Mary once again.

"Well," Jasmine began. "I can honestly say I don't know where he is right now," stammered a very nervous Jasmine.

"Well, when he left, he was chasing you," injected a now agitated Toni.

"Oh my God, he was in my bathrobe, too!"

"Well," Jasmine began and then paused. The evening played back in her mind like an awful soap opera; Luke's face as the policeman cuffed him, and the way he stared into her eyes just before he was taken away. She sat there and watched the man she loved get hauled away by the police and she did nothing. Suddenly, she knew what she needed to do and explaining herself to Mary and Toni was not it. Jasmine reached for her purse as she sprang to her feet.

"I've made a horrible mistake, and I have to leave right now."

Jasmine ran through the door, down the steps, to her car. In a flash she was speeding down the road. She just kept repeating to herself, *what have I done, what have I done.* Jasmine guided the speeding car through the dimly lit streets of town, all the while searching for the words to somehow explain her actions. *How could I have been so stupid,* she berated herself? *He is a wonderful man, so kind, so generous, and always looking for ways to help.*

A hard left then a quick right, Jasmine's foot slide over to the brake pedal. The car crossed the slight dip in the road and bounced into the jail's parking lot. The car's headlights sweep across the lot as she slowly turned looking for just the right parking spot. The darkness seemed more like dusk as the orange glow of a single lamp tried, in vain, to illuminate the area. Jasmine's car crept forward slowly. Her mouth was dry and she could hear her own heartbeat as the car sought out a place to park.

Empty spaces were everywhere but the jail was not a place Jasmine frequented, and an uneasiness settled over her. She needed to park somewhere she would feel safe. Jasmine was not quite sure why she was so uncomfortable, perhaps it was the cold granite of the building, or maybe the serpentine walkway leading to the door, or perhaps it was just the look of those high fences capped with a tangled mess of shiny razor wire. *Why would anyone try to climb a fence topped with that stuff*, she thought to herself. *Duh, guess that is the point isn't it.* The walkway was lined with single lamps, each one casting its round patch of light onto the walkway. A lone lamp hung over the door. The entire scene was like something out of a movie. All that was missing was a rolling mist.

She reached over and slid the shifter into park, released the brake and turned off the ignition. A silence fell over the scene as she stared at the door. *How could she have allowed this to happen? Whatever possessed her to allow them to take him away? What would he say when he saw her?* All manner of questions flooded into Jasmine's brain as she gazed across the parking lot towards that uninviting door.

With a deep breath, her hand reached for the car door just as the jail door flung open. A man's hand held the door and out walked a woman, tailored dress, heels, hair freshly styled, and perfectly formed. This was a woman of means. She somehow fit right into this scene from a murder mystery. The single lamp struggled to illuminate her face, but somehow her beauty shone through. She was followed closely by the man who had held the door. He was a tall man with broad shoulders.

The pair seemed to belong together. Jasmine watched intently as they paused outside of the jail. He turned to her, and they embraced. The scene was like that of an old Bogart movie, the jail in the background, dim light reflecting off of the chain link fence behind them. A cool mist would be hanging in the air. Jasmine could almost hear Bogey speaking, his low snarly voice taking complete charge of the situation.

She watched as they held each other. Jasmine was reminded of how it felt when Luke held her. A tear came to her eye as she continued to observe the couple. They broke their embrace and he held her hands in his then slowly raised each to his lips and placed a deliberate soft kiss upon them. *These are not strangers* she thought to herself. Once again, they embraced, and she watched as the woman's hands clasped behind his back. The embrace was tight, just like Jasmine loved, and they swayed side to side as the embrace lingered. Soon, it was over and the two turned to navigate the serpentine walkway. The couple moved slowly, but deliberately, along the walkway. They approached and entered another circle of light. Jasmine's heart stopped.

There, illuminated in the darkness, was Luke. *Who was the woman he was with?* Jasmine could not control the rage that welled up from deep inside of her. *That bastard! That two timing bastard!*

Jasmine turned the key, slammed the shifter into gear and hit the gas. The engine roared to life. Tires screamed as the car shot backwards throwing Jasmine forward into the steering wheel. Smoke from the burning rubber enveloped the car like an eerie fog. Her eyes welled up with tears as she struggled, in vane, to cope with what she had just witnessed. Suddenly, the back of the car launched into the air and the next thing she knew, she was surrounded by bushes; the dashboard lit up like a Christmas tree, and the engine fell silent.

"And that was the J. Geils Band performing their classic, Love Stinks. Up next is Nazereth with Love Hurts". Jasmine slammed her fist into the radio out of disgust. A loud whooshing sound was the last thing she remembered as the car reached out and punched her. She felt a stabbing pain in her face and her world went dark.

The Recovery

Jasmine was aware of a familiar touch on her cheek. Her mind was somewhat foggy, and a throbbing caused her eyelids to squeeze shut tightly. She was not sure where she was, but for some reason, the touch made her feel safe. Jasmine's mind began to struggle as she fought through the pain to open her eyes. Her struggle was not without reward because as she did, she became aware of a hand grasping her own - a strong hand gently squeezing hers as the world came into focus.

"Sis, here comes the ambulance. Wave them over here," the familiar voice directed.

It was a powerful and confident voice. One that Jasmine knew well. Her mind was more at ease as she fought for consciousness. Finally, she succeeded, and her eyes fluttered open. She scanned left, and then right, as things began to come into focus.

Suddenly there was a bright white light, forcing her eyes shut. She could hear voices, and the lights were interrupted by strobes of red. Her body was jostled, and the familiar grip released her to the unknown.

The cool touches of latex covered hands were now upon her. Jasmine felt a squeeze around her neck as something tightened and forced her chin upwards. Latex covered fingers forced her eyelid up and a spot of light pierced first her left then right eye. She felt hands moving over her arms and legs. Fingers were touching her, and not in a pleasant way. Jasmine attempted to get her bearings, but her struggle was in vain. She just could not move her head.

"I've got some minor bleeding of the forehead. Pupils are equal and reactive. No obvious fractures. Can you hear me? What is her name?" the voice said with the cold efficiency of someone who had done this sort of thing before.

"Jasmine, her name is Jasmine," a soothing familiar voice replied.

"Can you hear me, Jasmine? You are going to be fine. Do you know where you are?"

Jasmine's mind was pushing the fog away as she attempted to recall the events of the evening. Her stomach began to flutter and her eyes once again filled with tears. *Did she know where she was? Of course she did. That two timing bastard did this to me,* she thought. But there was something that didn't seem to fit. *Did she hear, sis? Who is sis,* she thought to herself.

Jasmine wished the day had been a dream, but it wasn't. She had endured enough pain for one lifetime this awful night.

"Jasmine, it's me, Luke," came floating across the cool night air.

"Will she be alright? Please tell me she will be alright," the powerful voice trembled.

Jasmine felt a familiar soft touch on her arm. She could feel the tremble as it gently stroked her. The touch warmed her; it warmed her deep inside as she struggled against her restraints to turn her head and make contact.

"Sis, this is a hell of a way for you to meet the woman I love."

He loves me! Sis? Oh-my-God, the woman was his sister. Jasmine quickly replayed the scene in front of the jail. *Could this be so? Could I have seen something that was not there?* Jasmine was grasping for a better reality and tonight it would not take much to find one.

"She's coming around," the voice announced.

"Let's get some oxygen on her just to be sure."

An unwelcomed mask was thrust onto her face. She fought to push it away.

"Luke, is that you Luke?"

Her chest heaved as she struggled to make the sounds come from her aching body. Jasmine knew she was hurt, but she also knew that her love was close by. What she needed most right now was her Luke. She struggled to sit up and pull the offensive mask from her face. Her head struggled to turn and scan the area looking for the one she needed.

Firm hands pushed her back down and held the mask in place. Jasmine's arms flailed as she fought against her captures. Her mind returned to the stories of her youth as she fought against the grip of the evil ogre. The princess would fight to her death to be with her knight. Somehow she found the strength to tear loose from the bonds, the veil was cast from her face and she broke free of the bindings around her neck.

"Oh, brave knight, you've come for me," she shouted.

"My lady, I'm here for you," was the response from her knight.

"Lady, you need to lie back down. You've been in an accident," a stern voice interrupted.

"Unhand me, you oaf. I will not be denied," and with that, Jasmine rolled into the arms of her brave knight. Luke cradled her and pulled her to his chest as he placed soft kisses upon her forehead.

"Lie down, my lady, and let the EMT tend to your injuries. I will be right here holding your hand every minute."

Luke placed her gently onto the gurney, his hands sliding ever so lovingly down her arm. His strong fingers gently entwined into her own as he placed another soft kiss on her still bleeding forehead. Jasmine surrendered to his desires and took a deep cleansing breath. Her head did still hurt and her muscles ached, but she began to relax as Luke caressed her. The EMT applied a bandage and continued his examination.

"Well, lady, let's get you to the hospital so the doctors can look you over."

"Oh-my-God, I don't need to go the hospital," Jasmine objected.

"Lady, you were out cold, and when you've been unconscious, its best to have a doctor look you over and make sure you don't have a concussion."

"I'm fine, I'll be just fine," Jasmine insisted as she stared into Luke's wonderful blue eyes.

"Honey, maybe you should go and let the doctors look you over," was Luke's encouragement.

"I said I was fine. There is only one place I want to be right now and that is in your arms. I said I don't need to go to the hospital and that is just what I mean," Jasmine insisted.

"Well, we can only advise, lady, but I really think it would be best if we transported you to the hospital."

Jasmine sat up and looked the EMT in the eye," I'm not going to the hospital and that is final."

She turned to Luke and smiled, reaching her arms out to him.

"Help me up my love. I really need a hug... a big hug".

Luke lifted her to her feet. They embraced as if they had been apart for ages. Luke's powerful arms encircled her and drew her tightly to his chest. Jasmine's head turned and she slowly nuzzled into Luke's powerful chest. She could hear the wonderfully soothing sound of his heart beating as she rocked her head up and down on his chest.

Luke placed his hand onto Jasmine's head; cradling it gently and lovingly against his chest. It had been a very difficult and puzzling day for Luke, but the feel of Jasmine against his chest brought a tear to his eye. The two continued their embrace as they shut out the EMT and the rest of the world. Luke's soft kiss upon Jasmine's forehead resulted in a muffled moan.

"Ma'am; you need to go to the hospital, and get checked over. Would you like us to take you there?"

The interruption was unwelcomed.

"I'm exactly where I need to be. Now leave me alone! I'll be alright," Jasmine snapped back.

Luke could hear the resolve in her voice and could feel her arms tighten around him. He knew what he needed to do.

"I'll take care of her. Go on, I'll make sure she is not left alone, and if she is feeling bad later, I'll take her to the emergency room myself. I think it best if you just pack up and leave. Sorry to have caused you to come out here for nothing."

Jasmine could hear the cold snap of toolbox latches as the EMT's packed up their equipment. She thought she heard a huff or two, but just nuzzled further into Luke's chest, and let the world around her drift away. It had been a horrible day and she just wanted to wake up from this nightmare and have it be over.

She felt the softness of Luke's lips on her forehead, as his arms tightened around her. The familiar subtle rocking began, and she could feel the calm flowing into her body. Jasmine shut her eyes and just let her lover take care of her. She inhaled deeply and filled her head with his wonderful scent. The fingers on her left hand began to flex ever so slightly as she stroked the powerful muscles of his back. Her right hand tightened its grip on his shirt. She was where she belonged.

"Deb, bring the car. We'll leave hers here for the tow truck."

"Sure, Luke."

Jasmine felt herself drifting away as she became lost in Luke's embrace. Her mind returned to the past adventures she so loved - the balloon ride, the picnic; it was happiness, true happiness she felt while snuggled in Luke's arms. She had entered her happy place, and she was determined to remain there as long she could.

The car rolled to a stop. Luke's sister got out, and opened the back door. Effortlessly, Luke lifted Jasmine from the ground. Her arms tightened around his neck as her man carried her to the waiting car. He placed Jasmine ever so gently onto the back seat and slid in next to her. She never left his embrace. She felt another soft kiss upon her forehead as Luke's powerful arms drew her tightly to him.

Jasmine felt the car lurch slightly, and they were on their way. She wasn't sure where they were going, and she didn't really care. Luke was back, and that was all that mattered.

"Could you drop us at home, Deb?"

Us...home, she thought. That just sounded so right to her. *Yes, take us home,* she repeated to herself.

Jasmine simply closed her eyes. Her head still hurt a bit, and the muscles of her back and neck were beginning to stiffen. It had been an extremely long day. Jasmine fought off the troubling thoughts that had filled her mind earlier that day. It was a battle within herself to keep the glass half full, but she was determined to win this battle.

She nuzzled her head into his shoulder as she felt the car navigating the streets of the town. It was late, and there were few cars out at this time of night. Jasmine simply cuddled in and enjoyed the scent of her man.

The car jolted over a bump, and came to a stop. Jasmine opened her eyes, and immediately recognized this place. It was Luke's home. Memories of the first horrifying ride to this place popped into her head. Jasmine recalled the fear and excitement it had brought her as she entered a man's home for the first time in so many years.

She remembered that first tour, and his nervousness. A smile came to her face as she recalled his hesitation to show her the master bedroom. She, too, was nervous that night. She was not sure what she wanted to happen, much less what would happen. He was such a gentleman. What happened that night was something so special that every moment was forever etched into her memory.

"I've got her sis, can you get the door?"

Luke once again lifted her into his arms and carried her to the house.

"Thanks for everything, Deb. I'll call you tomorrow."

"It was nice to meet you Jasmine. John has told me so many wonderful things about you. I hope you feel better in the morning."

"Thank you so much for helping. I look forward to meeting you again under better circumstances."

"Let me tell you, I wouldn't have missed it for the world. We will all laugh about this one day I'm sure. The site of John, in that pink fuzzy robe, black socks and dress shoes was something. He was standing in the corner of the cell with that monster of a man. What was his name again? Bubba, yes that's it, Bubba. Well, John, that image will keep me in stories for years. I think he really liked you. Where would you like your robe?" she chuckled.

"Oh, just drop it anywhere. I'll get it back to Toni another day. You know, sis, you really are one sick lawyer," Luke chuckled in response.

Jasmine struggled to keep a straight face. She simply placed a soft kiss onto Luke's cheek as she held tightly to him. Luke's sister left, and he turned towards the master bedroom. Jasmine loved the feel of his powerful muscles as he carried her though the house. Luke laid her gently onto the bed. Jasmine settled in while never taking her eyes off of Luke. Jasmine winced as she became aware of the stiffness in her body, but there was something much more important on her mind than a little stiffness. Her wincing did not go unnoticed as Luke's caring eyes remained fixed upon hers.

He slowly slid his hands down along her left leg, lifting it ever so slightly into the air. His skilled fingers unhooked the strap of her heel, and effortlessly slipped the delicate shoe from her foot. Slowly, he brought her bare foot to his lips - placing a soft kiss upon it. Luke then returned her leg to the bed, and gently lifted the other. Again, his fingers stroked along the calf until they cradle her foot. Jasmine was lost in his touch as the second shoe fell to the floor. She felt his moist lips placing an ever so subtle kiss upon her foot. Luke returned her leg to the bed with the reverence an artist gives his masterpiece.

"I'll be right back," Luke said in his wonderfully soft tone.

He disappeared, but soon she heard the water running. At first, Jasmine thought he was washing up, but soon realized that he was drawing a bath. A smile came over her as she recalled just what it was to be bathed by him. Luke returned, and sat next to her on the bed. The soft mattress compressed under his weight and she naturally rolled towards him.

Luke's eyes were filled with love and care as he deftly reached for the top button of her blouse. He had undressed her many a time, and she cherished each one. A smile came to her face as each button fell open with the slightest touch from his soft hand. His eyes never left hers. The two of them were lost in each other.

He continued as she felt the top button of her jeans release and the zipper slide effortlessly down. He rose and stood next to the bed. Never taking those magical blue pools off of her, he slowly removed his own clothes, until he stood before her in all of his naked beauty. Luke was like a Greek God posing for a statue. His chiseled body, with a form that would take the breath right out of any woman, worked to fan the embers of the passion building within her.

He reached out and pulled her to a sitting position. His soft hands brush her blouse from her shoulders. He drew close to her as his fingers stroked along her upper torso, finally, coming to rest on the hooks of her bra. Jasmine turned her head and placed her cheek upon the few soft hairs of his chest. She inhaled deeply, filling her head with that drug that was his scent. She felt the release as he unhooked the clasp. His fingers moved to her shoulders as he gently nudged the straps away. The straps of the bra slid down her arms. He gathered the delicate garment and set it aside. His eyes returned to hers. He stepped back, and lifted her to her feet.

Luke leaned down and slowly brought his lips to hers. The kiss was soft and loving. His soft lips moved ever so gently across her tingling flesh. The feeling was wonderfully familiar. Her lips ever so gently stroked his. The sensuous touch, fanning the glowing embers of their passion as the two lovers embraced. She could feel her now naked nipples touching his chest as his loving touch continued. Luke slowly slid down her body, his hands stroking along her back, until he came to rest on one knee. He looked up at her as his hands began to tug her jeans downward. They seemed to resist slightly until Jasmine wiggled her round bottom. The jeans fell to the floor. Luke lifted first her left, then right foot from the crumpled fabric.

Jasmine was trembling now and her chest heaved with excitement. She never tired of the way he made her feel. She was beautiful and he made her feel that way. She stood before him in her white lacy panties, a confident, sexy, woman, who desired, yes desired, this handsome man. She was his woman and she knew it. His thumbs slid beneath the waistband of the panties. With a tug, they too dropped to the floor. He rose, holding the soft lace in his hand. He looked into her eyes as he brought the treasure to his cheek rubbing it softly. He then smiled at her and dropped them onto the bed.

Luke scooped Jasmine into his arms and carried her to the tub. Candles flickered everywhere driving away the darkness, and replacing it with a soft warm glow. The water was steaming as he stood her in the tub. It was quite warm, but not hot. Luke held her hand while slowly lowering her into the water allowing her body to acclimate. He stepped into the tub behind her and lowered himself into the water, his powerful legs stroked along hers.

"Lie back my lady. I'm sure your muscles ache after the accident. This will help you relax."

Jasmine did just that. Her head on his chest as the water rose to her chin. She let her arms come to rest upon his knees as she simply floated, weightless in the steaming water. Luke's hands never stopped moving. He took the soft cloth, and stroked along her neck. The soothing water caused beads of perspiration to form on her forehead. They would no sooner form, before Luke would gently kiss them away.

It was like being lost in a dream. Time seemed to stop as she enjoyed the attention. Jasmine slipped momentarily into her dream world reliving all of the wonderful days they had spent together lost in each other's embrace. Jasmine was not sure how long they spent in the tub, but Luke's soft voice brought her back to reality.

"My lady, it's time to get out."

Luke kissed her ear as he slowly pressed her forward. Jasmine felt totally relaxed. Luke stood, stepped out of the tub, reaching for one of the plush towels he kept on the shelf. Jasmine watched intently as he toweled himself off. His large hands moved over his firm body as she watched. Her desire began to build. She could not help but notice that all of the stiffness from her body had apparently gone to his.

Luke reached his hand out to her. Instinctively she placed her hand into his. Jasmine loved the way he would take her hand; it made her feel like a princess. He slowly lifted her from the soothing water. Luke's hand steadied her as she stepped out of the tub onto the soft floor mat.

He took another towel from the shelf and began to dry her. She felt no stiffness as he took first one arm then the other drying them thoroughly. Jasmine was lost in the feeling of his hands massaging her back as he wiped the dampness from her naked skin. Luke's hands seemed to mold themselves to the roundness of her bottom as she imagined him dropping the towel and simply gripping her in the powerful way he did when he was about to take her.

Jasmine's daydream ended replaced by Luke's gentle touch guiding her as she rotated. The softness of the towel caressed her shoulders. Jasmine could not help but let her head fall back, exposing her long sensuous neck to his attention. The fluffy towel glided across her, drawing each bead of water from her tingling skin. The towel moved further down her body, until the sensations of the soft cloth were replaced by the soft, moist kisses she so loved.

Feeling Luke's warm breath on her freshly bathed skin took her breath away. The towel swirled around the curves of her breasts as Luke's hand lift each one. She savored the way he paid attention to every part of her body. Luke would sometimes spend hours softly caressing every part of her. He had such a loving touch that she would sometimes simply lie in his lap allowing his hands to roam lovingly over her beautiful body. This was the type of touch she was feeling tonight.

Jasmine watched in amazement as this naked, Godlike form, tended to her most basic of needs. Once dry, Luke took Jasmine's hands in his, looked deep into her eyes and softly whispered," Will you sleep with me tonight?"

Jasmine could see the emotion in his eyes and feel it in the grip of his hands. Her mind began to stray as she recalled the events of the day. She began to wonder how he could possibly want her after everything that happened. Her pause caused his hands to begin to tremble and she quickly pushed the thoughts aside.

"Yes, my love," were the only words she could find as she guided his hands around her.

Jasmine pressed her form to his. Her arms drew him tightly to her as she laid her head upon his shoulder. Her eyes started to well up with tears as she realized he wanted her in his life. She could feel the passion between them as the hug continued. They were both in their most basic of form, naked, warm, and vulnerable. These two lovers needed each other, not in a sexual way, but in the spiritual way one person needs another. The two retired to the bedroom and held each other tightly as they slept. They spent the night lost in each other. If one would stir, the other would tighten their grip and reinforce their need for one another.

Now What

The sun shone through the small slit in the curtains, falling across Jasmine's closed eyes, nudging her out of the slumber she was enjoying. The birds outside of the window seemed to be singing directly to her. The luxurious sheets caressed her body as the weight of the down comforter gave her a feeling of coziness. She rolled to her back and stretched an arm towards Luke. There was a slight stiffness in her and instinctively she began to stretch. Her leg muscles tightened as did her arms. A smile came to her face as she felt the warmth and tingles that every woman feels the morning after the night before.

How did she ever find such a man? What could she possibly have done to deserve someone so handsome, wonderful, and oh, what a lover? She reached towards his pillow, expecting to snuggle into his warm sexy body. The further she reached, the more awake she became, until finally she sat up. There, next to her, was only empty space. She quickly scanned the room, beams of sunlight filtering through the gaps between the curtains, shown like spotlights in the otherwise dark room.

Where was Luke? This is not what she wanted to awaken to. Jasmine sat there in the bed wondering what had happened. *Why would he leave her here alone? What time is it?* Jasmine then noticed the single red rose on the pillow next to her with a note tucked underneath. She picked up the rose, and held it to her nose. The sweet fragrance was wonderful. Jasmine let the soft petals of the flower caress her cheek while thoughts of Luke filled her head. She picked up the note and read:

My love, I watched you sleeping ever so soundly this morning. I just could not bring myself to awaken you from your slumber. Please forgive me for not being here as you greet the new day. When you are ready, put on my robe and join me.

All my love, Luke

Jasmine clutched the note to her naked chest. He loved her. *After all I've put him through, he still loves me.* With that thought, Jasmine slipped from beneath the covers and placed her feet onto the soft carpet. She rose from the bed, and reached for Luke's robe standing guard at the bed post.

Jasmine pulled the heavy terrycloth robe from the bed post, and slipped first one arm then the other into the sleeves. She gripped either side of the robe and pulled it tightly to her face. Jasmine drew in a deep breath. Luke's scent filled her head. It was almost as if he were standing before her. The feeling she was having bordered on euphoria as she spun and pranced around the room as if she and Luke were dancing in some grand ballroom. She was on her toes as the steps just seemed to flow joyously. This day would be a celebration of the love in her life and the man that infused that love into her.

Jasmine finally found her way out of the bedroom and began the search for Luke. The cool hardwood of his floors caressed her feet as she moved from room to room. Finally, soft melodies came floating from the far side of the house. The soothing sound seemed to draw her to its source. Jasmine reached out, slid the heavy wooden doors open, and stepped into Luke's study. There he sat at a massive wooden beauty. The intricate carving made the desk more of a piece of art than a place to work. His back was to her as he worked. She paused, and just watched as his fingers flew across the keyboard. He looked almost majestic as he sat there in his high back chair, leaning ever so slightly into the desk. Luke's large hands, the same hands that had touched her so delicately, seemed to take on a new form while he nearly pounded the keys while putting his thoughts into the document. Suddenly, Luke's fingers stopped, and he turned towards her. A smile filled his face as he leapt to his feet.

"Good morning, my love. Did you sleep well? My goodness, my robe has never looked so good," Luke said as he walked towards Jasmine.

He gathered Jasmine into his arms and pulled her tightly to him. She felt like a rag doll as he took control and seemed to move her at will. His long arms wrapped around her. The kiss that followed was soft, loving, and passionate all at the same time. Jasmine could hardly breathe as she felt herself go limp in his embrace. His fingers slipped into her hair as the kiss slowly ended, and she placed her head upon his broad shoulder.

The couple continued to embrace as if this was their first time. For Jasmine and Luke, every embrace was like their first. This was something that Jasmine could not explain and long ago quit trying. When they came together, the world disappeared. They were all that mattered. Luke guided the couple in this impromptu dance. Slowly, at first, they began to sway. Jasmine lifted her head from his shoulder, and looked into those deep pools of blue. She loved the way he looked at her. She could feel him deep in her soul as they became lost in each other's gaze. Jasmine found that she had to look away in order to breathe. She took a deep breath, slowly closed her eyes, and let her head settle upon his shoulder once again. She drew in another breath and filled her head with Luke.

The tempo of the dance increased as the two moved gracefully about the room. Jasmine watched the world go by as they did so. Through the windows she saw the deck and the chairs they had often sat upon while holding hands, and sipping wine as they watched the birds clustered around the many feeders. She saw the beautiful bookshelves he had made himself, a place to display the things he had collected in his travels. The antique radio he had restored and the wonderful oval mirror he had rescued from a dumpster. Beauty seemed to follow Luke's touch. The mirror, tattered and worn, but under his skilled touch, was reborn into a wonderful antique anyone would be proud to display.

Jasmine noticed how they looked in the mirror; this large powerful man holding her so tightly. She felt the warmth of her man and then it happened. She could not help herself. Her focus shifted from the beauty of the scene to the woman in the mirror. There she stood, her hair flying in all directions, a bit of white gauze taped to her forehead, no makeup, and this extremely unflattering man's robe that seemed to just hang off her body. The spell was broken as she stopped the dance.

"Oh-my-God, look at me!" she exclaimed. "I look a mess."

Luke just laughed.

"I need to get to the shower. My goodness my hair! I look like, like, well not like something you deserve!" Jasmine said excitedly.

Luke simply pulled her back into his embrace and kissed her. He kissed her in mid-sentence. His fingers running through that hair she was so embarrassed about. Once she quit trying to speak, he broke the kiss and moved his lips over her face. Soft kisses fell upon her cheeks, her forehead; he even placed soft kisses on her eyes. She loved it when she closed her eyes and he placed feathery kisses upon them.

"You are beautiful, my dear, and I'll not allow anyone, not even you, to say disparaging things about the woman I love."

With that, a smile returned to Jasmine's face.

"What have you been doing?" Jasmine questioned.

"Well I figured you would need something to wear, so I threw your clothes into the washer and then came in here to get some work done. Your clothes should be nearly dry, but personally I like this outfit much better," Luke said as he stepped back, raised her arms, and looked her up and down.

"I especially like the way it seductively falls open giving glimpses of those sexy legs and that, well, you know," stopping himself mid-sentence.

Jasmine loved the way Luke noticed everything. He could make her feel beautiful and sexy with only a look. She felt like a woman whenever he was around. The ladies at the salon could not understand what this felt like. She had tried on several occasions to explain it to them but none would believe her. She knew where they were coming from. She, too, had been cynical about compliments from men. They would cast them in the direction of women the way a skilled fisherman casts a lure to a hungry fish. Women, starved for attention, would grab the lure. The man would then play her until he got what he wanted. It was like watching the fisherman fighting the fish, wearing it down until it surrendered to him. Once he had gotten what he wanted, he would toss them back into the water and disappear. Jasmine could never convince them that Luke was not like that; every compliment he bestowed on someone came from his heart with no expectations of something in return.

"Can I cook you some breakfast?"

Just then, the grandfather clock in the hallway began to chime. In Jasmine's subconscious she counted each tone as it floated through the house.

"9:00!" she exclaimed. Mary is going to kill me. Today is regular's day."

"Regular's day?" Luke questioned.

"Today is the day my friends all come in to get their hair done. Mary is buried and probably ready to kill me! I'm sorry, my love, but I really need to get to work."

"Jasmine, you were in a car wreck, remember?" Luke asked with a level of concern in his voice.

"Maybe you need to take it easy today? Maybe you should just call in sick?"

"Call in sick! Luke, I can't call in sick; Mary needs me! My customers need me! Besides, I feel wonderful, thanks to you, my love."

Jasmine pulled in close to Luke and began to rub herself against him. Her arms reach around behind him and she gave his wonderful bottom a playful squeeze. Jasmine smiled at Luke and watched as the corners of his mouth turned up.

"I've called the tow truck and had your car taken to my mechanic to be checked out. He'll call me later and let me know if there are any damages, or if you need something repaired. I guess we better get some clothes on if I'm going to drop you at work."

Luke looked deep into Jasmine's eyes as he leaned in for a kiss. He could not resist her. Even after the craziness of the night before, all he wanted in his life was her.

"You go hop in the shower, my love, and I'll get your clothes from the dryer. You better wash your hair or all of your friends will know what you've been doing." Luke said with a chuckle.

He turned her around, gave her nice round bottom a love tap and sent her on her way. He headed the opposite way to retrieve her clothes. Luke pulled them from the still tumbling dryer. He quickly folded her shirt, smoothing out any wrinkles as he stroked the fabric. Next were her pants. Seam to seam, folded neatly. Once again, he used his hand to smooth out the few wrinkles that appeared. He then retrieved her panties from the dryer. He held them up and smiled.

He had a thing for sexy panties, and Jasmine never disappointed him. They were minimal. The lacy triangle seemed to reach up to the waistband; a piece of elastic adorned with yet more lace that stretched around to a smaller lace triangle. The two triangles were joined together by yet another piece of lace. His mind wandered to a mental picture of Jasmine wearing them. She looked so feminine, so lovely when she stood before him. Luke loved feminine, and Jasmine was his goddess. He folded the delicate panties and laid them on the dryer. The machine was nearly empty except for the bra and socks. He smiled, noting that all matched. Jasmine always matched. Luke quickly folded the last items and headed back to his master suite.

As he approached the door, he could hear his Jasmine humming in the shower. She sounded so happy; he had to pause and just observe the silhouette on the shower curtain. His desire was to strip naked, enter the shower with her, and share in her joy. His hands would take the shampoo and lather her hair, his powerful fingers would glide through her locks as their naked bodies touched, and the hot water would stream around them as they performed the intimate bathing ritual they had come to know.

The sound of Jasmine dropping the soap jerked him back to reality. He knew that if he entered the shower, she would never get to work, and he understood her concern for her friend. Luke took one last look at her silhouette, and turned back towards the bed. Carefully, he laid out her clean clothes, and then returned to the shower. He may not be able to join her, but darn sure could welcome her out.

The shower fell silent, and Luke reached for one of the plush bath sheets he kept on the shelf. He let it fall open and awaited her exit. The curtain slid open, and there she stood, his Jasmine. Her hair slicked back, and beads of water clinging to her soft skin. He immediately wrapped the huge towel around her, over lapping it in the front and tucking it back onto itself. He then grabbed another towel and began to dry her hair.

Jasmine just stood before him, gazing at this special man as he tended to her. She loved the feel of his fingers moving through her hair, firm, yet somehow tender, as he worked to dry her silken locks. Once done, he wrapped her head and then tucked the towel around her neck. He then opened the bath sheet ever so slightly and began to caress her body. She watched as he took the time to dry every part of her. His hands gliding over her as the bath sheet collected every droplet of water. Luke gently lifted her breasts and dried under them before turning her around and continuing on her back and legs. Jasmine trembled as his terrycloth covered hand moved up the inside of each leg and then flattening as it dried her most private of places. He even lifted one leg, then the other and dried her feet.

When he was finished, he wrapped the sheet around her once again and pulled her to him. Their lips met in silence as they embraced. Jasmine was tingling with excitement as she pressed into him. She could also feel his arousal as they embraced. His powerful arms wrapped around her, Jasmine's own arms struggling to match the intensity of his embrace. Finally, they released each other, eyes fixed on eyes as they spoke silently. Their lips inched closer, until, finally, they touched, and the kiss began. Jasmine loved the way Luke kissed. His lips were soft and sensual. He always seemed to begin his kisses the same way. Skimming over hers ever so softly until they were moist, then pressing ever so slightly until the passion began to burn. Luke never gave her a peck. His kisses were always deliberate and meaningful. She loved everyone .

"This will have to wait, my love," Luke said with a tremble in his voice.

"I'm so sorry, my love. You know I don't want to go, don't you?" Jasmine returned.

"Yes, and one day, we will be together always," Luke reassured her.

Jasmine looked towards the bed and saw the stack of clothes neatly placed there. The pants folded neatly at the bottom of the pile, hung over the edge of the bed, while the blouse lay folded neatly atop them. Next came the bra then the panties folded into a perfect triangle. The pile was topped with the socks. It looked like something from a movie where the butler lays out the clothes for his charge.

"Oh, thank you so much for laying out my clothes," Jasmine said with a smile. "You treat me like a princess."

"You are a princess, my love; my princess."

Luke took Jasmine's hand and walked her to the side of the bed. He then pulled her to him and gave her a soft loving kiss. He held her delicate hand in his as he looked into her eyes. Jasmine smiled when she saw the desire in his gaze. She could feel herself slowly leaning into Luke. Her mind was calculating exactly how long it would take her to get to work. Luke was a wonderful driver. He would drive fast, but could he drive fast enough, she thought. Maybe no one showed up at the salon, and Mary was simply killing time. Jasmine sighed because she knew what needed to happen, and what would just have to wait.

"I very much want to stay, Luke, but I really have to go. Please understand," she pleaded with that cute little whine women get.

"I know, my lady." Luke replied.

With that, he slowly dropped her hands to her side. and then slid his hands up her arms to her shoulders, leaned in, and gave her a soft kiss on her cheek. He also knew she needed to go. Her customers were waiting, and if there was anything Luke did understand, it was business. He remembered when his businesses were young. Before he was able to turn the day-to-day running of them over to someone else. Now, it was only Jasmine that he needed.

Jasmine began to reach for the neatly folded panties. Luke quickly captured her hand and held it in his.

"Let me," was all he said.

Luke released her hand, and retrieved the delicate lingerie. With one hand, he released her towel while allowing the soft triangle to unfurl. Jasmine could not help but smile as Luke crouched to one knee before her. The towel lay in a circle about her feet. He took her delicate foot and lifted it slightly as he slid the silken panties over her now pointed toes. He set that foot back onto the floor and nudged the other into the air as he slid the panties further onto her. She reestablished her stance as he began to guide the panties up her legs as he rose before her.

Jasmine loved it when Luke dressed her, and her desire not to be dressing right now seemed to amplify the tingles from his touch. She rocked her hips side to side as he tugged the panties into place. Next he reached for the matching bra. Luke took one last look at her breasts and slid the bra up her arms until each strap was properly placed on her shoulders. He then moved around behind her, letting his fingers trace across her skin as he moved. She could feel the slight tremble in his hands as he drew the strap tight and fastened the bra. Jasmine then felt his hands glide to her shoulder as his warm breath caressed her neck. Moist lips followed as she shuddered under the wonder of his touch.

Luke's hands never left the soft skin of her shoulders as he moved around to face her once again. His eyes gazed into hers as he reached for the shirt lying neatly on the bed. Luke opened it, and slipped it onto her left, then her right arm, and pulled it shut over her now heaving breasts. Slowly, yet deliberately, he began to button the blouse. His soft hands smoothed the fabric as the blouse clung to her. Once again, Luke knelt before her as he retrieved the pants from the bed. Jasmine placed her hand onto Luke's shoulder to steady herself. One foot rose from the floor as he slid the pant leg over it. A pause, then the other foot was gently guided into her pants. She could feel Luke's hot breath moving over her legs as he slowly slid the pants into position. His ritual was not something that only Jasmine loved, Luke also drew incredible emotion from the dressing of his woman.

He cherished Jasmine, and wanted the horror of the previous night to disappear from his consciousness. This intimate ritual was just what he needed. He knew that something had triggered the "Jasmine moment," but he was just glad to have her back. His arms encircled her as he pulled his precious lady to him and held on for dear life. She knew he needed her and her own arms joined in the embrace. Two lovers, who knew they had strayed, were back together, and each wanted the other to know just how much they were needed.

"I'm so sorry, my love, but I really must get going," Jasmine whispered.

"Relax, Jasmine. I know, and I do understand"

Luke released her, and slowly stepped back, allowing Jasmine to finish. He knew that sometimes life gets in the way. He understood the paradox. One must work in order to support themselves, and those who depend upon them. The father has to work to pay the rent and buy the food; as a result he misses his son's football game. A horrible thing, but sometimes, there is just no choice. In his past, he had often let his personal life suffer in order to fulfill the requirements of his business life. Luke had come to a point where his business successes could give him independence, and he was thankful for that.

The cool blue digits of the alarm clock caught Jasmine's eye; 9:55 was its message to her. She could only imagine what Mary was doing with all those ladies there. Maybe she had started one of her stories and had all of the women on the edges of their seats. A smile came to Jasmine's face as she recalled the last story told. The shop laughingly referred to it as, "The Tale of the Poop."

"I really need to get going, Luke. Can you please turn off that devilish charm of yours, and take me to work? Please?"

Luke smiled, raised Jasmine's hand to his lips, and kissed it ever so gently. Holding the back of her hand to his lips, he looked her in the eye, winked, and smiled. Jasmine knew he was messing with her. She jerked her hand back and gave him a playful whack on the shoulder.

"You are just awful, Luke! Now stop it. Stop it right now. We have to leave."

Luke laughed. He did know how to drive her crazy, and he just loved doing it.

"Ok, hon; let's go."

What Will the Girls Say

Mary looked up at the clock and then at the front door. This was just not like Jasmine. The night before had been a tumultuous one, and Jasmine's absence this morning was beginning to worry Mary. The "girls" were all here, and were being patient so far, but Mary knew that if Jasmine did not arrive soon, the natives would become restless. All of the regulars were here today. Over the years, this day, the third Thursday of the month, had become known as "Regulars" day. These four ladies, Madge, June, Robin, and Tina, would book the first four appointments of the morning. It was as much a coffee clutch as a beauty parlor appointment. Jasmine learned long ago that these four ladies, with all of their antics, would take up the entire morning, so she just blocked out the morning for them. It was a welcome and amusing break in the normally hectic month.

"Where is Jasmine this morning?" Tina asked in her naturally inquisitive voice.

"Probably trying to recover from a night with that Luke guy she keeps talking about," Madge said with a chuckle.

"She's had that "glow" about her the last few times I've seen her. You know, the one a woman gets when a woman is getting what she wants."

"It's been so long since I got what I wanted; I'm not sure what it is I want anymore." Robin chimed in sarcastically, and then laughed.

"The last time I had what I wanted was my daughter's wedding night," June said with a longing in her eyes.

"You kinky woman!" Madge said with a laugh. "I'll bet that poor boy never knew what hit him?" she continued laughing loudly as only Madge could.

"Madge, you are terrible. You know what I mean. Your mind is always in the gutter. I had so much fun getting all dressed up, and dancing. Seeing my daughter in her wedding gown brought back such wonderful memories. When my husband held me in his arms, it was like we were 30 years younger."

"Yes, a wedding will do that to you" Tina said with nostalgia in her voice.

"Well, I just loved watching all those young butts. There is just something about a firm butt in a suit that gives me chills," Madge said in her normal deviant tone.

Madge had never met a butt she didn't appreciate, and all of the ladies knew it. She could even get a bit out of control, as she had on several occasions when she added alcohol to the mix. Over the years, Madge had given her opinion about each of their husbands' butts. All of the ladies knew she was all talk, and tolerated her openness, and occasional advice, about just what to do with those butts.

"Yes, I bet you did Madge. Did you stop by the store and pick yourself up a fresh set of batteries on the way home?" Mary said with a chuckle.

The whole group started laughing as Madge reeled from the comment. Even Madge laughed. Mary needed to keep them distracted. She knew Madge could talk about sex all day. Mary looked out of the window again wondering what was keeping Jasmine. Suddenly, she dropped her comb as she watched a tow truck drive by. Mary ran to the window and looked down the street as the tow truck, and the car hanging helplessly from its hook, disappeared from view.

"That was Jasmine's car!" Mary exclaimed.

She ran to her purse, fumbling for her cell phone.

"Where the hell is that thing?"

Mary continued to dig and dig. She began tossing things onto the counter in an effort to locate the phone among all of the essentials in her purse. Finally, her fingers located the cell phone, and ripped it from her purse like a magician pulling a rabbit from his hat. Frantically, she punched the buttons and placed the phone to her ear.

"Hi," came blurting out of the phone, and Mary started talking.

"Are you OK? I just saw your car go past on a tow truck, and" Mary stopped mid sentence as she heard the rest of Jasmine's message.

"I'm sorry, but I cannot come to the phone right now. Your call is important to me, so at the tone, please leave me a message, and I will return it as soon as I can. Have a great day."

Mary waited impatiently for the tone, and began to speak.

"Jasmine, are you OK? Where are you? What is going on? Call me right away!"

Mary turned towards the ladies. The salon had fallen silent, having overheard the message, as each woman felt the panic sweeping over Mary. Her hand moved slowly towards the counter, dropping the phone into the debris of her purse explosion as if it were a used tissue being dropped into the waste basket. It is dangerous to give one woman, much less a group of women, a morsel of seemingly bad news, and let them stew. Mary was highly skilled at creating detailed scenarios of doom, whether they were justified or not.

She slumped back against the counter as her fertile imagination began to construct the scene. She could see Jasmine lying in the street motionless. Blood oozing from a gash on her forehead from where her head was bashed into the windshield. Her breathing labored, as pain coursed through her body. What would she do without her friend? A tear welled up as the scene played out.

The night before had been insane. The anger she felt for Luke was so intense, she nearly shot him. Jasmine herself slapped his face. We still don't know what happened to Luke or why Jasmine herself bolted without an explanation. Now her car is on the back of a tow truck. *What if SHE murdered him? Maybe she ran him down with her car?* Mary's mind was on overdrive now. Her palms were wet with anxiety. *What if, what if,* Mary didn't dare complete her thought.

Just then, the door flung open and, as if delivered by an angel, there she stood. The mid-morning sun at her back cast a glow around her. For an instant, Mary wasn't sure if this was Jasmine or the ghost of Jasmine.

"Well, where have you been?" came Madge's scratchy voice, snapping Mary out of her daydream, or more accurately, nightmare.

"Hi ladies, sorry I'm so late. I overslept," said Jasmine in a somewhat breathless voice.

Just then Luke stepped through the door. The salon fell silent as the girls got what they had been waiting for all these weeks, a look at what had to be Luke.

"I'd like you all to meet Luke, the man in my life", boyfriend seemed juvenile to Jasmine.

"Luke, this is Madge, Robin, June, and Tina.

"How do you do, ladies?" Luke replied in his normal gregarious fashion.

The ladies looked Luke up and down as each one appraised him from their perspective. They had heard so much about him, and each one wondered if he truly was deserving of all the hype. Madge immediately began moving up and down his form, undressing him with her eyes. Robin stood up, walked to him, and stuck out her hand.

"Hi, I'm Robin."

To her shock, Luke took her hand, raised it ever so slowly to his lips and kissed the back.

"Glad to meet you, Robin."

Madge rose, and she, too, walked towards Luke. When she came face to face with him she extended her arms and drew him in.

"Well, I'm a hugger. Hope you don't mind."

Madge pressed her body to his and Luke returned the embrace, just not with quite as much enthusiasm as Madge. Jasmine saw her hands beginning to slide down Luke's back and she knew exactly what was coming next.

"That's quite enough, Madge."

Jasmine captured Madge's roaming hands, and rescued Luke from the clutches of the Madginator.

"That is quite enough, Madge!" Jasmine scolded in a semi playful tone.

Jasmine had heard enough stories about Madge and her butt obsession that she knew exactly where her hands were going. Jasmine's hands were the only ones she wanted to see on Luke's wonderful butt.

Luke looked over at Mary, and smiled. She wasn't sure how to react. The night before had been outrageous, confusing, and, at one point, terrifying. Luke walked over to Mary, took her into his arms and hugged her gently. Mary could feel the sincerity in his embrace.

"Thank you for taking care of Toni last night. I really needed to find Jasmine and get this all straightened out. You are a great friend." Luke whispered to Mary as he tightened his embrace.

Luke released Mary, and gave her a soft peck on the cheek. He then smiled, and turned back to Jasmine.

"I'll check on your car later. Could I pick you up around 5:00 tonight?" Luke asked questioningly.

"I won't have time to go home and change, oops, guess I couldn't get home anyway. Sure, I'll be here, waiting."

Jasmine took Luke's hand, and walked him to the salon's door. All eyes were on the couple as they waited to see how they would say goodbye. The romantics wanted a kiss, and they would not be disappointed. Luke gathered Jasmine into his arms loosely. The two looked deep into each other's eyes. The salon fell silent as everyone waited. As if viewing a movie, the group watched as Luke's head tilted to one side ever so slightly. He began to move closer to her. On cue, Jasmine's head also tilted. Her eyes slowly closed and her lips parted ever so slightly. Luke's lips touched hers; his own eyes grew heavy, and slowly joined Jasmine in the privacy of darkness. Their lips gently formed to each other. As the ladies watched, their arms tightened drawing them even closer to one another.

You could have heard a pin drop as each of the ladies relived their last romantic kiss. For some, it had only been a few days. For others, it had been decades. Still others had only read about such kissing in the romance novels where they sought the passion missing in their own relationships. Here, before all, was the real deal, the thing every woman sought. The love that was on display for all was pure, beautiful, and inspiring.

Luke's eyes slowly opened as he began to withdraw. Jasmine followed suit and they broke the kiss. Luke leaned in, and whispered something into Jasmine's ear. Each lady strained to hear, but all failed. Jasmine's smile and slight blush was all they could see. Their arms extended as Luke moved towards the door straining to maintain their touch until the very last second. Finally, Luke's hands fell to his side.

He turned, waved to the ladies, and, in an instant, was gone. Jasmine stood, frozen in time as she watched him walk down the sidewalk, get into his car, and speed away. With a smile on her face, Jasmine turned to face the audience. The silence was deafening as she suddenly became aware of the eyes focused upon her. Her face turned crimson, and she began to stammer.

"What?" finally escaped her mouth.

Jasmine made her way quickly to her chair trying to act as if nothing had happened.

"Who's next?"

The ladies would have none of it. This was something very special, and they all knew it. Jasmine would not get a pass from this group.

Mary looked at Jasmine and said "What? What the hell do you mean what? You spill it, and don't leave out a single sigh, detail, or."

"Moan," Madge blurted out. That is one hot man!"

Jasmine took a seat in the styling chair as she began to tell the story of the bizarre night just past. Each lady was on the edge of her seat as the story played out. There were gasps, tears, and even some laughter as she shared the craziness of the night before. Even Mary, who had been there for most of it, could not take her eyes off of Jasmine as she wove her tale.

This would be a day the salon would remember for years to come. Each of Jasmine's friends knew they were privileged to have been a part of it. As the ladies took their turn in the chair, each one shared something of their own life, something sweet, romantic, and wonderful. Even Madge was able to let down her rough façade and expose the soft woman of her youth. That day turned out to be very special indeed as each lady, in turn, cancelled whatever plans they had, and waited at the shop. They all watched the clock in eager anticipation of Luke's return. It was as if each one of the women were being picked up by their suitor. Finally 5:00, arrived. Jasmine sat in her styling chair awaiting Luke's return. Mary had given her a touch up and even a manicure so she could look her best when he arrived.

On time to the second, Luke pulled up in front of the salon. Jasmine leapt to her feet to meet him at the door. She threw her arms around him. The day had served to build the excitement for Jasmine and she could not contain herself.

"Well, I'm glad to see you, too," was Luke's response with a chuckle. "We need to hurry. I have a very special night planned for us. Are you up for it?"

With that, Jasmine tossed her smock into the chair, smiled at Mary, winked at the ladies, and was gone.

A Change in Course

Jasmine clutched Luke's arm in barely controlled excitement while they walked to his car. They continued walking while Luke turned and gave her a soft kiss.

"So, where are we going, my love?" Jasmine asked in her sweetest voice.

Luke enjoyed surprising Jasmine, and she loved the way he would work to make even the most mundane things exiting. They could be going to the grocery store for all she cared. She was with Luke, and that was all that mattered to her. Luke glanced down and took notice of Jasmine's shoes.

"Good, no heels. I couldn't remember if you were wearing heels at my house last night. We needn't rush, but we don't have a lot of time. Would you like to stop by your house and pick up a jacket? It may get a bit chilly after the sun goes down."

"No, I'll be fine as long as you hold me tightly."

Luke opened her door, and helped Jasmine into the seat. This was a ritual they repeated hundreds of times. There was something so elegant and old fashioned about it, but Jasmine never tired of taking his hand, and being helped into the car. He gently closed the door, and soon was seated next to her, pulling away from the curb. Jasmine gazed upon this amazing man. She leaned towards him, closing the space between.

She slowly reached out and placed her hand gently on his thigh. This simple touch sent chills through her. Jasmine stared at him, taking him in as the car moved through town. She enjoyed looking at Luke, really looking at him; the way his soft lips merged into his cheek, the way his mouth seemed to naturally turn up into a smile. Luke could bring a smile to anyone's face and he did it without effort. The line of his jaw showed strength, and guided her gaze towards his wonderful ear. Her mind wandered back to last night. The feel of her lips on his neck, and how her tongue had played with his earlobe. Her heart was racing now as her fingers began to slowly stroke his thigh. Jasmine's slender fingers had minds of their own as they crept further and further into his inner thigh.

Luke turned to Jasmine with a smile on his face. He knew what she was thinking. He glanced back at the road, then Luke leaned into Jasmine for a quick kiss. Even the silence in the car was exciting for them. Luke's eyes returned to the road as he guided the car towards the destination only he knew. She loved his spontaneity. Jasmine continued her gaze and wondered if there was anything about Luke she did not love.

She continued to look him up and down as her mind went through their entire relationship. There had been a few bumps in the road, she thought to herself. A smile came to Jasmine's face as she recalled the night before. *I must have lost my mind she thought. Maybe he lost his too, and will forget what happened,* she thought, then had a laugh she kept inside.

"So, what is the surprise tonight?"

"Surprise may be an overstatement, I guess, since we've done this before. I just like to keep you guessing." Luke chuckled.

"Let me ask you something. Jasmine. Did you really think I was cheating on you?"

"Well…"

"Jasmine, I thought you knew me better than that. You are everything I could ever imagine in a partner. I love you."

Jasmine squeezed his thigh and sighed. She knew what he was saying was the truth. She couldn't rationalize what had happened. The past had crept into her present, polluting her thought process. She knew she had misread things and driven herself to a place that was not good. How could she answer his question? To be honest, would expose the pain and mistrust she carried from the past, and perhaps, damage this wonderful thing she had found. To lie to him would taint the wonderful trust and closeness she felt with Luke.

"I know, Luke. I know." Jasmine paused to see if perhaps he would take that and let the past go.

"What did I do, my love, to make you think such a thing? I've never lied to you, have I?"

"It's complicated. Things in my past sometimes creep into my present, and derail my thinking. I had no idea your "friend" was your ex-wife, and when I found out, my imagination took over. We've never spoken of her before, and rather than ask you about it, I assumed the worst. I'm sorry, my love. Please forgive me."

"Jasmine, there is no need to forgive you. I just need to know how to keep us from going to that terrible place again."

"It's not you, Luke, it's us. Our relationship is totally new territory for me. Never in a million years could I have dreamed of something like what we have. We need to keep ourselves from a place like that. We are a couple, and can do anything when we do it together," Jasmine replied.

"Guess we still have much to learn about each other, don't we." Luke said with a slight chuckle.

"Yes, we do, and it will be fun to learn all of it," Jasmine said as she gave his thigh another squeeze.

"So, what is with the shovel in the backseat?"

"Oh, I may need to do some digging tonight."

Jasmine looked at Luke. He had a mischievous smile on his face, one she had never seen before. She noticed that they had left the city and were well into the countryside. Jasmine had been gazing at Luke the whole time, and now she was not sure where they were. The roads kept getting smaller and it had been quite some time since she had seen a house.

"Where the heck are we?" Jasmine inquired.

Luke looked at Jasmine. A muffled laugh she had not heard before escaped him. She sensed that tonight's adventure was very different from those they had taken in the past.

"You don't recognize this? You've been out here before."

"I just love the countryside." Jasmine said with a sigh.

Luke looked over at Jasmine and smiled. She knew something was up. Jasmine had come to recognize Luke's mannerisms when he was weaving something special, but tonight seemed different. She wasn't sure what it was, but judging from Luke's nervousness, she knew this was something really special. She thought she caught glimpses of him lost in thought, perhaps even troubled. *Was he still thinking of last night, she wondered? What digging could he possibly need to do at night?* Momentarily her hand lifted from his thigh. Her imagination once again began to run wild, but this time, she would not allow herself to be derailed. Her hand quickly returned to his thigh as she took a deep breath, and pushed all questions from her mind.

The car suddenly began to slow. Luke was right, Jasmine had been here before. As he turned the car into what was now a gravel drive, her mind went back to that beautiful sunset and the wonderfully romantic evening they had spent out here together. The opening in the brush had widened and was much more inviting then the last time he had brought her here. There were many things different this time though. There was a wood chipper standing watch over a large pile of chips. Much of the wild brush had been cleared, giving the area a more manicured and inviting appearance.

The lily pad covered pond glistened in the setting sun. The creek meandered along and the old chimney remained as a sentry proclaiming, "Welcome back." The huge willow tree seemed to wave a personal welcome to her. Luke brought the car to a stop and looked to Jasmine.

"Now do you know where we are?" Luke asked with a 'cat ate the canary' look on his face.

"Of course, honey, I will never forget the day you showed me this wonderful place."

Luke opened his door, grabbed the shovel from behind the seat, and headed around the car. Jasmine couldn't take her eyes off of him as he walked around the front of the car carrying the shovel. When he was in the front, silhouetted by the setting sun, he paused. Luke's blue eyes seemed to glow as he gazed upon her. Jasmine could not help but return to the craziness of the night before. As Luke leaned on the hood, staring at her, her heart was suddenly in her throat.

What was he doing? Jasmine worked to chase the ugly memory away and smiled as she watched him. A smile slowly came to Luke's face, and soon he continued around the car to her door. She looked at him as he pulled the door open like he had a hundred times before.

Luke's eyes locked onto Jasmine's as his hand took hers and paused momentarily. This time it was somehow different. His hand was trembling. She didn't feel the confidence he normally projected. Luke was uncharacteristically nervous tonight. She couldn't put her finger on it, but something was different. She felt the gentle tug on her hand, and he lifted her from the car. There was definitely something going on. She couldn't quite put her finger on it, so she chose to just enjoy. Jasmine rose from her seat, and Luke kept hold of her hand as he drew it to his chest, then, leaned in, and gave her a gentle, yet passionate, kiss. She savored his soft moist lips pressed to hers. No one had ever kissed her like Luke, and they just kept getting better.

Jasmine wasn't sure how long the kiss lasted, but when he broke it, his fingers were entwined in her hair, and he drew her head to his chest. The two lovers embraced, and Jasmine was not sure what was happening here, but she could sense this was not a normal kiss. Luke seemed to be overwhelmed with emotion, and while she did not understand what was happening, she felt truly special as she shared in his release.

Luke softly kissed her forehead and whispered "I've loved you from the first moment I laid eyes upon you, Jasmine."

"I love you too, Luke. What is going on? Are you ok?"

"Come with me, my lady," Luke said as he led Jasmine along, never releasing his grip on her delicate hand.

Luke used the shovel as if it were some sort of staff as he led them towards the knoll near the willow tree. Once they got to the top, Luke paused, stabbed the shovel into the ground and turned to face Jasmine. The sunset painters were at work, and the warm hues began to fill the sky as the sun sunk lower.

Luke looked into Jasmine's eyes and began to speak.

"Jasmine, my life has never been the same since I met you. You've shown me a level of joy I could never dare to imagine was even possible for one person to give another. Often times, throughout my life, I've felt insecure, sometimes, even fearful, of personal relationships. Oh, I've succeeded in business, but my personal life often times caused me to put on a facade so as not to show just how frail my heart was. I've always tried to live a good life, help those who need help, and be honest with those around me. The craziness of last night made me realize just what is important in my life. When I was sitting in that jail cell, I tried to be angry with you. My head just kept returning to the police officer cuffing me as I watched tears streaming down your cheeks."

"Oh, Luke" Jasmine started, but she was quickly cut off.

"No, Jasmine, please just listen." Luke said with a tremble in his voice.

Jasmine could see the hurt in his eyes as he spoke. Her stomach cramped and her heart began to sink. Tears welled up in her eyes. She suddenly became fearful of what may come out of his mouth next. She glanced over at the shovel wondering what he needed with a shovel. Jasmine wasn't sure if it was the chill of the evening that caused the goose bumps on her arms, or the thought of where Luke may be going with this train of thought. Jasmine could no longer look Luke in the eye. She questioned whether she deserved such a man. It really didn't matter what he may be thinking, she was feeling as though she was not worthy of such a wonderful man. She often wondered what she had done in her life to deserve Luke.

Luke reached out and lifted her eyes to his. A smile spread across his face as he continued.

"I sat there in the jail cell thinking, reliving everything since I first laid eyes upon you. I remembered the awe that came over me as you approached me that first night in the pub. I closed my eyes and recalled the tremble in my hand as

I slowly inched it across that table until it touched yours. I relived the electricity that coursed through my body as my outstretched fingers first connected with yours. I could feel you looking all the way to my soul as our eyes locked. I remembered the feel of wonder as our spirits joined that first day. Jasmine my spirit soared to new heights right from that first day. I knew God was showing me the path to my total happiness. You were my treasure, and all I needed to do was prove my worthiness."

Jasmine's heart began to lift, and her stomach settled as she felt his fingers slowly slip from her chin, stroking gently down her neck as he continued his gaze. She realized that this was indeed a special moment. It was not the confrontation for her craziness the night before, but rather a continuation of the wonders that were Luke.

"I love you Jasmine. I've always loved you. I brought you to this place before, hoping you would appreciate it. Now I bring you back here hoping that you will share in my love."

Luke's eyes began to well up. Jasmine, too, could feel the mixture of joy, and something she had never seen in Luke; fear. Her heart was lifted as his words floated into her soul. She could control herself no more. She wanted, no needed to feel him in her arms. Her own eyes began to tear. Not tears of pain, but rather, tears of love and joy.

"Sshh," she whispered as she placed a soft kiss upon his cheek.

Jasmine could feel the emotions erupting out of her man. She held him tightly and guided his head to her shoulder. Her fingers stroked through his curls as she held him. This was new territory for Jasmine, but her instincts told her that there was nothing to fear. Her hand stroked gently up and down Luke's back as she worked to comfort him.

"I'm here, my love. Here, where I want to be," Jasmine whispered.

She could feel Luke tremble in her arms. His chest swelled as he drew in a deep breath, and suddenly, the Luke that she knew returned. The confident and powerful man that had swept her from her feet many months before seemed to appear before her eyes. Luke stepped back. His arms extended as he held her hands, and a smile came to his face. A twinkle sparkled in his eye. The setting sun glistened off the calm waters as the frogs continued to croak. A loon could be heard, invisible in the distance. The scene had become almost surreal. He gently squeezed each of her hands as he paused to look deep into her soul. Jasmine became frightened as she suddenly realized what was about to happen.

"I think this is a place where your beauty, and our love could flourish and grow unimpeded by the things around us," Luke said in his powerful yet loving voice.

Jasmine began to tremble as she watched Luke. His left hand slowly and deliberately lowered, releasing her right hand

Jasmine's whole body began to shake as Luke slowly dropped to one knee. *Oh my God,* Jasmine thought to herself. *Is this really happening?*

"Jasmine, when I awaken in the morning, I want to breathe you in. Ten minutes cannot pass during the day without you filling my head. Nothing in life seems to matter anymore except making more time to be with you. You are my life, Jasmine, and I love it."

Luke took a deep breath. Jasmine could hardly breathe. She watched as Luke's left hand began slipping into his pocket. It wasn't until this moment that she saw the outline of what was there. Sharp corners defined the shape, a shape she had seen before. She watched his fingers moving inside until the object was cradled within his large hand. Jasmine could not breathe as he slowly withdrew his hand, and the small box. Every woman knows what a box like that means.

Luke slowly, and gently released her left hand. Time seemed to stop as he carefully tipped the lid back and reached inside. Placing the now empty box at her feet, he reached out to her as he had done hundreds of times. His strong fingers hooked her left hand and gently raised it. Jasmine's eyes rose to meet his. She had been lost many times in those pools of blue, but this time it was different somehow. Her heartbeat somehow synchronized with his.

In the most natural of movements, Luke slipped the ring onto her delicate finger.

"Jasmine… my one true love; will you marry me?"

Jasmine could feel a ring slipping effortlessly over her limp ring finger. The silence was deafening. The loon stopped calling. The frogs quit their croaking. The world held its breath awaiting her answer as the two lovers remained consumed with each other.

Luke's face began to change as Jasmine's silence continued. *Had he made a mistake? Had he misjudged her feelings for him?*

Jasmine suddenly leapt into Luke's arms, and with tears streaming down her face, whispered, "Yes, my love. Yes, yes, yes, I will marry you!"

Luke lifted Jasmine off the ground as they twirled in the night air. His lips found hers and they kissed like never before. They laughed together as the world came to life around them. The loons called out. The frogs croaked louder than ever before. Luke captured her hands, and the two began to dance in what could only be described as pure joy.

"Jasmine, will you share something with me?"

"Anything, my love, anything."

"This was the place I would come as a boy when I needed to feel good. It was my secret place, my hideout. I would come here and fish in the pond, listen to the creek, I would even camp here some nights. I came here to escape everything and everyone. This was a sanctuary from those who would laugh and make fun of me. It was a place of pure joy. When I grew up, I turned to other things to make me feel safe and proud. Success in school and business became the cloak that protected me from the ridicule of others, and this wonderful place slipped into the shadows of my memory. When I met you, I realized what true joy felt like. In you, I found joy that was without limits, joy that was as pure as the joy I felt as a child sitting here, alone."

"I love you, Luke. Thank you for sharing this place with me."

"Jasmine, I bought it. I own all of this."

"You own it?"

"Yes, my love."

Luke reached out and grabbed the shovel. He swung it around in front of them and placed the point of the shovel atop the ground.

"Jasmine, will you break ground with me. I want to build our new life together upon this place."

With that, Jasmine placed her foot on one side of the shovel; Luke placed his on the other. They looked at each other, and drove the shovel deep into the earth, and with a simple turn of the shovel, the perfect couple began their perfect life. As they stood there, arm in arm, the sun slowly set on the first day of Jasmine's new, perfect life.

The End